Write-on Antholo

A Collection of Stories, Poems, Songs and Other Writings

Write-on Group

Póilín Brennan
Joyce Butcher
Helena Clare
James Conway
Frances Dermody
Joanne Dowling
Frank Fahy
Molly Fogarty
Bill Geoghegan
Deirdre Anne Gialamas
Elizabeth Hannon
Mary Hawkshaw
Mary Hodson
Ciara Keogh
Seamus Keogh
Thomas MacMahon
Josephine McCann
Anne McManus
Grit Metsch
Anne Murray
Anne O'Callaghan
Nollaig O'Donnell
Richard O'Donnell
Kathleen Phelan
Jutta Rosen
Brenda Silke
Mary Rose Tobin
Geraldine Warren

First Published 2024
Frank Fahy Publishing Services
5 Village Centre
Barna, Galway
Ireland
www.write-on.ie

All characters and events in this publication, other than those clearly in the public domain, are fictitious, and any resemblance to persons living or dead is purely coincidental.

The Publisher wishes to thank the Write-on members and guest authors for permission to use copyrighted material:

© 2024 Póilín Brennan
© 2024 Joyce Butcher
© 2024 Helena Clare
© 2024 James Conway
© 2024 Frances Dermody
© 2024 Joanne Dowling
© 2024 Frank Fahy
© 2024 Molly Fogarty
© 2024 Bill Geoghegan
© 2024 Deirdre Anne Gialamas
© 2024 Elizabeth Hannon
© 2024 Mary Hawkshaw
© 2024 Mary Hodson
© 2024 Ciara Keogh

© 2024 Seamus Keogh
© 2024 Thomas MacMahon
© 2024 Josephine McCann
© 2024 Anne McManus
© 2024 Grit Metsch
© 2024 Anne Murray
© 2024 Anne O'Callaghan
© 2024 Nollaig O'Donnell
© 2024 Richard O'Donnell
© 2024 Kathleen Phelan
© 2024 Jutta Rosen
© 2024 Brenda Silke
© 2024 Mary Rose Tobin
© 2024 Geraldine Warren

Cover photograph:
Connemara National Park © 2024 Professor Chaosheng Zhang, University of Galway.

Illustrations © 2024 Nollaig O'Donnell

ISBN: 9798884101098

Imprint: Independently published by Frank Fahy Publishing Services, Barna, Galway.

The Write-on Group wish to thank Galway County Council for helping to fund our various publications and activities.

Comhairle Chontae na Gaillimhe
Galway County Council

The moral right of the authors has been asserted. No part of this publication may be reproduced, stored in a retrieval system, or transmitted in any form, or by any means without the prior permission in writing of the Publisher. The views expressed by the authors are not necessarily the views of the Publisher. The Publisher is not responsible for websites (or their content) that are not owned by the Publisher.

DEDICATION

This Anthology is dedicated to the Write-on members, past and present, who gather with enthusiasm every Thursday evening on Zoom to explore the realms of their writings and imaginations. This collection would not be possible without the tireless dedication, camaraderie, and encouragement that each member extends to the others.

We thank you for your unwavering support and for inspiring one another to keep writing, even if it is only a few words each week. It is this collective spirit that propels Write-on forward, and together we will continue to flourish into the future.

CONTENTS

Introduction xii

Gone the Heather – Gone the Hawthorn Helena Clare *1*

The Hunter Seamus Keogh *13*

Tapestry in the Ladies Club Kathleen Phelan *14*

Lady in a Blue Dress Mary Hodson *16*

Fragility In Life Thomas MacMahon *19*

Constant Companions Deirdre Anne Gialamas *20*

Uncle Jim Elizabeth Hannon *22*

The Rise Póilín Brennan *27*

The Bird James Conway *28*

Life Story Molly Fogarty *30*

The Life and Times of Jimmy Mullins Mary Rose Tobin *32*

Churching Kathleen Phelan *41*

A True Mayo Man Anne Murray *42*

Sweet Citrus Fruits Deirdre Anne Gialamas *46*

New Girls Anne McManus *47*

Worlds Apart Josephine McCann *54*

The Postcard James Conway *59*

The Patience of Ordinary Things Mary Hodson *60*

Maidin Póilín Brennan *63*

Breaking Altitude Frank Fahy ***64***

I Will Sleep Seamus Keogh ***68***

The Site Joanne Dowling ***69***

A Falling Mary Hawkshaw ***76***

Chubb James Conway ***77***

The Write-on Christmas 83

Ho, Ho, Bloody Ho! Joyce Butcher ***84***

Christmas in Renvyle Thomas MacMahon ***88***

The Turkeys Mary Hodson ***89***

Death in December Geraldine Warren ***92***

The Magic of Believing Mary Rose Tobin ***94***

In a Picture James Conway ***100***

Nativity Elizabeth Hannon ***102***

The Colour Of Snow Brenda Silke ***106***

The Blanket Mary Hodson ***107***

All Souls Póilín Brennan ***111***

The Shiny Red Couch Deirdre Anne Gialamas ***112***

After Christmas Anne Murray ***114***

A Gamble James Conway ***117***

Pastures New Thomas MacMahon ***123***

A Traveller Woman in Ireland's Past Mary Hawkshaw ***124***

A Kind of Revenge Mary Hodson *126*

ABCs and Nursery Rhymes Deirdre Anne Gialamas *129*

Seeking a Cure Frank Fahy *130*

TV Junkie Josephine McCann *160*

The Good Old Days Elizabeth Hannon *162*

My Earthly Ties Mary Hawkshaw *166*

Daisies and Strawberries Mary Hodson *167*

Piecing It All Together Kathleen Phelan *170*

Discrimination Seamus Keogh *171*

Echoes of Friendship Mary Rose Tobin *172*

The Watcher Mary Hawkshaw *192*

One Field Once More James Conway *194*

A Mother's Dilemma Kathleen Phelan *195*

St Bridget Nollaig O'Donnell *198*

Bheith Gheal Póilín Brennan *199*

Smelling of Roses Frances Dermody *200*

The Discovery of the Death of a Goose James Conway *201*

Perfect Passings Deirdre Anne Gialamas *202*

Bamboo Wings James Conway *212*

Love is – 'Chips' Thomas MacMahon *213*

Piano Man Mary Rose Tobin *214*

Burdened Bog Deirdre Anne Gialamas *227*

The Poet who Sat beside me on the Train Anne O'Callaghan *228*

Nora's Journey Mary Hawkshaw *230*

Big Hair Deirdre Anne Gialamas *241*

Oxford Dictionary Kathleen Phelan *242*

Hearth Póilín Brennan *245*

Huggles – A Love Story Mary Hodson *246*

Nobody Told Me Geraldine Warren *249*

What Words Can Do Mary Hawkshaw *250*

Keeping the Piece Frances Dermody *251*

A Bouquet of Words for Mary Elizabeth Hannon *254*

Tobernalt Mary Hodson *256*

The Niedermayers James Conway *260*

Circles Deirdre Anne Gialamas *261*

Hysterectomy Kathleen Phelan *274*

Imagination Unleashed Mary Hodson *275*

I Long to Hide Geraldine Warren *277*

No Regrets Anne McManus *278*

What Lies Ahead Anne Murray *283*

What if? Deirdre Anne Gialamas *284*

A Normal Couple (extract) Olga Peters *286*

Power of Rural Electrification Josephine McCann *298*

Old Loves Deirdre Anne Gialama*s 300*

A Step Too Far Mary Hawkshaw *301*

The Stolen Kiss Elizabeth Hannon *309*

If the Prom could Talk Josephine McCann *310*

Mug of the Month 312

September Keywords – HIDE and STEAL 313

October Keywords – WILD and WONDER 319

November Keywords – LIKE and BOSS 325

January Keywords – TUNE and FINE 331

February Keywords – TIME and TIDE 335

March Keywords – PITCH and GROUND 341

April Keywords – WALK and LIE 347

Songs 353

Everything is Grand Bill Geoghegan *354*

Friends Grit Metsch *356*

Christopher's Journey Mary Rose and Peter Tobin *358*

Call Me Tomorrow Frank Fahy *360*

About the Authors 362

Introduction

Welcome to *The Write-on Anthology 2025*, a collection of stories, poems, memoirs, and songs that showcases the best of our group's creative work over the past year. This anthology marks our sixteenth publication since the group's inception in 2017, reflecting the dedication and talent of our diverse membership.

The Write-on Group is more than just a gathering of writers; it's a community united by a passion for storytelling. Over the years, we've navigated various challenges, from the isolation of the Covid-19 pandemic to the shifting landscape of technological innovations. Despite these hurdles, we've continued to thrive, producing work that resonates deeply with readers and reflects the breadth of human experience.

In this anthology, you'll find a carefully curated selection of pieces that range from poignant memoirs to evocative poems and compelling short stories. Each work offers a unique perspective, drawing you into the author's world and inviting you to explore their imagination and experiences.

The collection features award-winning stories and those written purely for the pleasure of writing, catering to all levels of literary craft. From Helena Clare's powerful exploration of memory and loss in *Gone the Heather – Gone the*

Hawthorn to Mary Hodson's beautifully crafted tale of love and identity in *Lady in a Blue Dress*, each piece sets a distinctive tone for the collection.

War and Resilience often bring turmoil and uncertainty, but amidst the chaos, stories of strength and determination shine through. The extract from Jutta Rosen's novel, *A Normal Couple*, takes readers into the harrowing experiences of a family during the first air raids of the Second World War. The story vividly portrays their fears, toughness, and the impact of the war on their daily lives.

Familial Bonds and Traditions form the cornerstone of our lives, providing warmth and continuity. Póilín Brennan captures the essence of traditional Irish life in her poem *Hearth*, where the kitchen hearth serves as a familial gathering place, a cornerstone of family life and a keeper of folklore. Deirdre Anne Gialamas takes us on a nostalgic journey with *The Shiny Red Couch*, a reflection on childhood Christmas mornings filled with excitement, joy, and familial love.

Personal Journeys and Reflections help us to shape our understanding of ourselves and the world. Deirdre Anne Gialamas's *What If?* playfully explores alternate realities and the whimsical possibilities of life's different choices, questioning the impact of existence and individual decisions.

Nature and Spirituality often intertwine, offering solace and connection to something greater than ourselves. Póilín Brennan's *Beith Gheal* is a lyrical homage to nature and connectedness, weaving imagery of the birch tree as a symbol of love and unity. Kathleen Phelan's *Tapestry in the Ladies Club* offers a poignant reflection on community and connection, further exploring the theme of shared human experiences.

Youth is a time of growth and change, filled with wonder and discovery. Elizabeth Hannon's *The Stolen Kiss* reflects on the fleeting joys of parenthood, encapsulating the emotional depth of a mother's missed moment and the transient nature of time and connection.

Life's Adventures and Discoveries are filled with excitement and wonder. Frank Fahy's *Breaking Altitude* invites readers to meet Roy and his family as they embark on a thrilling and unforgettable Halloween adventure in the Texas skies, blending excitement with the warmth of familial bonds. As is Frank's style, the ending will take many readers by surprise!

Memoirs that provide intimate glimpses into the authors' lives are well represented in the anthology. Deirdre Anne Gialamas's *Constant Companions* is a touching tribute to the enduring bonds of friendship, and Elizabeth Hannon's *Uncle Jim* paints a vivid portrait of family and legacy.

Interspersed among the stories are poems that capture the essence of fleeting moments and profound truths, adding depth and variety to the collection. The anthology concludes with a collection of new songs from our talented song writers and the hope is that readers will be encouraged to seek out the audios on our website www.write-on.ie.

Introduction

Our commitment to fostering a supportive and collaborative environment has been instrumental in bringing these works to life. Weekly meetings on Zoom, every Thursday from 7pm to 9pm, have provided a platform for members to share their work, receive constructive feedback, and draw inspiration from one another. While we primarily meet virtually due to our geographically diverse membership, spanning Australia, Germany, the US, Greece, Dublin, Kilkenny, Westport, Leitrim, Galway, and beyond, we cherish the occasional in-person gatherings for special occasions like *The Mug of the Month Competition* or member visits to Ireland. This spirit of camaraderie and mutual encouragement is at the heart of everything we do.

In addition to celebrating our authors' achievements, we also honour the memory of Anne O'Callaghan, who sadly passed away before she could see her poem, *The Poet who Sat beside me on the Train* published in this anthology. Her work about President Michael D. Higgins, and the kindness extended by the President in contacting the family and sending his Aide de Camp to attend her funeral, reflect the profound connections that literature can foster and the solace it can bring in times of grief.

We hope this collection brings you as much joy and inspiration as it has brought us in creating it. Thank you for being a part of our journey, and we look forward to sharing more stories with you in the years to come.

Frank Fahy
Chairperson
The Write-on Group

Gone the Heather – Gone the Hawthorn

Helena Clare

'You know about puts and calls, don't you?'

'No, Christy. I've only ever had savings in mutual funds.'

He sat up in his armchair. 'It's quite simple really; a put option gives the buyer the right to sell an asset at the strike price before a certain date.'

By the time Christy started on the call option, I had lost concentration. This was the umpteenth time that he'd started down that 'puts and calls' road. While I usually encouraged him, today I was just too worried to give him my attention. I was expecting Ed, Christy's landlord, to ring the doorbell any minute.

***

Christy was my father's first cousin, an only, long-awaited child of elderly parents. He and Dad grew up in a small village in Connemara. Christy spent many of his childhood years in Dad's company, looking to him as a big brother; they were close all their lives. They both did engineering, Christy choosing electrical engineering. Later he emigrated to the US and became an expert on hydroelectric stations. As children, we would hear stories of him and see

Helena Clare

his postcards from different countries. Poughkeepsie was his final project, and even now, when I hear the name that took me ages to be able to pronounce, I think of Christy's brilliance.

Every other year, Christy would return to the west of Ireland for a visit and take in some trout fishing with Dad. Together, the two would visit their long-ago home and fish in one of the nearby lakes, but there was a ritual before they started. I know it by heart because it's the same ritual that we all followed whenever we visited Dad's childhood home. I can see them in my mind's eye, climbing the hill as far as the old cemetery and saying words of remembrance as they laid their hands on their friends' gravestones. Then on to the holy well where they would drink that pure mountain water and leave coins for anyone who might need them. They would turn then, look down over the village and bay, and breathe deeply. The season's fishing could commence.

Fishing the familiar lakes around where they used to live, was partly to do with practising the art of fly fishing, but I think it had more to do with renewing memories. I imagine they used this time to fortify their images of home – the crunch of heather underfoot; the scent of furze and hawthorn; the sound of frantic bees with too many wildflowers from which to choose, the smiles of old friends they met in the pub and their soft Connemara accents. Christy, though gone from there for well over forty years, never lost that way of speaking.

When I first moved to the US, Christy and I had an annual date. He would get tickets for a

Gone the Heather – Gone the Hawthorn

Broadway show, and afterwards, we would go out to eat. Over dinner, he always asked about home.

'Who did you meet? How is Packey? Their son is a priest, you know.'

'Yes, we met the Joyces, and they wanted to be remembered to you, Bridgey especially. She spoke about your mother, God rest her. Will you go home next year, do you think?'

'Yes. Soon.'

But he didn't; he hadn't been home since my dad became housebound. He would ask about him, and that was about it. I never took the lead in these conversations; I was very much in awe of him, he was so confident, so well dressed. I can still picture him in his tan Brooks Brothers duffle coat, cavalry twill slacks, highly polished oxfords, and gleaming white shirt with a tie. He had always been the well-dressed gentleman; my mother described him as dapper. He held the door for every woman; he wouldn't seat himself until the 'lady' was seated. Put that together with knowing his way around Broadway and city restaurants, and he was in a different league entirely from the relatives at home.

A very easy subject to bring up in conversation though, was his known plan to retire home.

'Oh yes, I've bought the suitcase; I just have to make the arrangements.'

'That's great, Christy. Dad will be thrilled; it will be like old times.'

I had no reason not to believe him. And we didn't go beyond the yearly meet-up. He stayed somewhat distant. We both did. But in retrospect, I know there was a great deal missing in the way we communicated – I didn't know

Helena Clare

anything about his life in the US, I didn't even know where he lived. All I had was a post office box and a phone number.

My husband and I moved all over – first to Pennsylvania, then down south, twice! Christy and I still exchanged Christmas cards; until we didn't. It's a good while ago now, so I can honestly say that I don't remember if I was the one who stopped writing. I can't imagine that being the case because I had to account to Dad, who would always ask about him.

Then some years later, the call came from a relative at home to check up on Christy. Apparently, he fell and wasn't doing well. I called him right away and was surprised that he didn't know who I was.

'I'm JP's daughter – Francey. They're all asking about you at home, Christy.'

There followed the usual questions and answers – How is everyone? What age is JP now? How is your mother? and then –

'Tell me who you are again.'

'I'm Francey – JP's daughter.'

I had to remind him who I was a few times during that call. I was confused by his forgetfulness, but at the time, Alzheimer's wasn't spoken about much, so I didn't make the connection. Also, Christy was just about 70 then, and in a family blessed with longevity, 70 is 'young-old'.

'I'd love to come to visit you, Christy.'

Getting his physical address was a challenge, but we made a date for the following Saturday. I found his home, a tiny two-room apartment over someone's garage. There was no answer when I

Gone the Heather – Gone the Hawthorn

knocked, so the landlord let me in – Christy had forgotten I was coming. He was lying on his bed on top of the much-admired Brooks Brothers coat – now worn and stained. The curtains were drawn to block out the sun because there was no air-conditioning. His hair was completely white, and he was very pale. He looked like a man who lived in a dark drab apartment that never saw the light of day.

He wasn't dressed, so I stepped into the living room to allow him the time he needed. The clutter in that space was unbelievable. Every surface, and there weren't many surfaces, was covered with bits and pieces of things that he could not bring himself to throw away – rubber bands, string, electrical cord, empty pillboxes, old batteries, small change, floppy discs, and cassettes. I could tell by how they looked that he handled everything frequently, and I pictured him picking things up and wondering where he should put them next. What surprised me most, though, was that there were no photographs of family members, no pictures of the beautiful place where he grew up, or of places where he had been.

There were piles of unopened mail tied neatly with string, and bags of recyclables, all well rinsed, waiting to go out with the garbage. One kitchen chair, one armchair, one small table, probably the first portable TV ever made, and an Osborne 1, the very first portable computer, completed the scene. There was nothing I could point to and say 'Oh, that's nice,' – except for Christy, of course. When he joined me in the living room, he very quickly fell into his

Helena Clare

gentleman routine. But I shouldn't call it a routine, because with Christy it was ingrained; it was who he was. Yes, Christy had deteriorated considerably since I last saw him, but I could tell from his surroundings that most of this was how he had always lived; he lived simply.

He tried to hide his condition with his perfect manners and said that we must go out to eat. We went to a nearby diner, and when we got there it was clear that everyone knew him.

'Christopher! Good to see you! Right this way!'

There were many calls of 'Christopher' from all who worked there, it was lovely really. Everyone knew and obviously liked him.

'I'll bring you your usual, Christopher.'

'Thank you. Tell me your name again.'

He didn't have to order; the waitress knew exactly where to seat him and what to bring him. They knew, what took me so long to learn, that Christy could no longer make decisions. He had been going to that diner for so long that they knew, without asking, what he wanted to eat.

'Christy, it's as if you're the mayor. What a welcome they gave you!'

I learned during that first trip that Christy never left the apartment alone. A friend, Jack, drove out from Brooklyn a couple of times a week to take him grocery shopping and to go out to eat. It was Jack who called Ireland and said that someone had to do something –

'Christy is deteriorating before my eyes.'

I had many conversations with Jack in the weeks to come, while I came to conclusions about what had to be done about Christy. One thing was clear; he had planned to return to Ireland. The suitcase in the room gave me my opening.

'That's a great looking suitcase, Christy. Are you close to making that move home?'

'Yes. Soon.'

'This would be a great time to go. Everything is in bloom – the heather, the hawthorn. Maybe even the fuchsia.'

He nodded: 'Yes, as soon as the cuckoo leaves, the hawthorn blooms.'

'We should go together, Christy.'

'Yes. Soon.'

All offers to help or make plans for him were politely declined. The distance that he maintained, that was always a part of him, was another reason for my delay in coming to grips with what I had to do about Christy; it seemed impolite to bridge that distance. In any situation where a choice was presented to him, he could not choose. Surprisingly, it took a simple trip to the supermarket, to buy toothpaste, for that reality to really sink in:

'Tell me again the difference between them.'

'Well, this one is for sensitive teeth, and this one is just regular.'

'What about this one?'

'That's the one for sensitive teeth.'

'And the other one?'

Three months and many weekend visits later, the suitcase in the middle of the floor remained empty. By now, I had met Christy's landlord, Ed, many times. He and his wife Tricia did what they could for Christy, but they were older than he was, and they were beside themselves with worry.

'You must take him away; we're afraid that something might happen to him. If you don't do something, we will call Social Services! We have to! We're afraid to go on vacation. Tricia! Tell her!'

'I can't climb those steps up to his apartment any more. Look, we love Christy, but we worry all the time. What if he sets the place on fire? What if he falls again?'

Their threat to call Social Services really frightened me. Lying awake that night, I added even worse 'what ifs' to Tricia's concerns –

'What if they put him somewhere awful?'

'What if this gentle person is disrespected?'

But all the talk and reasoning I had done with Christy had achieved nothing; he would not leave with me. What could I do? I couldn't physically drag him to the airport.

I called Ed and told him that the only solution was to evict Christy. It was cruel, I know, to both of them, but I could think of no other way. Together, we made a plan for the following Saturday.

'And Ed, it's important that Tricia be there too.'

Tricia broke in – she must have been on the extension, she said that of course she would be there.

***

'Sorry Christy, what is it you were saying about the call option?'

I could hear Tricia and Ed on the steps, and though I was expecting them, I jumped from fright when the doorbell rang. To this day, I remember every word, every facial expression, and every movement during that heartbreaking event, the eviction that I had orchestrated.

Gone the Heather – Gone the Hawthorn

Ed, his voice as unsteady as his hand, gave the letter to Christy saying: 'This is an eviction notice. You've got 30 days to vacate the premises.' Christy's face went from smiling to disbelief and confusion. He tried to stand but fell back into his chair as the shock slowly set in. 'No! No! This is my home. Why would you do this to me?'
Tricia, kneeling now close to Christy, took his hand and gently stroked his cheek. Waiting for his eyes to meet hers, she spoke quietly and lovingly, saying: 'Christy, you know that Ed and I love you, but we're older than you are, and we cannot look after you anymore. Francey here will bring you home to your own family in Ireland. Won't that be nice?'

I tried to take his other hand, but he wouldn't give it to me. My heart sank and tears filled my eyes. I persisted, though, with 'Just think of what it will be like at home, Christy. Everyone will be so glad to see you.' He was quieter now, thanks to Tricia, but still mumbled 'No. No.'

Jack called him later that day, and Christy told him what happened. The hurt cut him to his core, he remembered it, he did not have to be reminded, he now knew he was leaving, and that he had to go.

***

I needed to have access to his accounts to pay for his long-term care and any other expenses that he might have, as well as unravel several years of unpaid taxes. It was fortunate that he had made good investments, funds would be the least of his worries. I was surprised at how easy it was to get Power of Attorney. It was a small mercy for Christy that he didn't know what I was doing. He had spent considerable energy keeping his affairs and life very private. Now here was I, seeing all of his assets, contacting his broker, closing and opening accounts, and speaking to his doctor. There was no more distance. I had crossed over and taken control. I had helped him, coerced him, and hurt that perfect gentleman.

I'd never been completely responsible for another soul, until this happened, and I wish that I had been smart enough to find a better way. Christy was so vulnerable; there came a time when he had to relinquish control to another, but surely it shouldn't happen by force. It's as if one spends one's younger years learning how to gain control of one's life and how to make decisions, only to give it all up at the end. And I don't mean that old adage about not being able to 'take it with you.' I mean the letting go before you lose your independence, the actively acknowledging that you need someone to take charge. The contentment that we associate with old age requires that this giving over be done freely, it also requires that you get something in return to replace what is lost. This could be inner peace, less worry, and hopefully a sense of security. Christy's disease cheated him of these return gifts. All he received was confusion and betrayal.

I felt his bewilderment and anger all during the return to Ireland when he asked me countless times:

'Where are we going?'

'We're going home, Christy; I'm taking you home.'

Gone the Heather – Gone the Hawthorn

'How dare you! How could you take me from my home where I was well cared for!'

His anger showed not only in his words, but in the way he sat, slightly turned away from me; in the way he both looked at me but avoided my eyes; in the way he walked, either slightly ahead or behind me. He was trying to re-create the distance that I had crossed, because I had brought so much upheaval into his life.

Thankfully, Christy settled down well in his new home, a nursing home close to family. I bought him new clothes, including a loden coat to replace the duffle – I wanted him to look the sophisticated gentleman that he was. I called often to speak to the staff – it turned out that Christy was a great dancer, and in a home with a dearth of males and with manners he hadn't yet forgotten, he was very much in demand with the ladies. And there was also the odd visit to the pub arranged when family visited.

Now, apart from the memories, all I have of Christy's are in a small box in my closet: his flute (seemingly he taught himself to play), a book of Irish ballads, his passport, and his engineer's license. I added a photograph of him with my father, sitting on a rock on the hill when they were young men.

I often wondered what it said about Christy that he didn't own anything. Did it mean he was free? He certainly didn't need things to give him the feeling of home; he brought those memories of home with him in his mind's eye, as he moved from place to place. But when the time came for that awful disease to take its terrible toll, then, gone the heather, gone the hawthorn and the sounds and scents of Connemara. Christy's home had been in his head, and Alzheimer's took that away from him.

The Hunter

Seamus Keogh

Winter morning stillness in the air
The hunter quickly covers ground,
Beneath his tramping heavy boots

Frost coated grass crunching sound.

The sun hazed winter morning
Dim shrouded sphere in the sky
Its hindered light in solemn grey.

A rising snipe leaves the rushes,
Like wind pressure through a funnel.
It cries, darts and turns, disappears.

The hunter lowers the shotgun.
It was not a day to shoot and kill.
Tomorrow is the start of Spring.

Let them have their final chorus.

As the ice melted and dripped
From the moss-covered walls
He turned slowly for home.

Tapestry in the Ladies Club
Kathleen Phelan

A spectrum of colour
in a cardboard box.
Cotton remnants
blended together
Waiting,
to replicate the marsh
outside our window
Where, at dawn,
the grey heron stands
statuesque
in the still water.
His keen eye watching
for minnow, frog or duckling.
Either one will do,
To take back
to the heronry.
To regurgitate
and keep the chicks
alive for another day.

Where bullrushes
stand proud
in their velvet coats
amid the marigolds,
iris, and purple orchid.
And the Fritillary
Butterfly hovers
on the pink

Tapestry in the Ladies Club

flower heads
of devil's bit.
To suck sweet nectar
and lay her eggs
on the underside
of a leaf.

Meanwhile,
back at the Centre,
the whirring
of the sewing machine
means all is well.
While a clanking sound
could mean trouble.
With a few drops of oil
and sighs of relief
we could depend
on the metal teeth of feed dog
to continue where it left off.
Finally
pushing
our tapestry
into existence.

Lady in a Blue Dress
Mary Hodson

In 1952, Kathleen Fallon's life was a pattern of rich, woven experiences, coloured by the vibrant hues of her blue dress with navy trim. This dress wasn't just any garment; it was a treasure chest of memories, purchased from the esteemed Smart-Ware shop on O'Connell Street in Sligo, nestled right next to the aromatic haven of the Ritz Coffee shop and restaurant.

Kathleen, with her apron tied snugly around her waist, was more than a waitress at the Ritz – she was part of its soul. Her days were scented with the robust aroma of freshly ground coffee beans and the tantalizing spice of cinnamon from the pastries that beckoned from the glass display.

'Would you fancy some more tea, Mrs. Banks?' Kathleen would ask, her voice as warm as the beverages she served. She knew her regulars, from the robust laughter of the country neighbours to the brisk, no-nonsense town's businesspeople who darted in and out during the lunchtime rush.

'Oh, Kathleen dear, just a splash more. And do tell me, how did you manage to get such a beautiful pair of shoes?' one of the gentry from Lissadell would inquire, their reserved table by

Lady in a Blue Dress

the window offering a view of the bustling street beyond.

'It's a keen eye for a bargain,' Kathleen replied with a wink, her navy leather shoes a perfect match to her dress.

The camaraderie of the staff was like a second family to Kathleen. Upstairs, where they lived, was a sanctuary of solidarity. They shared stories that danced through the air, mingling with the laughter and occasional sighs of dreams yet to be realised.

'And then he said, "I'm no Gene Kelly, but I can hold my own on the dance floor!"' Kathleen recounted, her eyes sparkling with the memory, as they lounged on their beds, legs tired from the day's work. Saturday nights were a jubilee of music and movement in the ballroom, where the Kilfera Céilí band played, their tunes coaxing even the weariest feet to dance. Kathleen, in her cherished blue dress, swirled and swayed, her high heels clicking rhythmically on the wooden floor. She lived for the moments when her country gentleman, shy but earnest, would arrive. Spotting his entrance, bicycle-clips removed, Kathleen's heart would skip a beat.

'I was wondering, Kate,' he stammered one night, his dark hair combed to a glossy sheen, 'if you might save a dance for me?'

Kathleen's laughter was a melody that matched the band's rhythm.

'I thought you'd never ask, Andy.'

Their first dance was a tale of two like minds finding their rhythm, a quickstep followed by a waltz, their movements a silent conversation of

Mary Hodson

tentative hopes and shared smiles. It was for her best friend May's wedding that Kathleen first chose the blue dress from Smart-Ware. The dress was a promise, paid for in instalments with the coins she earned, each a testament to her hard work.

'Oh, Kathleen, you look like a dream!' May exclaimed as Kathleen twirled before the mirror, the dress hugging her figure just so. Andy, ever the gentleman, only came for the evening celebrations, his eyes never leaving his Kate in the blue dress that mirrored the twilight sky.

'You look... mighty,' he whispered as they danced, the music enveloping them in a world of their own.

Decades later, the blue dress was more than a garment – it was a legend within their family, a love story that spanned over fifty years. The grandchildren would gather around, their eyes wide with wonder as they pointed at the photograph on the mantelpiece.

'Tell us again about the lady in the blue dress, Granny,' they'd plead, and Kathleen, her eyes misting with the tender sheen of reminiscence, would begin the story anew.

'The lady in the blue dress,' she'd start, her voice soft as the embrace of dusk, 'is a tale of love, of dances and dreams, and how a simple dress can hold the heart of a lifetime.'

In this way, the legend of Kathleen, the lady in the blue dress, would dance through the generations, as timeless as the memories woven into the very fabric of the dress itself.

Fragility In Life

Thomas MacMahon

Fragile are the building blocks of life
Choose your partner wisely to avoid strife
From true love do not run
Blossom you will with the right one

Harmony sings a pleasant note
Kindness always gets the vote
Always share and do not lie
And when time gets tough do not fly

Union gives strength to all
Catching one another before they fall
Work hard from the start
And you will be forever in her heart

Constant Companions
Deirdre Anne Gialamas

He danced at his niece's wedding
Bounding to the call
The bright eyed, white smiled uncle
with companion took the floor

He danced at his niece's wedding
Carefully tracing each step
The haunting Greek zeibekiho
Affirming his very being

He danced at his niece's wedding
Floating on clouds unseen
His partner kept the rhythm
More often fell out of line

He danced at his niece's wedding
Limbs flailing about
Eyes salted with sweat and tears
The music his scrap of life

He danced at his niece's wedding
Enthralling those who knelt around
Clapping and shouting 'OPA'
At the inseparable pair

He danced at his niece's wedding
His aura swelling the hall
Trickling through the silted hearts

Constant Companions

Of those who gaped in awe

He danced at his niece's wedding
Knowing he could not walk away
No operation nor medication
Had rendered the two apart

Yet, he danced at his niece's wedding
Spirit soaring above the crowd
While Mr Parkinson was left bereft
Floundering below on the floor

Uncle Jim
Elizabeth Hannon

Gran's dad, Martin James, who lived in Dougha, Co. Mayo was married twice. His first wife was Brid of Aillban and they had two children: Maire and a son, Jim. Sadly Brid died when giving birth to Jim in 1903.

Martin Jimmy, as the old man was called locally, got married again to Mary from Collmor. A really loving couple, they had four daughters Brid, Flora, Sheila, and Ann.

Jim and Maire lived with their stepsisters on the small farm with four milk cows, a few bullocks and some sheep on the mountain. Across the road from the picturesquely Irish, whitewashed thatched cottage, two fields of meadow land bordered a lovely lake where old Martin Jimmy occasionally shot ducks for the table with a single barrel shotgun.

Above the cottage was a stile on a wet ditch that led to a boggy field where the young grandchildren picked sellstrom to use as sail boats on the little burns, happy as the birds and butterflies that loved that wild place.

Time passed. Maire, who never married, emigrated to Chicago and kept in touch by letter until her death in her eighties.

Ann married Pat (nicknamed by Martin Jimmy, Pateen Easog,) and they lived in beautiful

Uncle Jim

Carran with their large family. Brid became a teacher and married a Garda. They lived in Lanesburgh and had eight children. Flora and Sheila emigrated to the States. Jim stayed in Dougha and maybe resented the fine time his siblings seemed to be having, both at home and in the states, while he, stuck on the farm, went nowhere.

Jim was sent with his teenage nephews, Brid and Ann's sons, to cut turf in Coolmore and bring it home to Dougha on the donkey cart. In summer the boys had to help save hay and other jobs on the grandfather's farm which they mostly enjoyed. None of them liked working with their uncle Jim, who apart from skiving off and not pulling his weight, was sarcastic and short tempered.

Then, in his middle fifties, totally bald, and the proud owner of one tooth in his top jaw, Jim decided it was time for him to get a wife. He wrote a letter to Mary Rose of Gleann Caoin, and asked his nephew, young Tony, to deliver it. In error the letter was given to Mary Rose's sister, Kathy. She opened the letter and assuming it was for her, stated categorically to her father,

'I'm not going there.'

Tony reported the father's reply.

'Do you want to sit there by the fire like a lump of cow shite all your life?'.

So Kathy, dressed in her best coat and hat, came to visit Jim, in a pony and trap driven by her father. Jim quite liked the look of her and decided he could do worse. The marriage was arranged. She moved in with her fortune/dowry to the home house with her in-laws. They seemed

23

Elizabeth Hannon

to do all right together.

It is said that Jim and Kathy made a strange sight taking a ride to town in the pony and trap, he in his bawneen and flat cap and she in her best hat, long dress and shawl from another era. His niece Eithne, a district nurse, recounted how she had the newlyweds in her car once and stopped at a garage to buy petrol. A friend passed and taking in the pair giggling and cackling in the back seat, asked Eithne who were the two. When Eithne said they were her uncle and aunt, the girl said, 'Yea, but seriously, who are they?'

Good humoured and welcoming, Kathy was renowned for making tea like tar, the taypot sitting on the side of the open turf fire all day long. Eithne, who always refused to drink a cup, insisted that all visitors and returned Yanks she brought to visit, have at least one refill. Most surreptitiously spilled the tea into a pot plant which miraculously survived, even thrived, on the onslaught, while they listened to Kathy's interesting chat and answered her questions.

Jim, who liked a drink or ten, was jovial and witty in the pub. But he was known to make life very difficult for his teetotal garda brother-in-law. Shouted insults were his usual currency if they met up when he was drunk, bad tempered and scurrilous. Once, uncharacteristically, the garda was heard by one of his sons to retort, 'I'll whitewash his brains against that wall,' as Jim loudly cursed him and his wife from across the public road. The nephews threatened to sort Jim out but were prevailed on to refrain for the sake of family harmony and local discretion.

In later years, his mother and stepmother both

dead, Jim lived with Kathy and his aging dad in the family home. His half-sister paid for renovations to the house, replaced the thatched roof and put in indoor plumbing. Then Kathy died, but his father lived to the great age of ninety-eight.

Time passed. Living totally on his own now, Jim when he wasn't in the pub, had a drink by his meagre three sod turf fire. During a harsh winter storm, a close-by farmer checking on him, found him tipsy and half frozen, dancing solo to Ceili Hour on the radio. The same neighbour offered to buy the farm at a reasonable price, but Jim arranged with a solicitor that in return for a plate of dinner to be delivered each day, a cute hoor neighbour who could not be depended on, would get the house and the land on Jim's death.

This, of course, did not go down well with his sisters and was much to the chagrin of his many relatives. Eventually Jim's health failed, and he went into the county Old Folks Home in Castlebar.

When word came of Jim's death, in 1978, his nephews at first refused to come home to attend. Their father insisted that for their mother's sake, they must turn up for the funeral. Dutifully they donned black, appeared at the church and lined up to carry the coffin. I believe Uncle Jim had a very uncomfortable journey to the nearby grave side, the coffin shook so much in response to the whispered ribald comments passing among the pallbearers. He is buried in Killeen graveyard in the family plot.

But strangely, no mention of him appears among the inscriptions on the tombstone above

Elizabeth Hannon

him.

I only wish I had met him.

R.I.P. Uncle Jim.

The Rise
Póilín Brennan

Of blood and bone,
and upturned cups
The petals glas 'is iontach.
Glistening drops on spiral stems
embracing pear ó chroí.
How willow séimh in wisdomed waves
he speaks of calmer days.
As seen before; it ebbs, it flows
a morning song – comh binn.
Oak leaves respond,
the magpies jeer; a raucous of the jester.
Who dares to sleep, stir soul dúisaigh!
Soft breeze speaks;
is mé d'anam.

The Bird
James Conway

The man shone in a dot of distance
his daily walk a panacea for loneliness
with the sand sticking to the soles
of his shoes, his gait leaning towards

the sea, it's then he heard a squeal
in the clouds, a bird flew high
it was long and pale, its wings out,
fighting with the wind, but it faltered

wobbling, circling now in the sky
tracing it with the journey of his eye
the man knew the bird was dying.
This great godly being, winged

in the colours of sea, sand and earth,
a vagrant maybe, wombed to be
alone on the ocean's edge. Like
a star falling from the night...

it was down, crumpled in a dune
the man bent to touch its feathers
soothing silk to his skin. Against
the odds, it was breathing, a cooing

mirrored memories, heightened
as shadows of its own purest time.
After in the warmth of his surgery

The Bird

the man gave it breath, linked little

sticks to its legs, bandaged its wings
and watered it, gave it life in newness
kept it near, whispered silent hymns
to the music of its heart, listened

saw it roll its head, happy, safe,
knowing it itched to fly.

Life Story
Molly Fogarty

All fluffed up, eyes shuttered, legs awry,
beak to the wall beneath the feckless window
and shivering until the whispering monster
comes
carrying a pool of hope and fear.

Shutters fly open:
tiny, round, young eye, to sad, old, monster eye.
Shutters close.

Later, monster hands put creature and slopping
pool amongst the warm top-stones
of an old wall where the breeze tickles baby
feathers in the laughing sun.

And later again, much later, monster fingers
spread perfect wings,
flinging out and long, whispering:
Go! Fly! I can't but you can...
And yet, all the same, all the while, over and
over, again and again,
creature glides silently, gracefully earthward,
unresisting, as if in wonder,
as if loving the coming embrace of the gentle,
mossy, forget-me-not grass.

At dusk, monster tucks creature into a padded
hanging basket

Life Story

cradled within the quiet twist and drape and
smell of wisteria.
And, in the morning, it's finally flown the nest.
It's gone.
Although its flattened, empty body lies there,
although – wings or no wings, young or old – it
couldn't escape lockdown either.

The Life and Times of Jimmy Mullins

Mary Rose Tobin

I was sitting in the Control Room when the phone jangled, breaking my reverie. The authoritative voice on the other end belonged to the Director-General.

'We need to admit a new boy from the courts.'

'We're at full capacity,' I replied, frustration creeping into my voice.

'You'll need to make space,' he retorted. 'Don't sigh down the phone at me. Send somebody home.'

'But there's nobody ready!' I bleated.

'That's too bad. You're in charge while I'm not there. These are the kinds of decisions you need to get used to making.'

He hung up.

I've worked at St Dermot's Secure School as Deputy Director, since it opened in March. My job? To provide a semblance of structure, discipline, and, if possible, a touch of compassion to the thirty teenage boys under our care at any given time. Navigating a ship through a never-ending storm.

It had been a long day so far, and I didn't need this. I needed to focus on the Christmas Mass and Dinner.

The Life and Times of Jimmy Mullins

For the boys of St Dermot's, Christmas was a big deal. Minding our charges was tough at the best of times but keeping their spirits up over the festive season was particularly hard.

'Will I be getting out for Christmas?' was the constant chorus. When the answer was 'No', even the most hardened boys would lash out, kicking lockers and spewing strings of curses. Dublin mothers insisted that their sons had special Christmas clothes; as one of them put it, they had to be 'new from the skin out'. If a boy didn't have permission to go shopping with his mother, she somehow managed to bring his new outfit to the school.

We rarely saw the fathers.

The boys did their utmost to push the staff to their limits. In school they threw pencil cases, overturned desks, and tossed books to the floor. Any staff member who tried to engage in a positive way had their words thrown back, laced with expletives. In the dining room, the housekeeping staff were driven to despair with food smeared on walls and trays discarded carelessly.

Yet, every Saturday, without fail, the visiting room was full. Mothers in worn-out coats disembarked from old buses or walked long distances, carrying special treats and hope in their eyes. They hugged their sons, ignoring the stares and whispers, their love evident and unwavering.

The air in the assembly hall, today doubling as a chapel, was thick with anticipation. The smell of pine needles and the sweet scent of the candles burning on the altar mingled with the

Mary Rose Tobin

smell of the boys' freshly laundered clothes. The sound of their shuffling feet and the occasional whisper of a joke filled the room. The warmth was palpable; light from the candles and the Christmas tree shimmered in the boys' eyes.

The priest stepped forward, raising his hands in a gesture of peace. As the first notes of the hymn began, the boys joined in, filling the room with a resonance that was powerful and unexpected. Their voices wavered at times, but the strength of their collective spirit was undeniable.

Glancing around the room, my eyes met those of a woman with tear-streaked cheeks. She clutched a handkerchief tightly, her gaze fixed on one of the singing boys. The handmade jumper and the carefully wrapped gifts at his feet spoke of a mother's love, a desperate wish for her son to feel the joy of Christmas, even in these circumstances. I fought back my own tears.

The priest nodded, and one of the boys, Jimmy, approached the altar. He clutched a piece of paper in his hand. Taking a deep breath, he began, 'A letter from St Paul to the C-C-Co...' He paused, collecting himself. Whispers of encouragement drifted from the back. With a determined look, he tried again.

'A letter from St Paul to the C-C-Co-Coalminers.'

The room was silent for a heartbeat, then a burst of spontaneous applause erupted. Boys cheered, some shouting words of encouragement, others clapping him on the

The Life and Times of Jimmy Mullins

back. The pride in his effort was spontaneous, their collective support evident.

As Jimmy shuffled back to his chair, I caught his eye.

'Well done,' I mouthed.

***

The Director-General's phone call had left me in an invidious position. When dinner ended, I made my way back to the Control Room, situated between the admin block and the secure unit. A reinforced glass window provided a clear view into the boys' quarters. On a central desk, radios and walkie-talkies stood ready in their chargers, their soft beeps intermittently breaking the silence. Alongside, a pegboard held an array of labelled keys, each representing a door or gate within the school. The polished floor reflected the room's overhead lights, while CCTV monitors on the wall continuously showed various parts of the school. It was the heartbeat of the institution, a blend of vigilance and order.

My mind turned to Jimmy. Though far from ready to go home, he seemed like the best option. He was a meek boy, well behaved, and out of place here. Had life dealt him a different hand, he might have been at home with his family now, preparing for Christmas with his brothers and sisters.

I contacted Tony, the social worker, urgency evident in my voice. Retrieving Jimmy's file, I dialled his home number, but the line echoed with a monotonous buzz. I quickly reread his admission report to refresh myself on the

Mary Rose Tobin

details. It was a catalogue of deprivation and abuse. His mother, dealing with addiction and personal demons, would sometimes disappear for days, leaving Jimmy and his siblings to fend for themselves. In his early days at the school he had flinched at the slightest touch, his eyes always darting around as if expecting danger from every corner. When he first arrived, having been convicted of a minor offense, I talked to him about it. I asked, 'Jimmy, why are you here? What did you do?' He replied, 'Well, me charge sheet says I was 'interfering with the magnificent.' I remembered this as I flicked through his file and saw the actual charge written on the sheet – 'interfering with the mechanism of a mechanically propelled vehicle.' I couldn't help smiling.

Despite his past, Jimmy had shown remarkable resilience. Over the last few months, he had begun to find his place, building trust with a few of the staff and forming hesitant friendships with some of the boys. It was heart breaking to even consider sending him back to the environment he'd so narrowly escaped.

As the Director-General's words echoed in my mind, I felt torn. The pragmatic part of me recognised the logistical challenge; we couldn't take in another boy without making space. But my heart resisted. These weren't just numbers; they were lives, each with its own story and potential. Who was I to be playing God, choosing one over the other?

Looking at the CCTV screens, I watched as Jimmy laughed at something one of the other

The Life and Times of Jimmy Mullins

boys said, his smile a brief moment of genuine happiness amidst the institutional gloom. The weight of my impending decision pressed down on me even more.

I walked down to the common room. The warm glow of the TV lit the area. Jimmy was engrossed in a snooker match.

'Jimmy,' I beckoned, voice softer than intended. 'You're heading home.'

His face lit up, eyes wide.

'Really? Now?'

There was a quiver of excitement in his voice.

We moved into the bedroom corridor. I unlocked his door and together we gathered his belongings. The familiar scent of his room, the muted colours of his clothes, the soft shuffle as we packed – every sensation amplified, a stark reminder of the impending void.

Tony waited by the van, its engine murmuring softly. As I said goodbye to Jimmy there was a catch in my voice. 'Stay out of trouble,' I whispered.

'I...I...I'll do me best,' he promised.

Later, as darkness settled, Tony returned, his face etched with exhaustion. He began recounting the evening's events. When they reached Jimmy's home, the curtains were drawn and an eerie silence hung in the air. After what seemed like an eternity, a neighbour peeked out, her face creased with irritation. 'She's in the pub,' the woman shouted, pointing an accusing finger in the direction of O'Reilly's. Tony nodded, thanking her, and took the boy to look for his mother.

Mary Rose Tobin

The pub was noisy, dimly lit, and reeked of stale beer. They made their way through the crowd, searching for Mrs Mullins. When they finally found her, she was hunched over a table, a drink in her hand, surrounded by raucous friends.

There were no tears of joy, no tight embraces. As Jimmy approached, she looked up, her expression a complex mixture of surprise, guilt, and pain. Her eyes barely recognised her son. Jimmy's hopeful gaze met hers, searching for a hint of affection. Her indifference, exaggerated by her intoxicated state, wounded him. The boy could barely hold back the tears.

'But I had to leave him there.' Tony went on. 'I bought him a glass of orange. What else could I do?'

***

The days that followed were a whirlwind of Christmas preparations. I found solace in the familiar traditions – wrapping presents, decorating the tree, and baking treats that filled the air with delightful aromas. The shimmering lights and cheerful carols almost managed to push the memory of the school and the boys to the back of my mind.

Having some long-anticipated leave, I decided to travel up to my parents' house in the countryside. It was a welcome break, a place where the cacophony of the city was replaced by the soft whisper of wind through the trees and the crackling of the log fire. For the first time in months, I felt genuinely relaxed, the weight of responsibility temporarily lifted. I lost hours sitting by the window, watching

The Life and Times of Jimmy Mullins

snowflakes dance in the winter air and feeling grateful for the homeliness and love that surrounded me.

But this peace was short-lived. One evening, while enjoying a glass of wine and browsing through a local newspaper, a headline caught my eye and cut through my festive haze. The familiar warmth drained away, replaced by a chilling realisation that the world outside was far from the idyllic scene in which I had lost myself.

> ### Teen Tragedy
> *Boy Perishes in Blaze, Companion Narrowly Survives*
> In a horrifying accident that has sent shockwaves through the city, a 14-year-old boy named as Jimmy Mullins became the victim of a catastrophic blaze that reduced an abandoned building to ashes last night.

The article painted a grim picture. Two runaways frequented an abandoned building with a few other local kids. It became their hideaway – a place where they'd share stolen cigarettes, recount tales of their escapades, talk and dream. The building was decrepit but offered a semblance of shelter and camaraderie.

The weather turned particularly bitter one evening. With nowhere else to turn, Jimmy and his friend decided to light a small fire to keep

Mary Rose Tobin

themselves warm. They believed they had things under control. They weren't to know the house had been used as a makeshift car-repair shop. The vicinity was laden with old rags, empty petrol containers, oil cans and other flammable debris. Within minutes, the entire place was alight. The other boy managed a harrowing escape, but Jimmy was tragically trapped.

My stomach lurched. Memories of that recent Christmas Mass flooded back. I pictured Jimmy's face, innocent and vulnerable, stammering at the scripture reading. The laughing eyes from the CCTV screen haunted my mind.

Christmas cheer was replaced by a heavy silence. Festive lights appeared dimmer; their twinkling overshadowed by a profound sense of loss. Overcome with a potent cocktail of guilt, despair, and accountability, I drained my wine glass and reflexively reached for another bottle.

Churching
Kathleen Phelan

It is quiet here.
The music has been
turned inside out.
And wisps of incense linger
on the haughty air.
It is all too smug.
My stillborn baby
and pangs of childbirth
count for nothing.
I have been to Calvary
twelve times
and the stations of the cross
are dripping with my blood.
I choose purification
Above shunning....

The priest greets me,
His rheumy eyes lingering on my face
like a hungry lion stalking its prey.
I hold the dripping candle.
Kneel for the ceremony.
An exorcism without evil.
'Now a prayer
for your baby
in Limbo,' he says.
With a wry smile, I comply.

A True Mayo Man

Anne Murray

Growing up in the shadow of Croagh Patrick, young Paddy would often climb The Reek. From the top of the mountain, he would look out at the three hundred and sixty-five islands in Clew Bay. The islands looked like sparkling diamonds in the distance, but there was only one that held his interest: Dorinish Island, a forsaken piece of land barely twenty acres in area. In 1967, John Lennon purchased Dorinish Island. He and Yoko had plans to build a cottage there as a hideaway retreat, far from the madding crowd.

A child of the swinging sixties, Paddy was infected with Beatlemania for most of his teenage years. He would tune the radio to the medium wave 208 Radio Luxembourg every time he got the chance. Records were a luxury, but he did odd jobs for the neighbours and saved his money. His communion money and confirmation money was all spent on Beatles records. His most prized possession was the Beatles' very first single 'Love Me Do'.

He longed for a pair of Beatle boots, but these were expensive and, anyway, wouldn't last too long walking the fields, mountains, and bogs around Murrisk. Often on his way home through the fields in his wellingtons, he would kick the cow dung and watch the dung beetles scurry for

A True Mayo Man

cover and think to himself, 'Will I ever get to see a real Beatle in the flesh?'

Beatle boots may have been out of his reach, but it cost nothing to grow your hair. His mop-top haircut was the cause of many a row.

'I'll get the scissors to that hair,' his mother threatened. 'You'll be expelled from school if you don't cut that hair.'

Nothing could break his resolve to look like a Beatle. When he looks back now at old photos, he gives thanks as he takes out his hanky to polish his head.

'At least I can say my hair never went grey,' he boasts.

Paddy looked up as the helicopter flew overhead on the day that John Lennon brought Yoko Ono to see the island, but he couldn't get a glimpse of his idol.

Time moved on, and so did Paddy. His dream of seeing the Beatles faded. After finishing his Leaving Cert in Castlebar, he started university in Galway. In 1972, he was the proud holder of a J1 student visa to work in the USA for the summer. Paddy got the dream job: a barman on a ship cruising from New York to the Gulf of Mexico, visiting the Bahamas, Jamaica, Puerto Rico, and Barbados.

First, there was a week's induction when the crew got to know the ship: first class, second, VIP areas, and crew quarters. Senior crew could access all areas, but Paddy was not one of them. He had clearance for first and second class only. He had done a bit of bar work in Galway at weekends, dispensing mostly pints of Guinness and bottles of cider. Here, he had to learn how to

43

Anne Murray

mix cocktails with exotic names: Sex on the Beach, Mojitos, Blue Haven, Bloody Mary, all the different whiskies, gins, and brandies, along with the appropriate mixers and glasses. He was appointed to The Windjammer Bar. As the name suggests, it was on deck and could be a bit windy at times. This didn't bother Paddy, a proud Mayo man; he was used to the rough weather around Clew Bay. He wasn't a bad singer. The punters loved him. He regaled them with a few old Irish songs like 'Danny Boy', 'Galway Bay', 'Skibbereen', and 'The Old Bog Road' as he filled the drinks.

He doubled up as a DJ in the afternoons and played music from Top of the Pops, playing tunes such as 'American Pie' – Don McClean, 'The First Time Ever I Saw Your Face' – Roberta Black, 'Lucille' – Kenny Rogers, 'Stand By Your Man' – Tammy Wynette. He enjoyed life in The Windjammer. But being an inquisitive Mayo man, he was eager to get a pass into the VIP area to see how the other half holidayed. When he got the chance, he slipped into the restricted area. A 'hippie' type sat alone, sipping a coffee. 'Enjoying a bit of peace?' says Paddy. The 'hippy' turned to face him. 'I detect an Irish drawl, a neighbour,' answers the hippy in his best Liverpool accent. For the first time in his life, Paddy was speechless! It couldn't be... It was... It really was... His idol, John Lennon. 'A nearer neighbour than you think,' quipped Paddy, recovering his composure. 'I'm from Mayo, just across the water from your Dorinish Island.'

They chatted for a few minutes. Paddy told him all about Croagh Patrick and about his record

A True Mayo Man

collection. As he made to leave, John stood up and shook his hand. 'Great to meet a fellow Mayo man,' he said. 'I'll see you around the ship.' 'Not likely,' says Paddy. 'I don't always have access to this area. Thrilled to meet you, though. A dream come true.' As he made his way back to The Windjammer, he was wild with excitement. He was bursting to tell his passengers about who he had met in the VIP lounge, but that would be disloyal to his 'friend' John. For the rest of the cruise, he shook the cocktails with more vigour than usual and, late at night, treated his guests to a few Beatles favourites. The guests smooched around the floor to the sound of 'Let It Be' and 'The Long and Winding Road'.

When the last day of the cruise arrived, Paddy couldn't bear to leave the ship without one last encounter with his idol. As the ship docked at Pier 88, the Manhattan Cruise terminal, he made his way to the departure gate. His luck was in. There, waiting to disembark, was John and his entourage. As Paddy approached, John saw him. 'My neighbour, the Irish man,' he called, stretching out his hand. Over John's shoulder, Paddy spotted a Limo pulling up on the dock. 'Sorry, John. Can't stop now,' says Paddy, indicating the Limo on the dockside. 'My car is just pulling up on the dock. Great to meet you, though. Here's my number. Keep in touch.'

Sweet Citrus Fruits

Deirdre Anne Gialamas

Once they stopped looking
They found each other
He had barely searched
If truth be known
Trepidation stalked his path
He trod perhaps too slowly
To bump into the fleeting one
She tore about
A March wind
Never pausing for the gentler
Side of life
Always dashing forth with
Projects which when completed
Gave birth to bigger plans.
At market in the fall
He wanted lemons but
Could not find them ripe enough
She whirled by arms laden
With juicy citrus fruits
And tripped in a most ungainly
Manner when one errant
Yellow fellow fell
He swept her up in awe
At the abundance of lemons.

New Girls

Anne McManus

My phone is ringing. It has to be my mum; it's 7 am. I love her dearly but not at 7 am on my day off. I'm tempted not to answer but she'll just keep on calling. What on earth is bugging her so early in the day? Should I sound sleepy or cheerful? I opt for sleepy.

'Hi Mum!' Two loud yawns. 'What's so important; it's my day –?

'You'll never guess who's on Facebook this morning.'

'Mum! It's my day off, it's too early. Couldn't it have waited?'

'No, no. Take a look now. It's that girl you were friends with in school — Emma, or was she Emily? She was a nice girl.'

'Mum, she was anything but nice.'

'What do you mean, Tracey? I always thought she was a nice girl.'

'Mum, I never told you the truth about Emily.'

'What do you mean?'

'Look, I don't want to go into that right now, Mum. It was a long time ago.'

'She's not Emily now. She's Jessica Aylward.'

'Okay, Mum, I'll check it out later. Have to go now.'

Anne McManus

Curiosity gets the better of me so I go into Facebook; and sure enough there she is — Emily; but she and I were never really friends. It's definitely Emily from our school days. We lost touch as soon as the Leaving Cert was over. She seems to have disappeared from our small town, never coming home. Now I'm wide awake.

Emily/Jessica has become an overnight success in London in G.B. Shaw's play *Saint Joan*. Her once blonde long hair is now black, cropped like a boy's. She's much thinner than I remember, almost skeletal, dressed in what appears to be a suit of armour; not bright and shining, more like something she put together with whatever was available to Joan on the farm where she grew up. There are rave reviews — this is Joan of Arc as a feisty young girl, rough in speech, brimming with conviction, nothing saintly about her; a performance of sheer physicality, towering over the men who condemn her.

There will be no going back to sleep now, so I lie in bed thinking back on how Emily and I first met.

We came to our new school on the same day, into third year; she from a boarding school, me from the city. She made no secret of the fact that she had been expelled, having had several warnings about her behaviour. The final straw was when she was seen in a pub with a much older man. Me, I was the child of a single mum who left the city to escape my violent father. For years she had put up with his drunken violence, finally getting a barring order which he constantly breached. Eventually, her social

New Girls

worker advised a move away from the city, which she found very hard to accept as all her family were there. In the end she left for my sake. I was glad to leave that life behind, to look forward to a new school, new friends. I was fourteen at the time, old enough to realise that my father was never going to reform, that he had damaged both me and my mum. We never wanted to meet him again and we never did.

Emily and I arrived into the school just after Christmas. The Head introduced us as 'The New Girls'. From that day on we were known as The New Girls. Because the others in the class had already formed friendships, Emily and I were thrown together. We were polar opposites. Emily brimmed with self-confidence, me, shy, diffident, but thankfully, smart. I guess Emily made a friend of me because the other girls hated her. Simple as that.

Her family lived in a large old house a few miles outside the town and were said to be rich. They had racehorses, which my mum said was a sign of wealth among country people. Me and my mum lived in a small council house in an alley in the town. To me it was heaven after the cramped, damp city flat where there was endless noise and often screaming. It was common to see drug dealing going on in the so-called playground at the back of the building.

Mum and I were so nervous about going to a strange place, but we knew there would be no life for either of us as long as Dad kept coming back to our house, often drunk, looking for money, shouting at Mum, hitting and kicking her. We had to leave.

49

Anne McManus

I settled into school much better than Emily which surprised me, she being a local. However, from the first day, Emily made it clear that coming to the local school was a come-down for her. She made no friends in our three years there – unless I counted. She had been sent at the age of ten to the school her mother had attended in England. Small wonder that she didn't fit in with her posh accent and her snooty attitude. She had been expelled for sneaking out at night to meet some local man, much older than her.

I visited her house on a few occasions where I met her father but never her mother. Once I asked where she was, but Emily shrugged saying, 'She could be anywhere; America, Italy, France, maybe England.' Her two older brothers were away at college so there was only Emily and her dad in this huge house. He seemed old to have a fifteen-year-old, but it emerged that he was her stepfather. Emily never spoke about her real Dad so I guessed he could have died or just left his family. Her stepfather seemed a nice man, calm, quiet, shy perhaps. However, she was rude to him and shouted rather than spoke to him. Emily was indeed a handful. From what Emily told me about her mother, I realised that she too was brash and loud, just like her daughter. I wondered why she married such a quiet man — money maybe.

I got a good Leaving Cert, Emily did not. That summer she disappeared from the town. Meanwhile, I got into college in Liverpool, graduated in business studies, and now work

New Girls

in a small importing company in Liverpool. I have a good life here, have made friends, and still play basketball. Mum comes to visit quite often. We get on well together. I wish she could meet a new partner, someone who would be kind and loving. She deserves it.

Because of Emily's success in London, I often find myself reflecting on my school days. I don't understand this, as Emily is not significant to me these days. It was ten years ago and thankfully I've moved on. There was one major incident that got me into big trouble. We were playing a basketball match against a visiting team. During the closing minutes, I missed a shot, causing us to lose by three points.

'Stupid cow, no brains like her streetwalker mother,' yelled Emily.

I just went for her, had her on the ground, thumping her in the face. The ref had to tear us apart; then the principal arrived and hauled us into her office. We spent the rest of the day there in sulky silence. Mum and Emily's stepfather were sent for. Mum turned up as I knew she would. He didn't.

I liked the principal; she was fair if strict but this time I was disappointed.

'We must make allowances for Emily,' she explained. Well at that Mum lost it.

'Allowances for that spoiled, stuck-up brat with her trendy clothes, more money than is good for her, driving around without a license, speeding through the town.'

She grabbed me by the shoulder and marched me out of the office. We were suspended for the rest of the week — two days.

Anne McManus

When Mum finally got me to tell her what had caused the row, she was all for going up to confront Emily and her stepdad. Somehow, I persuaded her not to. At that stage, there were only a few months left to the Leaving Cert. I just wanted to get on with my schoolwork.

***

Now and again I check Emily on Facebook. Plaudits on all sides. The production will be going to New York. The London critics are certain the production will take Broadway by storm. Mum follows Emily on Facebook, sending messages almost every day. We had a row about this when I told her she was acting like a silly teenager over the latest boyband. She didn't call me for a whole week after that.

Now she's hinting at coming to Liverpool so both of us could go to London to see Emily on stage. After the show, I would introduce myself to the security staff as an old school friend of Emily's, which would be sure to gain us access to Emily's dressing room. We could even get her autograph! Mum was on a roll alright.

Then the bombshell fell.

'Hi Tracey, it's Mum. Have you seen the latest about Emily?'

'Mum, I'm not interested. Surely by now you...'

'Emily is taking her stepfather to court for child abuse.'

'What!'

'You heard me, Tracey.'

'I don't believe her. She'd do anything for attention, Mum.'

New Girls

'No Tracey. You've got it wrong. It seems playing Joan of Arc has given her the courage to take the case.'

'Mum, Emily sees herself as a martyr, like Joan of Arc. She's let this whole thing go to her head.'

'Well that may be, but she's determined to go ahead although the stepfather has denied all accusations.'

'Has her mother made any statement?'

'Oh yes indeed. She says it's all about – revenge because of her awful childhood. Calls her an ungrateful bitch.'

'Mum, I think I should go to the police here in Liverpool or else get in touch with the Guards in Dublin.'

'Keep out of it, Tracey. Much and all as I admire Emily, they're not our kind of people. They would swallow you up in court.'

'But Mum, I feel what she's doing is all wrong. I can't believe her stepfather is guilty of such a crime.'

'Well, you'll have to make up your own mind Tracey. With any luck the whole thing will fizzle out. Talk to you soon.'

I need to look at my motivation. Do I honestly believe Emily's stepfather is innocent or am I taking his side to get my revenge on Emily for her nastiness to me all those years ago? The worry of it is keeping me awake so maybe I should listen to Mum.

I agonised for another few weeks, took Mum's advice, and am sleeping better now.

The case will be heard in six months' time. I will certainly attend.

53

Worlds Apart
Josephine McCann

Susan

They took me out of that cellar and put me into a large room, a very large room. There were about forty people in there, dying, if not already dead.

The overwhelming stench from within these four walls stalled her other sensory perceptions. The sound of a steel bolt being slid across an iron door soon brought her back to reality.

Locked in and far, so very far, from the safe security of home.

A red-bricked two-bedroomed townhouse, in Crooks Lane, Chilhurst, Kent, has been her home and refuge for the past five years.

With a shudder, Susan realised that she had just now eased her cheek off the cold belly of the same corpse she had tripped over.

'What the...?'

As she looked at the body stretched out on the floor, the sound of sombre silence returned and echoed around the dark dismal chamber.

'Well, I'm not going to be another one,' uttered Susan in a quiet resolute voice.

Taking a few deep breaths was her usual way to calm down, but now she struggled to regain an element of composure. Determined to focus,

Worlds Apart

Susan held her hands to her eyes and attempted to take a shallow breath...

...felt her pounding heartbeat calm a little and

...ease back from crashing into her ribcage and

...as a little space for composure emerged, questions surfaced.

Where am I?

Why am I here?

Who has put me in here?

Struggling for answers, she heard the sound of a cat's screech, quickly followed by running, the sound of feline paws scratching on a metal grid in the room. Susan was now distracted with thoughts of her own cherished cats, awaiting her return.

Right now, though, a more important question was demanding an answer.

How the hell do I get out of here?

As her breathing regained its rhythm, harmonising with the cruel throbbing pain in her head, Susan lifted her damp hands to discover them covered in blood, her own blood, sticky, almost dried.

That warmth she felt clinging to her legs was blood, her own blood, oozing from a large gash on her thigh.

Despite the increasing intensity of her headache, her mental fog started to lift. The events of the day so far were little by little revealing themselves to her, yet Susan didn't like to be reminded.

How could I have been so stupid?

Josephine McCann

Khawla

Khawla appeared to be looking out the window as the train's engine eased the locomotive out of the station, but in fact, she was examining the reflection of the passengers, passing up and down the aisle of the carriage. She did not want to risk direct eye contact with any of her fellow travellers.

Dropping her weary eyelids, she heard the seats opposite being sat upon and luggage squashed under legs. The surge of passengers soon subsided, and the sound of the engine started to strike a steady rhythm.

Khawla was no longer pretending to be asleep. A deep sleep had taken over, the deepest she'd had for a very long, long time.

Susan

'Anybody see Susan?' asked Meagan.

'Last I saw of her was she was heading to the Ladies, hoping to sneak a vape before boarding the train,' Kathryn offered.

'Ah, she always does things at the last moment,' wailed Sally, glancing around to see how many of her group of eight friends had managed to source seats on the overcrowded train.

'What chaos!' exclaimed Meagan, almost immediately forgetting about her missing pal.

'Just our luck, the airport being closed. All we wanted was a weekend away and now we have to return over land and sea to England.'

'I'd heard there was a refugee crisis in Europe, before we left England,' murmured

56

Kathryn. 'I know now what they were talking about.'

The early morning call was beginning to take its toll, and she was drifting to sleep and thinking of Alan's warm welcome, waiting for her on her return. She knew from past experience that, having taken the day off work, he would have a special meal ready with a thoughtful bottle of wine for them to enjoy while she shared with him the news of her weekend away.

Khawla

As Khawla slept, her mind suppressed not only the memory of the arduous walk she had endured for the last sixteen days, but also the terror that was felt as she and her fellow refugees tumbled over the troubled terrain.

Just for now, she wasn't recalling the murders she had witnessed before her home was ransacked, or the horror of watching her younger sisters being raped before being dragged away.

But buried deep in her subconscious was her most recent and most daring act.

Days earlier, Khawla had lost contact with the other refugees from her village, but she wasn't alone in seeking shelter. She was never without companions, as groups, big and small, were converging, all going in the same direction.

As they approached the train station, Khawla's eye caught sight of something glistening in the morning sun – a Michael Kors medallion on a black handbag. Her brief

57

Josephine McCann

flashback to a similar bag she had herself only three years ago, was quickly erased as the security forces stepped in, herding people to cram deeper into the heaving crowd at the train station.

Moments later, while the stiff security guard was shouting at an elderly man to stand up, Khawla managed to slip away to the Ladies' Room. There, catching her breath, Khawla was startled to see on the shelf the same handbag that had caught her eye only moments earlier.

Looking around, she saw nobody else, and only one booth door was closed. Clearly visible in the open bag, she saw a passport, air tickets, a wallet, and train tickets.

SURVIVE, her only thought.

With the contents safely in her pocket, Khawla dumped the handbag in a litter bin outside the Ladies' Room, and then quickly distanced herself. Showing the train ticket to the collector, Khawla boarded the train and took her seat to freedom.

The Postcard
James Conway

You would have picked
the postcard up from
a street seller, the colours,
the peace, saying this is
heaven.

Yesterday, I picked it up
from a scattering of memories
its gloss face quiet amongst
the pain of your loss...

'Come on,' they said 'it is time
for the sea,' once in you felt
the fear, 'further' they cried
and that's all you remember

their Nordic figures, tall, shining
bringing you to the shore, you cried
wanting the song of the blackbird
in echoes the flicker of home

caught your sweet spirit, 'blackbird'
you sang in sleep and its feathers
came to you, giving you mystery
but how I wished I was there!

The Patience of Ordinary Things

Mary Hodson

'Ah shure, why would you bother buying those firelighters?' my father often mused. 'Look, all the kindling you need is right there in the hedge. Firelighters were never part of your upbringing.'

I always held a deep admiration for my father, who, undeterred by the allure of modern conveniences and gadgets, continued to gather kindling. He meticulously dried the sticks in a vintage USA biscuit tin, nestled in the oven of our trusty Stanley 8 range. These carefully preserved pieces ignited our day's first fire.

Each morning, before anyone else, my father would rise and switch the wireless from Radio Luxembourg to Radio Éireann. He would anticipate, almost with a child's eagerness, the day's first news. In contrast, my nights were filled with the latest tunes from Elton John, The Rolling Stones, and Cliff Richard on Radio Luxembourg. My father had little patience for such music, facing the daily chore of retuning to Radio Éireann. A familiar ritual to my still-drowsy ears was the wait for the seven o'clock news: Beep, Beep, Beep, followed by the headlines.

The Patience of Ordinary Things

Lying in bed, I would soak in the comforting sounds from the kitchen: the news broadcasting on RTÉ Radio 1, the clearing of ashes, the crisp snap of kindling as it was broken into smaller, manageable pieces. Then came the striking of a match, its brief flare igniting the prepared kindling. On stubborn mornings, a slice of an old Wellington boot would join the kindling, the peculiar aroma of burning rubber mingling with turf smoke permeating the house as my father coaxed the fire to life.

The seasoned turf, saved by our family during the summer, combined with the kindling and the wellie piece, ensured the fire's endurance throughout the day. It was a source of warmth, from dawn till dusk, in a house devoid of back boilers. The kitchen, radiating this warmth, stood as the heart of our home.

The kettle's reassuring whistle, the simmering cabbage and bacon, and the bubbling pot of Kerr pinks – these were the soundtrack of our daily life. Homemade soda cakes – brown, white, and currant – would bake in the oven, all part of the simple yet profound rhythm of ordinary things.

That same fire also nurtured life, warming day-old chicks in makeshift incubators and reviving premature calves swaddled in recycled Odlum's flour bags until strong enough to re-join their mothers. These animals, essential to the seasonal cycle of our farm, contributed to the family's yearly sustenance.

The fireside was more than a source of warmth; it was a hub for family gatherings.

Mary Hodson

Political debates, local news, and light-hearted teasing of relatives who returned speaking with newfound accents – all these unfolded by the range's glow. Sometimes, for extra warmth and comfort, we'd open the fire-box and oven doors, the latter serving as a toasty footrest on chilly winter evenings.

Despite the advent of convenient firelighters and logs, the memory of collecting kindling remains vivid. My father's dedication to this ritual, amidst rapidly changing times, is a constant reminder of the enduring beauty found in a life of simplicity.

Maidin

Póilín Brennan

Hanging clothes, cold toes, the call of morning
on flapping wings ar gaoth an lae.
Refrains of chirp-rustled harmony
in candle flicker at break of day.

How soft and soothing morning spideog
'aft aisling caoineadh – Badb did come.
Mo shuan síochánta in breath returned
h'eis a d'imigh an bandia caoineadh – slán.

In love and honour, glacadh iomlán
of myth and ancestral presence here.
In visioned message: i mo dhúiseacht
fáilte file, sí, 'is cailleach.

Breaking Altitude
Frank Fahy

Every Halloween, there's a whisper of magic in the Texan air, a subtle rustle through the yellowing oaks that foretells adventure. But this year was different, the whisper turned into a shout, as Roy, my daredevil of a husband, decided it was the right time for our kids to break altitude.

Roy was a skilled helicopter pilot, his heart divided between the skies and us, his family. He believed that the horizon broadened perspective and fostered bravery. It was a chilly morning, the sun just winking in the sky when he disclosed his plan over a cup of coffee.

'Carol,' he said, his eyes sparkling with excitement, 'I've got a surprise for the kids. I'm going to take them up in the chopper this Halloween. Imagine the view, the whole of Texas stretching out below, pumpkin patches dotting the earth. It's going to be epic.'

I choked on my coffee, the words stumbling out in a rush. 'Are you out of your mind, Roy? That's against every rule in the book. It's dangerous. They're just kids.'

'Oh, come on, Carol. I've flown in the worst of weather, in dangerous zones. The sky is home to me. And I've done this a thousand times. What could be better for my kids than to experience what I do, see the world from above?'

Breaking Altitude

I knew arguing with Roy was a futile endeavour when his mind was set, but the mother in me couldn't let it go. 'Roy, they are just eight and ten. What if something goes wrong? I can't even bear to think about it.'

He came over, his hands gently holding mine. 'I promise you, nothing will happen. I'll keep them safe.'

His reassurances did little to quell the storm brewing within me. But I saw the gleam in Emily and Timmy's eyes when they were told about the trip. Their laughter filled the room, their imaginations soaring high with each passing hour.

The day arrived much sooner than I wanted. As they stepped out, the morning sun cast long shadows on the driveway. Roy, in his army fatigues, looked like a hero from the kids' bedtime stories, ready to whisk them away on an adventure. Emily and Timmy couldn't contain their excitement, their faces bright, cheeks flushed against the morning chill.

I stood there at the doorway, the house suddenly echoing with silence and the emptiness gnawing at me. The hours dragged on, my mind imagining the worst. I busied myself in the kitchen, the aroma of pot roast filling the house, a feeble attempt to drown my fears.

As the day bade adieu, casting long, haunting shadows, the distant thud of the helicopter blades cutting through the cool evening breeze reached my ears. My heart leapt with a blend of relief and joy. I paced around the kitchen, the seconds stretching out like

65

Frank Fahy

hours until at last, the front door swung open and in they burst, the setting sun casting a warm glow on their faces.

I hugged Emily first, her tiny frame engulfed in my arms. 'Oh, my baby, you're back,' I whispered, my words trembling against her soft hair. She giggled, squirming out of my embrace, the thrill of adventure still dancing in her eyes.

Timmy jumped into my arms next, his laughter ringing through the quiet evening. 'Mama, it was like touching the sky, like holding the clouds in our hands!' His words tumbled over each other, the excitement bubbling out. I held him tight, his innocent joy a balm to my jittery nerves.

Roy stood there, a smug smile curving his lips, his eyes meeting mine with that 'I told you so' gleam. 'See Carol, nothing to worry about. It was just a little Halloween magic, a tale they'll tell for years.'

I wanted to hold onto my annoyance, but the relief washing over me was too strong. I let out a shaky laugh, 'You're incorrigible, Roy.'

We walked back to the dinner table, the children's chatter filling the rooms that had been hauntingly quiet just a few hours ago. They raced each other to the table, their laughter echoing through the hallway.

As we settled down, the aroma of pot roast mingling with our tales of mundane and adventure, I felt a peace I hadn't felt the entire day. The clinking of the cutlery against the plates, the sparkle in Roy's eyes, the children's animated gestures, it was a snippet of normalcy I had craved.

Breaking Altitude

Just as I was beginning to relish the ordinariness of the moment, a loud knock reverberated through the room. With a sinking heart, I opened the door to find two stern-faced officers. The world around me blurred as their words cut through the evening haze, shattering my reality into a million pieces.

'We're sorry to inform you, ma'am,' the officer said, his voice a distant echo, 'There's been a crash. Your husband and children...'

I Will Sleep
Seamus Keogh

The unholy Demon's cowl melts
Like black candle wax, it spills,
Pouring over a frightened mind.
I am inconsolable; I am doomed.
The running tide recedes in flow
Leaving rock pools in its wake
With green weed covered stones,
Spiny crabs, ugly crustaceans,
Weaving between sea and shore.
Secret shells vacated, scattered,
In sand troughs 'mid sand ridges.
I will sleep deeply and long tonight.
There is no rush to wake to pain.
Death – its curse cannot be undone.

The Site

Joanne Dowling

I passed this road many times before when I was going somewhere else. I never had reason to come here. But today, we saw a sign on the main road advertising a site for sale down this way. Along the route, there were lavish dwellings and spacious lawns, the driveways big enough for two, even three cars. I imagined us living here, a swing on the front lawn, a puppy running around, and children's shouts coming from the back. Then we were in a tunnel. Trees had come together above us, blocking out the sun. In the car, the sound of the engine became more pronounced. Moments later, we were out again, out to a shaft of sunlight and open fields. Sheep roamed, and a small herd of cattle sheltered under an oak tree.

'This is so lovely,' I cried, 'it's just like home.'

'No sign of a house,' said Brian from the driver's seat.

'It must be up there beyond that hill,' I said.

'Will we take a look?'

'Of course we will.'

We went up a long narrow lane surrounded by fields and hedgerows. We came to the crest of the hill, and I looked back to see the view, but I only got a quick glimpse of trees. Now we were on the other side, spinning downwards, ahead of us a bungalow, a typical farmhouse

Joanne Dowling

with a turf shed and stables and cows wandering in a paddock. The car slowed. Then I saw the small sign attached to the fence beside the front wall.

'There it is,' I cried, 'that's the site there.'

Brian stopped the car.

'Oh, it's absolutely fantastic,' I cried. 'Brian, what do you think? Don't you think it's the best one we've seen so far?

Brian looked at me with a smile. 'It's a fine site,' he said, 'I have to agree with you there.'

'It's massive.'

The big square must surely be more than an acre. There were no other houses in the vicinity except for the farmhouse. I imagined where our house would be and the garage to the side and the trampoline at the back, the swing of course, at the front. In the distance, there were open fields, and I could see myself walking through them, the puppy at my heels.

'Beware the dog,' said Brian.

'What?'

I stared at him. He was pointing at the house.

A black dog had appeared in the front garden. His front paws rested on the wall, and he was glaring at us contemptuously. Then, the silence at an end, he began to bark. The sound became louder and more intense. Bile assembled around the mouth dripped onto the wall. I stared at the dog, transfixed. Then, sensing a movement, I looked up and saw a man standing on the path, a bit of a smile playing around the corners of his mouth. I waved, but there was no response. Surely, he should be calling off his dog. The man was still

70

The Site

one moment and then he moved in a flash. He strode down the footpath and, lifting his right leg, kicked the dog in the stomach. The barking became a howling. The dog, bereft, stumbled away without giving his master a look. I leaned on the wall and tried to breathe. Brian grasped my hand.

'Should we just go?' he whispered.

'No, no, we can't. Think of the site.'

Brian sighed.

'Tis the site ye're after, is it?' the man inside the gate said, his gravelly voice mocking in tone.

'We're just driving around looking at a few,' said Brian.

'Sure, come in for a cup of tea and meet the mother,' the man said. 'Are ye from these parts?'

'No. We're from Galway.'

'Come on in anyway,' he said. He stood back, holding the gate open.

Brian looked at me. 'Will we go in for a few minutes so?'

I rushed ahead of him and headed for the front door. Inside, blinded by the darkness in the hallway, I had to put out a hand to feel the way. There was a wall, the hinge of a door, and then the door itself. I came to a large room with a kitchen table near a window and a television on a small table. A sofa had a brown rug thrown over it. Beside the range, a woman sat on a chair. This must be his mother. She wore a shiny apron. She looked at me nervously and gave me a smile that vanished soon after. The smell of stale food mingled with cigarette

71

Joanne Dowling

smoke, and there was also a whiff of the stable that might have come from outside or from his clothes.

'That's the mother,' he said. 'Sit down there now. Ye'll have a cup of tea.'

'Oh no, thank you,' I said, looking at the dirty mugs on the table.

'You'll have a cup of tea now, and that's it. We're very hospitable around here.'

He sat down at the head of the table and took up a knife and fork. Food left on the plate must be the remnants of his dinner. Fat had congealed around chunks of bacon, and the cabbage and potatoes were meshed together. He plunged the fork into a bit of the meat, topped it with the potato, and thrust it into his mouth.

'Please don't go to any trouble,' I said.

'No trouble at all.' Grease oozed from the pores of his skin, made visible by the sliver of light beaming through the net curtain. He beckoned to his mother and then looked at Brian. 'Sit down, will ye, for God's sake,' he said, his mouth full. 'Ye're giving me a crick in my neck looking up at ye.'

I sat on one of the chairs, and Brian sat on another.

'That site is a beauty, isn't it?' the man said.

'It is,' said Brian, 'and is there's planning permission?'

'You betcha.'

His mother, who had gone to a glass cabinet, was fumbling with the catch.

'Can you not open it?' he bellowed.

She didn't make a sound.

72

The Site

'I declare to God,' he said and slammed his knife on the table. 'I have to do everything around here myself.' He scraped back his chair from the table. 'What's wrong with bloody mugs?'

I got there before him. She stood back so I could reach the cabinet. At first, I too struggled to open it, but then the catch gave way. Then, about to return to my seat, I saw that she was waiting there without moving. She pointed at the china cups and nodded at me encouragingly. Then I understood that she meant me to remove them, that she wanted me to help her. I took four cups that had roses on them. I brought them to the table. She came behind with four matching saucers.

'Oh for God's sake,' the son said, 'we're only having a cup of tea. Mugs would have done us.'

'I'll get the milk out the back,' she whispered. 'The water is in that kettle there on the table. You can put it on to boil.'

'Lord God, you're making a big job out of a cup of tea,' he said, heaping the remains of the bacon onto the fork. 'I can tell ye now, I've had a lot of interest in that site. It won't be there long, I can tell you that.' He crammed the food into his mouth.

'Yes, I suppose there's a lot of interest,' said Brian, giving me a quick glance.

'You'd want to hurry up, that's all I can say,' he said, looking at my husband. 'What's the name?'

'Oh...my name is Brian, and this is Cathy, my wife.'

'Brian who?'

Joanne Dowling

'Finnerty.'

'From where?'

'Renmore. But we've lived abroad for years.'

'Terry is my name. Terry O'Malley.'

I busied myself boiling the kettle and adding tea to the teapot. She settled the cups on the saucers and added spoons. From a drawer, she removed a doily that looked handmade from crocheted lace and put it on a china plate. On this, she arranged a circle of chocolate digestives. Then she went back to the range and sat again on her chair.

The two men were talking about the water scheme. Unfortunately, there was no scheme at present, Terry said. However, one was on the way, and we were the lucky ones because by the time we would have the house built, we'd be connected. He himself had to have a well constructed. Of course, we would have to pay to join the scheme.

'Twenty-five thousand,' he announced, 'that's what I want for the site, and that's what I'll get.'

'That's an awful lot of money,' said Brian.

The figures ratcheted up in my head. I looked at the man sitting in the corner. Inwardly, I cursed him. I looked at her. Her eyes rested on the floor. When I passed her the tea, she beckoned for me to put it on the range. She smiled. I poured for the rest of us. Brian lifted a biscuit and took a bite of it.

'And I'll want about five thousand in cash,' this Terry said, grasping the china cup with huge fingers. 'Ye can give it to me outside the solicitors' office.

The Site

'Is that so?' said Brian, looking at his biscuit.

'Do ye have any kids?' he asked.

'Yes, we've two boys and one girl.'

She gave Brian a mischievous gaze, like a mother looking at her little boy home from school whom she had to humour to do the few jobs around the place. She looked at the range, and her finger dabbed at the corner of it. I saw my mother before me. The same look, the same nervousness, the same apron. Any minute now, she'd get up from that chair and go to that dresser for her prayer book.

I rose from the table.

'Do you not want another biscuit?' said Terry. 'Be God, there's plenty there.'

'No, thank you, Mr O'Malley,' I said, heading for the door, determined now not to look at her again.

'Where are you going with your Mr O'Malley?'

I kept going. As we went down the footpath, I heard Terry mention the solicitor's office and where it was located and where we'd meet beforehand. He wanted the money in an envelope, the five thousand. I got into the car and so did Brian. Terry shouted for the dog. He waved as we drove away.

A Falling
Mary Hawkshaw

There was a time.
A time of love and peace.
A land of olive groves, and leafy vines.
Skies of blue, and sunlit streets.
Butterflies with wings of gold,
Fluttered round our children's feet.
Then,
Evil came in human form.
To our peaceful land
in a deep black swarm.
No mercy has she by her side.
She swoops down to shatter lives,
And roars through blackened skies.
We run, but we can't hide.
Her sword of death shines in our skies.
And plunges deep to pierce our sunrise.
In darkness she spreads her vengeful wings,
And in homes where children's songs once
filled our dreams.
Our hearts now cracked, our blood runs cold.
Our shrouds in death she firmly folds.
In darkness we die alone.
The world has turned to stone.

Chubb

James Conway

'Come on Chubb, let's head for the shelter,' Richard says running through the rain along Dun Laoghaire's pier.

'This Irish rain is so oppressive,' Chubb replies.

'You're beginning to sound like old Whitley, our English teacher,' Richard answers.

'Wasn't there some bit of Irish in him?' Chubb asks.

'Apparently he had a Galway great grandmother, but he's English through and through.

'Anybody but him, old man, please,' Richard replies.

The two teenage boys continue to run in the heavier rain.

'What about a bite to eat?' Richard asks.

'Great, I'm starving,' Chubb replies.

Chubb looks famished. His thin English face shows traces of an unpleasant journey across the Irish Sea. His pencil figure is drenched.

'See that cafe over there, Rita's, they do a lovely mixed grill,' Richard says.

Chubb's eyes light up. 'Sounds terrific, but is it expensive?'

'Not a bit. Have you a shilling?'

James Conway

Delving into his pocket, Chubb retrieves a shilling with the King's head on it and announces, 'I've got one.'

Seated in Rita's cafe, the two boys order their meals and chat.

'Lord, that tea is good,' Chubb sighs with relief.

'All the way from India, China or some such exotic place. It's so much better than the pee we get at school,' Richard concludes.

'I suppose they have to satisfy their customers. Does a tidy little trade, our Rita, that's her over there at the till,' he adds, eyeing her up.

'Do you know her?' Chubb enquires, then thinks everyone knows everyone in Ireland.

'Yes, mother comes here occasionally, she brought me when I was younger, always an ideal haven from the rain,' Richard says.

'Rains a lot in Ireland doesn't it?' Chubb prompts.

'It's the favourite pastime, that and getting sloshed,' Richard replies.

'Anything bizarre to report on your crossing?' asks Richard, yawning.

'Oh, just the usual motley crew; drunks, people snoring and the odd shy girl looking sheepishly at one.' Their conversation continues.

'Pass the mustard that's a good fellow, will you?'

'English or French?'

'English of course, what would I want with that froggy stuff?'

'We eat French at home, It's cheaper sometimes.' Richard admits. He considers it time to annoy Chubb.

Chubb

'Good God, Chubb, you've sailed through those chips.'

'I love chips, proletarian I admit, but that's how it is, the greasier the better,' Richard's little English friend replies, his thin face almost swelling into normality.

'Gives you pleasure, does it? A trifle sexual?' Richard laughs. Chubb peers at him in a strange way.

'All simple fun, sex and chips,' Richard continues to jibe. 'What a strange little boy you are!' He edges on.

'Oh do shut up Dickie that woman is beginning to stare.'

'All right, let's be civilised. Almost ready to go? Don't forget your raincoat, me auld English mate.'

After paying, Richard hands two *Fox's Glacier Mints* to Chubb. Rita always had a few extras for customers.

Chubb replies, 'That's rather posh for an Irish cafe after a fry.'

Richard's mind has wandered. He still hasn't convinced his mother to give him the money to join the Theatre Company travelling to Egypt the following summer. He has been offered a prop's position, much roughing stage bits around and the possibility of sleeping with some of the chorus girls. Some chance, he thinks. Mostly Catholic, afraid of getting pregnant. Still he is determined to go, even if he has to kill for it. He wonders if his surgeon father would cough up. Such parents, dour, tight and rude!

Chubb is concerned about Richard's mental state, but he loves his trickery. Now, it will soon

79

James Conway

be time to land in Booterstown, to meet his volatile, unstable mother. Last time he visited all was well for a short time, having tea and cucumber sandwiches served up. Fine china cups held strong tea, but he couldn't help noticing the cups had a series of cracks. The wallpapers showed signs of staining and one of the legs of the mahogany hall table was dented like it had encountered a tank. Otherwise, a lovely vase full of large, colourful flowers brightened up a carefully disguised house. Hints of a minor war having occurred patched themselves about one's vision. Was daftness to be the order of the day?

After their meal, Chubb and Richard catch the tram to Booterstown. On the way, a sign says 'Boycott British goods' while some latent loyalist had apparently stamped an image of 'Old Vic' onto it giving it the distinct sense of duality. Further on towards the coast, bathers bounce about in the lively water. Slim girls in one piece bathing suits and fat men, their liberated stomachs hanging down as they enter the waters dash about. Couples frolic. Children scream at the shock of the ever cold Irish sea. The waves come and go, white necked of foam.

'Let's play a game,' Richard suggests. 'As we approach the next Catholic church, you must rush to bless yourself before the tram full of Catholics do it.'

Chubb looks at Dickie perplexed. 'Wouldn't that be provocative?' he asks.

'Yes, but what fun!' Richard replies.

'You're a bit of a pagan proddy alright. Aren't you?' Chubb responds.

Chubb

In no time a tiny church appears. Above it an ornate cross lurches towards the sky. 'Ready now little Chubby?' And with that the long and bony hand of Richard crosses himself in lightning speed.

'Sweet divine!' One lady exclaims. 'You blessed yourself with your left hand,' she says in horror. Richard explodes into furious laughter. He gets steely looks. Chubb is afraid to laugh.

'Laugh up, why don't you man?' Richard encourages. Mutterings grow, insults are close.

After getting off the tram, they arrive at Saint Helena's Road and Richard presses the bell. The door is opened by a large woman with wild, red hair wearing a green dress which is by now tight. Her verdant eyes meet Chubb. She takes his coat, shows him in, while a tasty maid sets about getting tea. Richard smirks!

The Write-on Christmas

To celebrate the Festive Season, we encourage our Write-on members to write stories and poems with a Christmas theme.

Every year, our authors respond with some fantastic memories from their own childhoods or with fictious events with a holiday motif.

The following pages contain some examples of these memoirs, stories and poems. We hope you enjoy reading them.

Ho, Ho, Bloody Ho!

Joyce Butcher

Christmas 1988 was supposed to have been the perfect day. Val and Will were new parents of one child, eighteen months old. Val was pregnant with their second, due in May. Their little darling was a very precocious, active child, excited by the Christmas tree, the lights and decorations.

As Val wandered out to the living room, the lights on the tree twinkled. It was early morning. The view from the large windows was of snow-capped mountains that ringed the desert valley in which Palm Springs sits. Despite the mountain snow, down in the desert, it was going to be another warm day. Val made a cup of coffee and some toast and headed back to the bedroom to mind the little one.

Her dearest husband, who insisted on keeping their ball of excitement in the bedroom with Val until he'd set the scene, went out to the living room to put the finishing touches on what he'd hoped would be a storybook Christmas morning. Val had already placed the presents around the tree well before their daughter was awake. She and Val waited in the bedroom, as Val tried to keep her occupied with a bit of toast and her favourite toys.

Much to Val's surprise, the wait was far longer

Ho, Ho, Bloody Ho!

than she'd expected, and there were worrying noises coming from the living room. A thump, a few errant expletives, and finally, the high-pitched whine of the smoke alarm.

Val opened the door and yelled out, 'What on earth are you doing? Are you okay?'

'I'm just, well... Damn! I can't get the smoke to stop!' his lordship yelled back.

'Do you want me to help?'

'No, I'll get it. Just wait,' he said.

The smoke alarm continued, which was very distressing for Ms Eighteen-Months-Old. The smoke had made its way back to the bedroom, and she was crying. Val opened the windows and did her best to comfort her. It didn't help.

He-who-tried-his-best finally admitted defeat and came back to the bedroom looking frantic, saying, 'I don't know what to do!'

Handing him their little bundle of screaming distress, Val went out to the source of the smoke. She yelled back, 'Did you forget to open the flue? We haven't used the fireplace in a year or so.'

He didn't have to answer, it was obvious he'd forgotten. Val used the fire poker to reach up and open it, which allowed the smoke to flow up the chimney. With the doors and windows open, it still took quite a few minutes for the smoke alarm to stop.

Father and daughter were in the living room by now, Little Miss 'I Love Christmas', once again besotted with the tree, the lights and decorations, then spying the wrapped presents. She quickly forgot all about the smoke and the noise; it was all systems go!

Val took charge of the little present-seeker as

85

Joyce Butcher

her beloved showed off the big surprise for his family – he'd bought a video camera, so he could record the magic of Christmas for all time. This was the first Christmas their daughter could really participate in the festivities. He thought one day, she would love seeing this 'video window' into her own past.

Somehow, they got through that very stressful and eventually, very sweet morning. The major efforts both parents had made paid off, even if Little Miss would never remember them.

***

Recently, Val gathered several old videos and had them transferred onto DVD format. That particular Christmas video was rather short, but brought back so many memories. It went something like this:

Husband: (from behind the video camera) Stand over by the tree so I can see her reaction to it all.

Wife: (through gritted teeth) Like this? (Annoyed look on her face as she stands beside the tree, while Little Miss reaches out for the decorations and the lights).

Husband: Wave to me! Come on little one, wave!

Wife: (Staring at the camera, looking as if her head is ready to explode.)

Little One: Hi Daddy! (At least someone is happy – blowing kisses to her daddy).

Husband: Let's let her open some presents. Pick that big one over there!

Wife: Okay! (flat voice, fake smile)

Little One: I want to open it. I want to open it! (rustling, ripping, unwrapping) Oh! Oh! Look,

Ho, Ho, Bloody Ho!

toys! (exclamations of delight on seeing the toy kitchen)

Husband: Wait, I didn't get all of that, can you put the paper back on it?

Wife: What? Are you crazy? (silence, followed by more paper rustling as more boxes and bags are ripped into, then fading to black...)

Val could clearly recall the seething annoyance she'd felt at the smoke, the waiting, being stage-managed. Not that it mattered, as the little one loved it, the dramas long forgotten. Soon all that was left was the happiness, presents, and a pile of paper and ribbons. A delighted child and her parents shared a salvaged morning which the parents laughed about later.

Unfortunately, none of that made it onto the video because the camera battery wasn't fully charged and cut out after that first couple of presents.

Christmas in Renvyle
Thomas MacMahon

Light dimming on a Connemara road.
Mirror lakes reflecting patchwork hills.
A toasty turf fire to banish the cold,
And a warm drink to ignite Christmas thrills.

Bright eyes and broad smiles from old friends,
Hugs, kisses and Christmas bells,
Food and song, happiness ascends.
That's Christmas in Renvyle House Hotel.

The Turkeys
Mary Hodson

My mother took immense pride in her flock of turkeys. 'They were hard reared,' she would say. At the beginning of spring, she would set off the five miles on her Raleigh bike with her clucking turkey hen in a cardboard box, its beak and tail protruding. This memory is particularly vivid as we watched her set off down the lane from the house on this delicate and important journey. We were particularly intrigued, as we were not told why the turkey hen was going for a spin on Mother's bike. Why was this turkey hen so special and going on an unexpected trip?

Sometime later, the turkey hen hatched out her baby turkeys. It was an exciting time in our house; we watched as the baby birds broke through their shells and tumbled out, their feathers wet. They were very unsteady on their feet. These baby turkeys were treated with great care, brought into our house, and either placed in an incubator – a little box with straw and a red lamp for heat, assembled in the back kitchen – or if very delicate, they were placed in an old USA biscuit tin under the range for extra heat. They were fed scrambled eggs initially, and when they were stronger, special baby turkey food. They stayed in the homeplace until they were strong enough to move out of the incubator and into

Mary Hodson

bigger pens in the outside turkey house, which was kept warm, clean, and only housed the turkeys.

They finally grew stronger, with white, majestic feathers, their necks held high. The turkey hens trotted around making little fuss, while the turkey cocks, with their long necks and distinctive turkey combs, made their presence known with their loud chuckling sound, dominating the farmyard. The hens and chickens gave right of way around the farmyard to these majestic birds.

The flock of twenty-four turkeys was well treated and cared for. They maintained a dominant position in the farmyard. They were fed twice a day and admired by the neighbours. Mother took immense pride in her turkeys. There was an unspoken, unwritten competition among the women of the neighbourhood regarding who had the best flock of turkeys. Indeed, it was an accomplishment to successfully rear a flock with a few thirty-pounders in time for Christmas. Most years, Mother had many 30lb turkeys to boast about to her neighbours.

These birds served many purposes; they were sold to help fund Santa and Christmas treats for the family, with the biggest one roasted for the family Christmas dinner. I also knew with happiness and expectation that Christmas was imminent when the ritual began of preparing the turkeys for posting to relatives in the UK for their Christmas dinner. This preparation started a week or two before Christmas. The turkeys for posting were identified, fasted, slain, and plucked skilfully by our parents without breaking the skin

The Turkeys

of any of the birds. They were then hung in the hallway for a day before getting them ready for posting. A sturdy cardboard box was sourced and lined with newspaper. Then, the bird, carefully wrapped in greaseproof paper and brown paper, was placed in the box, covered with strong brown paper, secured on all sides with Sellotape, and then tied with strong twine, the knots sealed with red melted wax.

My mother would write the address, including the all-important postcodes of the recipients, many times on the box. Then it was labelled with the sender's address. In all, four boxes would be posted to the UK with the Christmas turkeys and a few treats added to the parcel for the families. Our father took immense pride in preparing these boxes, and my mother was always anxious to get the parcels posted in time to avoid any Christmas delays.

This exciting part of Christmas preparations ceased when the UK had an unexpected postal strike. On that Christmas, all the turkey boxes arrived in the New Year with untold damage to the enclosed birds. Christmas that year was spoiled. This upset my parents, and they no longer posted the turkeys abroad.

However, my mother continued for many years to rear a great flock of turkeys for her large family and friends, all of whom received an oven-prepared turkey at Christmas. We look back on this time with very fond memories of the special place the turkeys commanded leading up to and including Christmas.

Death in December
Geraldine Warren

How can I not matter
When I know each and every sinew
Every nook and cranny
Every crease and fold of you
the taste of you

The way your eyes twinkle
When I made you laugh
The way you push your glasses
Back on your nose
The smell of you

Who knows you like I do?
Do I still not matter?
Did you not serve my head upon
a platter?
Does she matter more than I
Was there nothing left to save?
Do you know how much I crave
Your voice?

Death in December

You had the choice
You took a unilateral decision
My pleas met with blank derision
Do you even remember
that cold bleak day in December?
'It's over' you said
And left me for dead.

I just didn't matter.

The Magic of Believing
Mary Rose Tobin

It was the first day of the Christmas holidays. Ricky, a lively 12-year-old with a head full of tangled curls, was playing football with his friends on the green outside their house. Their roars and shrieks could be heard from a mile away.

In the middle of the game, Ricky felt something odd in his mouth. He reached in and pulled out his loose tooth. Holding it triumphantly, he yelled, 'Yay! Two euros!' The other boys, a mix of ages but all older than him, exchanged glances before bursting into laughter.

'Two euros? For a tooth?' one boy, Sean, said between chuckles. 'You're not serious, are you?'

Ricky nodded enthusiastically. 'Yeah! The tooth fairy always leaves two euros under my pillow.'

The laughter intensified, and a few of the boys started to jeer.

'Ricky still believes in the tooth fairy!' shouted another boy, Liam, his voice laced with mockery. 'Grow up, Ricky,' Sean added, shaking his head. 'There's no such thing as a tooth fairy. That's just a story for babies.'

Their words hit Ricky like a cold wave. His joy turned to embarrassment and hurt. He ran home, tears streaming down his face, feeling the sting of their ridicule.

The Magic of Believing

Bursting into the kitchen, he found his mum. She was on one of her rare days off from the hospital. They happened less and less often since Dad left. She looked up from unloading the dishwasher.

'Mum!' Ricky shouted, his voice shaking. 'You lied to me!'

She turned, surprised by his outburst. Seeing his tearful eyes and the tooth in his hand, she looked puzzled. 'What do you mean, Ricky?' she asked gently.

He confronted her, his hands trembling. 'And that letter! You wrote it, didn't you?'

He was referring to a letter she had left under his pillow once, pretending to be from the tooth fairy, chiding him for not brushing his teeth enough.

Mum knelt down, trying to meet his eye. 'Yes, Ricky, I wrote the letter. And... there's no tooth fairy,' she admitted, her voice filled with regret.

'Why did you lie to me?' he demanded.

She tried to explain, her voice quivering. 'It wasn't a lie, love. It was a bit of magic, a story to make childhood more special.'

'But I believed in it! You made me look stupid!' Ricky wiped his eyes, feeling angry and foolish.

'I'm sorry, Ricky. I never meant to make you look stupid,' she said, her eyes brimming with tears.

He whispered, barely audible, 'I wish you hadn't.'

She watched him struggle with a dawning realisation. His emotions boiled over. 'I suppose next you'll tell me you're Santa too?'

Mum's heart sank further. 'Oh Ricky,' she

95

Mary Rode Tobin

began softly, 'Santa Claus is a wonderful story, a beautiful tradition... but he's not real, not in the way you think.'

'Not real?' Ricky repeated, his world upending. 'What are you saying? No Dad; no tooth fairy; and now, no Santa?'

'Parents tell these stories to make Christmas special. But it's really us. We put the presents under the tree,' she explained.

'So, all of it... the whisky and Christmas cake, the carrot... it's all just... a lie?' he asked, struggling now.

'No, not a lie,' she insisted gently. 'It's a story we share, a way to celebrate the spirit of giving and love.'

'Why didn't you just tell me?' he asked, not knowing whether to be sad or angry.

'We wanted to give you the joy of believing in something magical,' she said softly.

'Mum, it's not just about believing in Santa. It's about... about trusting what you say,' Ricky, near to tears, replied.

'I'm so sorry, Ricky. I never wanted to hurt you or betray your trust.'

'I suppose... I'll just have to grow up, then,' he shouted. Ricky stormed out of the kitchen, slamming the door behind him. He could sense Mum's heartbreak in the silence that followed.

He pounded up the stairs, his emotions raw and overwhelming. He banged around his room in a storm of anger and disappointment. Then, he came back down, holding a PlayStation console. 'This! This never worked properly!' he yelled at Mum. 'You said we couldn't send it back to the North Pole. Now you can just go and exchange it

The Magic of Believing

for one that works!'

Mum, trying to stay calm, replied, 'I can try to fix it, Ricky. Or we can see about getting it exchanged.'

'You said Santa's elves made it, but they didn't, did they? It's just a broken game from a shop!' His voice was thick with anger and betrayal.

'I'm sorry, Ricky. I know this is hard for you. I really meant to get you another one but there's been so much going on,' she said, her own emotions swirling.

He looked at the console, then back at her. He placed the console on the kitchen table, his shoulders slumping. He felt awful for shouting. He knew she was just as upset as he was. He knew she had to work so hard to keep everything together for him and his brothers.

'I just want things to be the way they used to be, Mum,' Ricky said quietly.

Later, Mum asked him to go for a walk with her. 'If you want to talk about that Santa stuff, forget it. I'm okay now,' he said.

Mum sighed, looking into his upset eyes. 'Still, we need to talk,' she insisted.

As they strolled towards the green, Mum began. 'Ricky, when you asked, "Are you Santa?" that was a good question; and the answer is no, I'm not Santa. There isn't just a single Santa.' Ricky listened, the crisp air around them seeming to stand still.

'I fill your stockings with presents and wrap the gifts under the tree, just like my mum did for me, and her mum before her,' she continued. 'And yes, your dad used to be part of it too, when he was here.' The path beneath their feet

97

Mary Rode Tobin

crunched with every step.

'One day, you might do the same for your children. And you'll love seeing their joy on Christmas morning. But doing it doesn't make you Santa.' Mum paused. 'Santa is more than one single person. He's a team of people, mums, and dads, all over the world. Santa's work is about teaching children to believe in something they can't see or touch. It's a big, important job.'

Her words hung in the air, confusing Ricky. They walked in silence for a bit, the sounds of the neighbourhood distant and muffled. 'Now you know Santa's secret. When we're young, he fills our hearts with joy. As we get older, we help him carry on the tradition. People like your dad and me, and now, you.'

Mum looked at him, her eyes full of love. 'We're on Santa's team, Ricky. We help with his impossible job. Santa is love and magic. He's hope and happiness.'

Ricky felt a lump in his throat as her words sank in. 'So, no, I'm not Santa,' Mum concluded. 'But I'm part of what he represents. And now, so are you.'

After a pause, Mum spoke again. 'Ricky, I have a big job for you tomorrow. Will you come into work with me?'

'What for?' Ricky asked.

'We're having a Christmas party for the children on the ward. We have presents for all of them,' Mum explained with a hopeful smile. 'Santa is coming to visit and I'd love you to be his helper.'

His expression changed from curiosity to surprise. 'Me? Helping Santa?'

The Magic of Believing

'Yes, you,' Mum said warmly. 'These kids need the spirit of Santa, more than most of us. They could do with some hope and joy.'

'What would I need to do?' Ricky inquired.

'Dress up, help hand out presents, talk to the kids a bit, make them smile,' Mum said. 'Bring a little bit of happiness to the ones who might be feeling sad.'

'I suppose... that's what Santa's really about, isn't it? Making people happy?'

Mum smiled. 'Exactly, Ricky. And by being there, by giving some of your time and care, you're keeping Santa's work going. You're keeping hope alive for the sick children.'

Ricky stood a bit taller. 'Okay, Mum. I'll do it. I'll be Santa's helper.'

Mum reached out, squeezing his hand gently. 'I'm proud of you, Ricky. You're going to make those children very happy.'

In a Picture
James Conway

That Christmas rusts
in a picture, the frame
silvered in a winter sun

the bodies are fading on
crumpled paper, the faces
like little orbits nearing

the coldness of the moon,
that day before closing, their
year coming to an end

all dressed up for Church
and crackers, all fired up
to live forever, to live for fun

the men were back from
England, the Queen's head
on their pockets of notes

and on floors spewed with
freshly smelt sawdust where
feet tapped into a whirling tandem

there's life still in that picture
her violet hat courts a velvet
ribbon, an ancient pin smiles

In a Picture

gold in the scuts of winter sun
she's standing in an awe where
happiness is hypnotic...

that day dancing with frost
crunching into secrets
silvered in a winter sun.

Nativity
Elizabeth Hannon

The choir rustled pages as they flicked through their hymn books for the *Adeste Fideles* the organist was rehearsing. They were preparing for the Christmas Tridium of masses. One beautiful, but quite elderly lady, glanced down from the organ loft at the traditional Christmas crib erected to the side of the altar. It looked the same. The star of Bethlehem at the peak of the thatched stable roof slightly askew; the shepherds and animals; Joseph and Mary and... the baby Jesus. It was so long ago but the memories flooded back....

Carmel was getting fidgety. 'Sit still,' hissed Mum. The seven o'clock mass on Christmas morning in the Claddagh church seemed to go on forever. She had made her first communion this year, so she was fasting. Starving more like. Mum and dad insisted that they attend mass first, then breakfast, then the opening of Santa and Christmas presents. 'The family tradition,' they said.

Her two younger brothers were misbehaving but only she got scolded by Granny who lived with them since she moved from Clawinch Island. It was not fair. The boys could do nothing wrong but as the eldest she was expected to 'set an example' for the others. At last, they all knelt for

Nativity

the final blessing, and the choir and congregation were merrily singing *Joy to the World.*

'Let's go up, see the crib, and say, "Happy Birthday," to Baby Jesus,' said Mum as she took Seamus and Joe's hands. Dad helped Granny up the aisle. They all waited behind the crowd that had gathered to admire the crib. Carmel saw a small gap and crawled under one man's legs to get to the railing. The teacher had told them all about Mary and Joseph. No room at the inn. The shepherds. The terrible bad King Herod. The angels. Everything. The shining star gleamed on the faces both in the crib and those gazing in awe at the scene.

The fearsome looking ox was lying still beside the shepherd holding a tiny woolly white lamb. The manger bed the baby lay in looked hard and cold to Carmel. The straw was scratchy, and he had no blanket! But the baby's big eyes looked straight at her and seemed to smile sadly. No one else seemed to notice that the baby was cold. Really cold. Not even Mary, his mother. Carmel shivered.

Her dad tapped her shoulder and pointed to the door. Mum and Granny were talking to some of the women sitting at the back left-hand side of the church, wearing the traditional Claddagh shawls. They all agreed – the young Dominican priest who gave the sermon was lovely.

'Wish I knew as little about life as him, God bless him,' said Granny, 'but yes, he's lovely all the same.' The family all moved towards the car, stopping to greet neighbours and returned friends not seen for some time. Carmel hung back. She turned and ran quickly to the front of

Elizabeth Hannon

the now almost empty church. Opening her new red coat that she got for Christmas, she quickly tucked baby Jesus inside. He was heavy, much heavier than any of her dolls. Creeping past the statue of Saint Martin, who seemed to look at her strangely, Carmel whispered, 'It's okay. I'll take good care of baby Jesus. I promise.'

Settling herself into the car's back seat, she tucked Baby Jesus under her feet. When the others arrived, Granny sat in the front passenger seat, Mum and the boys squeezed in beside Carmel in the back. Joe whined, 'Carmel is taking all the space, I'm too squished.' Mum took him onto her knee and promised breakfast and sausages would be ready and waiting for them – and then it would be time to open the presents!

In the rush to get into breakfast, no one noticed Carmel slipping into the sitting room. Baby Jesus would be warm and snug behind the sofa with cushions and her coat wrapped around him. Maybe he would like some toast?

Santa was brilliant that year! Seamus got a train set, Joe a toy circus and Carmel a beautiful doll and pram with a pillow and blanket. Her sock hanging from the mantelpiece had a mandarin orange and a pack of animal playing cards. It was not till all the presents were opened and admired that Mum, picking up the discarded packaging, noticed the breadcrumbs and the red coat on the floor. Ready to scold, she stooped to pick it up and discovered what was under it.

'Oh my God! What will we do? She's stolen the Baby Jesus!'

'Carmel what have you done? What in heaven's name were you thinking of?'

Nativity

'He was really cold. I only wanted to be kind to him. It's his birthday!'

Dad's face was really a picture. He was shocked, amazed, half smiling, slightly proud, trying to be stern, needing to support his wife.

'Come, Carmel, we must take it back before the Prior discovers it's missing, or you will be in serious trouble. I know you meant well, but he must go back where he belongs. You can put one of your doll's blankets about him.'

Back at the church, the Prior was at the door to the sacristy, looking towards the crib, scratching his head. Still watching, he said nothing as a little girl, snuffling through tears, carried the infant Jesus statue, up the central aisle. She solemnly placed it back in the manger, kissed it and arranged a pink blanket about it.

Her dad bent down and gave her a hug. 'Come, there's a big girl. Let's go home. Its nearly time to carve the turkey.'

Winking at the Prior, with a big grin on his face, he said, 'All's well that ends well. Merry Christmas.'

The Colour Of Snow

Brenda Silke

Under healing white light,
A snowflake is gently laying herself down on her
destiny bed in anticipation.
Lady Dolomite's femininity revealed in pink
hues under the rays of the midday sun.
My outstretched hand believes it can touch her
essence.
Gazing at her beauty, I find myself
contemplating upon the memory of stone.

The Blanket

Mary Hodson

The package, a gift from America, found its way to our doorstep just in time for the inaugural Christmas in our new house. Excitement buzzed through our home, not only for the festivity but also for the imminent arrival of our firstborn, due in a few months. The parcel, adorned in glossy brown paper with secure edges, proudly displayed distinctive American stamps – stars and stripes marking its origin in North Dakota, a Northern state where some of our ancestors had settled following the waves of emigration from our homeland in the late 1800s and early 1900s.

In the 1901 census, our ancestral home housed thirteen residents – daughters, Margaret, Mary, Kate and Hanora, and sons Thomas, James, John, William, and Andrew. The household, reflecting the era's Irish family structures, also included Catherine, the sister of its head. Mary and Kate, accompanied by their brothers, William and James, would later embark on a journey to the United States, seeking a better life and leaving behind their family and ancestral home. Kate met her life partner, an American, in Boston and subsequently settled in North Dakota.

Mary Hodson

This was a bleak period in Irish history. The aftermath of the great famine was still evident. Between 1845 and 1851, one million emigrated while a further one million died. Ireland lost a quarter of its population during those terrible years. It has been estimated that over six million Irish people emigrated to America since 1820. The west coast of Ireland was the worst affected. In Mayo, the population declined from 389,000 in 1841 to 274,830 in 1851.

Emigration to North America, in particular, was seen as an opportunity to support families back home and to improve the life of the emigrant. A distinguishing feature of this emigration period between 1856 and 1921 was the large numbers of young single women who emigrated to the United States. In the years 1886 to 1905, the ratio of male to female was 175:100. A startling statistic demonstrates the continued effect of this mass emigration. In 1991 the population had reduced to 110,000.

As a child, our father shared tales of his aunts and uncles who undertook this significant migration, tinged with a touch of sadness for those who never returned. The 'yanks' as they were affectionately called, became mythical figures in our family narrative, their stories conveyed with love, affection, and a hint of wonder. Despite the geographical distance, the stories of those Irish emigrants in America lingered in our hearts.

The Christmas parcel, a connection to those early emigrants, arrived from Kate's direct descendants. One day, an airmail letter, bearing the unmistakable American stamp and script,

The Blanket

arrived on our parents' doorstep. It was from Harry, Kate's son, who sought to reconnect with his Irish family, particularly his first cousin, our father, Andrew. In 1969, sixty years after Kate's emigration, Harry and his American wife, Dorothy, visited the ancestral home. The excitement was palpable as they unveiled a letter they'd found hidden behind a picture following the death of his mother, Kate. The letter offered details, names, and addresses of her family in Ireland and a vivid description of her life at the homeplace. She had never shared this information during her lifetime with her American family.

The emigration experience was fraught with challenges, and sometimes compelled Irish emigrants to conceal their identity, even altering their surnames to evade discrimination in the post-famine United States. Kate, influenced by her brothers, changed her Irish surname, guarding her Irish heritage to protect her family.

Harry's emotional reunion with his cousin and his large Irish family in the ancestral home was marked by stories, tears, and laughter. They retraced the footsteps of their ancestors down the bog road, exploring the derelict stone cottages that once housed the community in Carrownagh, later known as Carnaugh.

The connection between our families endured, with Harry and Doherty expressing a particular interest in me, the eldest of nine. Their offer to bring me to Dakota for education, seen as a gesture of assistance, was ultimately declined. Over the years, our families stayed in touch, and in 1977, that special parcel arrived to mark our

Mary Hodson

first Christmas as a married couple. A beautiful green hand-crocheted baby blanket was enclosed, later used to swaddle our son. This heirloom has passed down through generations; seventeen years ago, our grandson was swaddled in the same blanket. It serves as a poignant reminder of our emigrant forebears.

Each Christmas, a handcrafted Merry Christmas decoration, a gift from Dorothy, adorns the window next to the Christmas tree. The story of our ancestors' emigration is retold each year at Christmas to the next generation. President Mary McAleese's words echo, encapsulating the emigrant's heart that beats to the rhythm of two different worlds, forging a bridge between the old and the new, a bridge strengthened by stories, memories, and the enduring thread of family connections.

All Souls
Póilín Brennan

A silent goddess sat in lotus,
within a circle of seeking souls.
An energy of vibrating woes,
a dancing veil, a smudge to heal.
Divinity stayed to hold the space
with compassion for their weary frames.
Their breath exhale in tearful sighs
all burdened tales returned to source.
With Meri Didi I sit enshrouded,
bestowing peace with love's embrace.
Buddha heals her from base to crown
releasing her glow in streaming light.

The Shiny Red Couch
Deirdre Anne Gialamas

The shiny red couch
still greets the Christmas tree
this mid-December night.

Pear-shaped and obese,
the tree's lights dance
with its redness,
their tango fervent,
soothing.

Across from them,
on an old armchair,
I sit and spy my name
on an oblong shape
nestling under the tree,
next to multicoloured,
ribboned bags and boxes.

My siblings join me
in a frozen frenzy,
half-clad and barefoot,
slumber clinging to their
childish bodies,
as they fight it,
squeaking and screaming,
ripping the paper off their
toys from Santy.

The Shiny Red Couch

Her tender eyes meet mine
as I claw the final cover
from my Crolly doll.

With dry throat
and my heart aflutter,
'Look, look what I got!
Oh, she's lovely!' I shout
to anyone who'll listen.

Up and down,
over and back,
I swing my baby,
her blue eyes coyly winking.

Then, I squeeze her to me
and know she loves me too.

The shiny red couch
beckons me with its
promise of comfort.

The Christmas tree flickers
on my past,
flirting with my memories,
as spring within me
mocks my autumn years.

After Christmas

Anne Murray

It's the last day of the Christmas holidays.

'We must take down the tree and decorations today,' says Mammy. 'You can help me after the little ones are gone to bed,' she whispers to Marie.

They gather all the ornaments and baubles from the tree and put them back in their boxes. The crib has its own box, and all the figures of Mary and Joseph, and the baby Jesus have to be wrapped separately and put in another box.

'I think you were happy with all your Christmas presents. Do you like the different sparkling nail varnishes, and the make-up mirror? You know you can't wear any of those going to school, strictly for weekends,' says Mammy. 'I'm sorry if I spoiled things a bit for you about the Santa business. I really thought you knew.'

'Don't worry about it, Mammy. I had to find out sometime.'

'The next big event now, Marie, is your confirmation. Once the New Year sales are over, we'll start to look for an outfit for you. I'm sure the date will be arranged as soon as the school holidays are over. Are you looking forward to the big day?'

Marie shrugs her shoulders.

'You don't seem very interested!'

After Christmas

'That's because I'm NOT interested,' Marie replies. 'I'm not going to make my confirmation.'

'But of course you are. You're in sixth class now. This is your last year in national school. Imagine you'll be going to secondary school after the summer holidays.'

'I'm NOT making confirmation.'

'What do you mean? Has someone said something to you? Are you in trouble with the teacher? Did the Bishop say something?'

'Nobody said anything. I'm NOT doing it. That's all.'

'You're tired. We'll finish taking down the decorations. I'll get Daddy to put them in the attic tomorrow,' says Mammy, trying to change the subject.

After Marie had gone to bed, Mammy rang Granny for advice.

'Teenage tantrums,' says Granny.

'But she's only eleven, not even a teenager. What is she going to be like in a year or two?'

'I'll call over during the week and have a chat with her,' consoles Granny. 'Don't worry, I'll get to the bottom of this.'

As promised, Granny calls over on Saturday morning.

'I need a bit of help with my shopping,' says Granny. 'I wonder, would you be free, Marie, to give me a hand? We could go to McDonald's for lunch after.'

The two go off to Dunnes and Marie helps Granny fill the boot of her car with shopping. Sitting in McDonald's eating their lunch, they get chatting.

115

Anne Murray

'How did Christmas go? Did you get everything you wanted from Santa? I suppose Emma and Tom were awake very early to check their presents.'

'There's no need for that now, Granny. Mammy told me the whole story about Santa. She thought I was only pretending, but I really, really, really believed. I'll NEVER in my life get caught like that again.'

'Well, Christmas is baby Jesus' birthday and parents like to get presents for their children to celebrate his birthday. It's just a little white lie to make it more exciting for the children,' Granny replies, trying to comfort her. 'Sure you're all grown up now. You'll be going to secondary school next September. First, of course, there's your confirmation. Will you let me buy your shoes for that? We'll go shopping together and you can pick them out yourself.'

'There's no need. I am NOT making confirmation.'

'Why do you say that? Of course you're making confirmation.'

'NO. I'm not. This God thing is just another made-up story. Just like Santa Claus.'

A Gamble

James Conway

She walks alone along the headlands, high up over the bay. From there she can view the whole episode of the morning, the panorama of the beach. Waves rush in as they have for some countless years. Their vibrant heads race with a terrier's impatience towards the shore, colliding in tenacity with the sharp arms of the cold brutality of the rocks.

She likes the privacy of the early hour. Regardless of the weather she is there. It is like she is related to the sea. The harsh grassy growth wraps round her ankles, tight and slim. This view is worth seeing. For the sea changes colour, changes mood from hour to hour. She often wonders, when the sea is cross, did something upset it. It may answer back with a splurge of anger or a timid grin.

Sounds so, make up her canvass of a whistling defiance, where winds cut through the grassy dunes, if the rain joins in, it is hard to breathe. And when thunder and lightning add their anger she rouses wild. She becomes like a bird almost able to fly. Her old gabardine becomes for the briefest of moments a furbelow, she shines bright, her garb something to marvel at in this concoction of elements. This makes her live.

Not many have seen her at this hour. The early driver or fisherman may have caught a quick

James Conway

snippet of her image. Like a rare fish she enters the net which is their eyes. But when they spoke about such a sighting, they seemed to be unsure of whether they saw her or not.

'She was there all right, but she was so hard to see and her age, it is difficult to say, it's like she played tricks with the light,' one all night lorry man once said.

'Ah Paddy, sure you are only making her up,' another said trying to rise him, poking him quickly in the ribs.

'So, ye think I'm fit for the funny farm, to be sent to the big house on the hill? Is that it?' Paddy replied crossly, knowing she was there.

During the last world war, an American plane got into difficulty off the beach as it attempted to land. It wavered and stumbled like a drunken figure unable to veer home. The plane wished to speak, its belly almost touching the high impatient waves of blue and grey. At least that's what people of the time said. Eventually, it disappeared. Some say it landed further up the coast, its pilot surfacing, then going down to the deep. But when asked who actually saw the plane meet its watery demise and who saw the pilot fight for life, struggling to push the cockpit open, nobody spoke up. It was even mentioned at Masses. The truth was sought. The authorities were determined to find out.

A set of trawlers ploughed the coast, but no plane was found. Some of the local fishermen offered advice, but their opinions were deemed not to make sense. The Americans had radars and deep probing experts to find the plane.

A Gamble

'Devil a plane will they find,' said Sean Mac, an old fisherman. 'It's a case of finding her somewhere out by Rockall, where the old sea swallows quick.'

In this part of Ireland, which was and still is under British rule, the Americans had aerodromes for their planes. The men needed company. It was said the Americans arranged socials. They had a sale of work for a church. They played music with Glenn Miller type tunes and held dances. The local girls were fascinated by the uniforms, the casual and modern talk, the cigarettes. A few of the girls married Americans, a few were put in the family way. Others were disappointed when what seemed like something was happening didn't happen. Towards the end of the war, the Americans left abruptly. One day they were in camp. The next day, they were gone. The planes no longer dragged their big bodies through the sky. Instead the weather was all that could be seen above in the clouds.

One girl had other intentions about her liaison with one of the Airmen, a pilot who was involved with bombing raids and intelligence. He knew a lot. He was fascinated with his new Irish Colleen. She was fascinated by his work. Her father had been a German who settled in Ireland and died young. Sentences like 'Hey, I really shouldn't be telling you this, ye know babe.'

'Arah, now Mike, when are ye hitting the Germans next, sure who would I tell?' And she'd giggle, her dancing eyes making Mike feel like he was in a grand old dream.

'Tomorrow, I am in the air, then we have to hit a big Jerry ship that's causing a bit of trouble.'

119

James Conway

And she'd smile.

'Out past Bloody Foreland in Donegal, that's it, isn't it?' she asked with a devious look.

Strangely enough, all these years later, there has been talk of this woman who nobody around here really knew. Someone asked was she still alive. And if so, where does she live?

'God only knows,' came the answer in the pub. Then the topic turned to politics and football on the TV.

Northerly, where red rocks rise, the remains of old summer chalets crumble. Maybe she inhabits one. If so, how does she live? She may live by theft. Or is she looked after by some kind relative who keeps her privacy in the secrecy it deserves?

The days of the airmen are vague now, just the aged speak of their presence. The runway they once used is now overgrown. Instead of a sheened surface, weeds grow high and merrily, showing off a sprinkling of purple and yellow heads. Occasionally, a rusted screw variegated in green turns up.

But in the mind of the woman who walks earlier than anyone else, such times could well live on. Could it be, she changes from an elderly woman into something supernatural? Now, that is stretching a tale into nonsense or is it?

'But where did you say she lives? Somewhere beyond a finding?'

'She lives where nobody goes. When I say where nobody goes, well there have been young lads who lead girls (who find them cool) into such strange places.'

Once, when intoxicated, one such ruffian brought a girl there. The woman sensed them,

120

A Gamble

wished, prayed, to put them off the track, to leave her be.

But such is superstition, is it not? Further on up the cliff walk, they slipped. Their drowned bodies were discovered along the beach a couple of days later.

But what of this woman, was she responsible for the downing of her lover's plane? How could this have happened? Did she gamble with death? Did she in her mind want him to return safely? This naive American pilot who seemed to love her charm and apparently, innocent ways. The little matter of his day's intentions being radioed to her foreign friends made it a gamble. A gamble that didn't come off. She thought his skill and luck would bring him home despite being tracked by the Luftwaffe. A dual loyalty perhaps?

As by irony, one of the local girls who married an American pilot is due to stay back here on holiday soon. Her marriage was successful, and she has three sons. One, Zachary, in particular is overzealous about the years when his father with his uncle were stationed in Ireland during the war. His father survived. His uncle didn't. His uncle's plane disappeared along the coast it was said.

Zachary has prepared a portfolio, assembled facts, listened to his mother who is weary with his questions. The fact that he is overly keen to find out about a certain plane that was lost near the end of the war bothers her. She offers a good old Irish solution when things can't be solved. 'Leave all this in the hands of God,' she says when no apparent answer is forthcoming about the plane.

James Conway

This will not impress or indeed soothe Zach's curiosity. His father, who is now an ageing, wealthy businessman, is more than determined to get answers and has urged his son to tease out proof where really proof is hard to find.

His father, Mister Archie Smith, entrepreneur, is considering using his strong Republican party links to press the Government to dig a hole in that god damn sea to raise his brother's forgotten plane. With that Zachary raises his Bourbon whiskey. His mother joins him. Then a strange look comes over her face... 'What is it, Maggie?' his father asks. Words grumble to the surface of her lips.

'Now it is all coming back to me,' she says. 'That bloody bitch, I wonder now...'

His mother's eyes scour time. She leans back and unreels years delicate in her mind, while Zach and his father wait with impatience in their eyes.

Pastures New

Thomas MacMahon

A peaceful spot in Stephen's Green
To share a seat with an old friend,
Reminisce and bury life's woe
And talk about the world flow.

Geranium blossoms colour the green,
Picture perfect the positive view.
The future and prosperity
And new horizons and sunny days

A Traveller Woman in Ireland's Past

Mary Hawkshaw

You grew up long before your time,
Thrown into a world you could not define.
Your day began as the day before,
Oblivious to the misty rain,
you went from door to door.
You held out your flowers with such pride
to every face at every door.
But your paper flowers
We promptly denied.
Every stranger you passed on your long road,
Turned away, indifferent to your heavy load.
You were of no importance a disgrace,
We passed you by, never looking at your face.

The church bells rang loud and clear,
But not for you, my wretched dear.
With your empty belly thundering in your ears,
You scurried past with dreaded fear.
We cast you out without any emotion,
And prayed aloud with deep devotion,
For the sick, the dead, and God above,
But you were not worthy of any love.
If Mother Nature is mother to all,
Where was our nature when you came to call?
We left you on the side of the road,
Cradling your children invisible to all.

A Traveller Woman in Ireland's Past

The sleeting rain as hard as ice,
Spilled from the raging skies,
The howling wind showed no retreat,
Beating hard against your feet.

Your shawl is pulled tight around your head,
Your life endures, your tears are shed.
The English have long since left our land,
The Irish now grab from your hand.

A Kind of Revenge

Mary Hodson

In the serene landscape of May 1986, a bright and promising young man, the youngest among nine siblings, celebrated his eighteenth birthday. With a heart full of joy, he embarked on his day's work alongside his father and brothers, their routine tasks in the wood proceeding seamlessly under the warm sun.

The wood, alive with the echoes of familial banter, witnessed a brief respite as the family paused for a break. Laughter and conversations filled the air as they enjoyed sandwiches and biscuits, basking in the camaraderie.

The young man, on the cusp of adulthood, revelled in the company of his family and the beauty of the horses grazing nearby. His world was one of contentment and anticipation. However, fate took a cruel turn. In a heartbeat, he slipped and tumbled from a fallen tree trunk, vanishing from view.

His father, the first witness to this abrupt accident, urgently alerted his brothers.

'Patrick is gone,' he cried, a chilling proclamation that hung in the air. Unaware of the gravity of the situation, his brothers initially questioned the meaning of 'gone'. It took their father's second desperate plea to comprehend the tragedy unfolding before them. Racing to the

A Kind of Revenge

scene, they discovered Patrick trapped beneath the encasing roots of the fallen tree.

Their father, with trembling hands, delivered the crushing news.

'There is nothing we can do for him now; he's gone.'

The heaviness of grief settled, and the family gathered, clutching their rosary beads, seeking solace in prayer as they awaited help and the arrival of the priest. The silence that enveloped the wood was deafening, broken only by the Hail Marys recited in disbelief.

The priest, Fr McEvilly, arrived. He was a respected figure in the community, and brought a sombre serenity to the unfolding tragedy. Patrick's lifeless form was eventually extricated, blessed by the priest, and transported to the hospital. A darkness had descended, and the world, once filled with the promise of the day, now bore the weight of an irreversible loss.

Following the ambulance, winding down the mountain foot road, they approached their home, where their mother, unaware of the tragedy, continued her daily rituals, lost in memories of Patrick's birth and the joy of his milestone birthday. Fr McEvilly entered the house. Mother, though sensing something amiss, welcomed him warmly. Anxious questions poured forth, each more desperate than the last. The news of Patrick's accident shattered her world, and in a chorus of despair, she pleaded with the heavens for answers.

The silence that followed was profound. Words eluded his mother's grief as she clung to the

Mary Hodson

prayerful invocation of 'Jesus, Mary, and Joseph'.

In the aftermath, those sacred words, once a source of comfort, became a haunting refrain – a kind of revenge exacted by a fate that had mercilessly torn apart the fabric of a once-harmonious existence.

ABCs and Nursery Rhymes
Deirdre Anne Gialamas

The plastic thing above the crib
Spun round and round
Relentlessly blurting out
Raucous tunes of
ABCs and Nursery Rhymes
The babe below
Half deafened
Thought only of almost
Silence and its mother's
Healing touch
It waited endlessly
To see its saviour's eyes
Beguiling
Reaching down
With outstretched arms
That whisked it up
To nestle next to her
White gold gushing from
Her globed pillow
Cocooned
The babe surrendered

To the nourishment and peace
Forgetting ABCs and Nursery Rhymes.

Seeking a Cure

Frank Fahy

In the early morning, as the sun cast its first light over Ballymore pier, Matt O'Reilly's day began not with the chirping of birds but with the quiet symphony of an ageing body. His bones creaked, and his joints sighed, a stark reminder of his seventy years and the fibromyalgia that whispered tales of agony throughout his frame. Each day, Matt faced the world with a resilience that belied his pain, his smile as warm as the morning sun.

With every deliberate step along the pier, the salty breeze offered a fleeting reprieve from his discomfort. Today, the sun seemed to play a game with him, kissing the wrinkles around his eyes and coaxing a squint that softened into a smile. The shimmering dance of light on the water was a view he cherished, a comfort for his weary soul.

From the corner of his eye, Matt caught a glimpse of Con's boat. It wasn't like the others docked at the pier – it had a character all its own. The boat, a sturdy fishing vessel, had a sail that spoke of many journeys across the waves. Its wooden frame, etched with time and the sea's touch, and the modest cabin within, spoke of a life intimately connected to the water and sky.

As Matt approached, the clatter of his boots on the wooden dock merged with the harsh sounds

Seeking a Cure

of Con's morning ritual. Amidst a fit of coughing and the unpleasant expulsion of phlegm, Con's head emerged from the cabin.

'Morning, Matt!' called out Con.

'Good morning, Con,' Matt replied. 'Seems that rattle in your chest is getting worse.'

'Just clearing the windpipes,' Con spluttered between coughs. Wiping his mouth with the back of his hand, he shrugged it off. 'Ah, it's nothing a bit of sea air won't fix.'

With an agility belying his age, Con hoisted himself up so that he could perch on the roof of his cabin.

Matt frowned. 'Con, that's your lungs crying for mercy, not just clearing your windpipes. It's those damned cigarettes. They're doing you no favours.'

The fisherman chuckled, his laughter blending with the distant cries of seagulls. Throwing his head back to feel the warmth of the sun, he said, 'Seems the sun still favours us old-timers, eh? Never forgets us.'

Then, in a more serious tone, 'How're you holding up, Matt? You look a bit more worn than usual.'

Matt paused, leaning slightly on his cane, an unspoken symbol of his battles. He hadn't told Con the full extent of his bruising encounter with Covid that had nearly cost him his life. Long Covid had continued to rage through his body, exacerbating the other health issues which limited his mobility. Only Jenny was aware of the absolute terror he had of ever catching Covid again.

Frank Fahy

'Ah, you know, the usual. But I'm still here, still standing. That's got to count for something.'

'Kathleen tells me that you were up in the big smoke recently?' Con inquired, his tone suggesting a mix of curiosity and concern. 'You'd wonder do they do any singing at all in that choir, with the gossip that goes on. I suppose Jenny told her the news?'

'No, your Jenny has more sense than to be spreading rumours. But my wife? There isn't a whisper circulating in the village that doesn't find a willing ear. Kathleen could tell you what Father Moloney had for breakfast.'

Matt nodded, his eyes reflecting a moment of introspection. 'Aye, I was above in Dublin alright. Dr Keogh told me something interesting. Said I should "look in the mirror" for the source of my pain. Suggested that my fibromyalgia might be more than just physical – that it could be rooted in stress, maybe something from the past, even psychosomatic.'

Con blinked, taken aback. 'Psycho... what? You know, Professor, the biggest word I learned in school was wheelbarrow. And you're here throwing around rocks of words like it's nothing!'

Matt's smile widened at the familiar nickname. 'I know, it's a bit of a mouthful. It means that the mind could be influencing the physical pain.'

Con nodded slowly. 'So he thinks it's all in your head?'

Matt sighed. 'Something like that. It never occurred to me that the mind could have such an effect on the body,' Matt continued, his gaze drifting toward the horizon. 'Dr Keogh reckons I

Seeking a Cure

might benefit from seeing a psychiatrist, delve into the psychological side of things.'

'Well, that's a journey and a half, Matt. You think you'll go through with it?' Con asked, stretching out comfortably on the roof of his cabin, the solid surface beneath him offering a makeshift recliner as he gazed out towards the horizon.

Matt let out a sigh, the weight of the decision evident in his posture. 'I'm considering it. I never thought I'd take that path, but if there's a chance it could ease this burden, it's worth exploring.'

Con nodded, his expression thoughtful. 'You've always been one to face challenges head-on, Matt. If there's a way to ease your pain, I'd say go for it.'

Matt smiled, grateful for the fisherman's support. 'Thanks, Con. It's a strange turn of events, but then again, life's full of surprises.'

With a nod of thanks, Matt continued his journey along the pier. Each creak of the wooden planks beneath his feet was a familiar language, a conversation between old friends. His fingers, once nimble on guitar strings, now rested quietly in his pockets. Yet the melody of his life – a blend of resilience, pain, and unwavering spirit – continued to play in his every step.

Matt settled into the well-worn armchair in his living room, facing the phone with a mixture of resolve and trepidation. The room was quiet, except for the ticking of the grandfather clock in the corner, its rhythmic sound a steady companion in the tense silence. He picked up the phone, its familiar weight a contrast to the

Frank Fahy

unfamiliar journey he was about to embark upon.

'Howard Clinic, how may I help you?' came the crisp voice of the receptionist.

'Good afternoon. I'd like to arrange an appointment with a psychiatrist. It's for... um, issues related to Fibromyalgia.' Matt's words stumbled out, each one heavy with a mix of reluctance and necessity.

'Of course, I'll put you through to our nurse,' the receptionist responded efficiently. A brief interlude of muzak filled the line before a click signalled a new connection.

'Helen Shaw here. How can I help?' The nurse's voice was softer, more soothing.

Matt explained his rheumatologist's suggestion, his fingers drumming nervously on the armrest. The notion of delving into the psychological aspects of his condition was daunting, yet a part of him yearned for any thread of hope. The nurse asked more questions and when she had a thorough understanding of Matt's condition, she set about arranging possible interventions.

'We can set up weekly one-to-one sessions at our clinic on Bridge Street,' the nurse proposed, her tone encouraging.

'How soon can we begin?' Matt asked, a fragile hope threading through his words.

There was a pause, the shuffling of papers on the other end. 'Well, we're looking at a six- to nine-month waiting list.'

Matt's heart sank. 'Six- to nine-months,' he echoed, the delay a heavy blow to his flickering hope.

Seeking a Cure

The nurse, sensing his disappointment, offered a softer tone. 'It's worth the wait. We'll take good care of you.'

Matt grappled with the reality of the long wait, his mind racing. The armchair felt less comforting, more like a holding cell. As he was about to respond, the nurse interrupted his thoughts.

'There's another option,' she began. 'Consider becoming an in-patient in the hospital in Dublin.'

The idea took Matt aback. The prospect of hospitalisation, of surrendering his daily routine and independence, loomed large and intimidating. Yet, the promise of immediate care, of not being just another name on a waiting list, was tempting.

'And if I choose that...,' Matt sought clarification, his voice a mix of hope and uncertainty.

'You would be looked after by a dedicated team geared towards your recovery,' Helen interrupted. 'You'd have the services of the chief psychiatrist, an occupational therapist, a psychologist, and a pharmacist all on site and working with you towards your recovery.'

Matt took a deep breath, the weight of the decision pressing on him. This was not what he had bargained for, but perhaps it was what he needed.

'You would be under constant observation,' the nurse continued, 'with the best team around you to monitor any new medicines they might recommend, or any other treatments that they might suggest.'

Frank Fahy

The agony of indecision yielded to impulse. 'Alright, let's do it. I can't live like this anymore. I'll check in,' he said, a note of resignation in his voice.

'That's a good choice, Matt. I'll arrange everything. You won't be alone in this.'

He found Helen's words comforting, easing the tumult of his racing thoughts. Maybe, just maybe, this was the first step towards a semblance of relief.

***

Matt checked his watch for the umpteenth time. It was now just after 5:00pm. The waiting room, a bland space with rows of chairs and outdated magazines, had become his world for the past four hours. He had arrived early, anticipating a prompt start to this new chapter at St. Jude's Hospital, but the clock had ticked on relentlessly with no sign of progression.

He watched as the receptionist shuffled papers, occasionally answering the phone with a forced cheerfulness that felt jarring in the silent waiting area. Matt had only been called once, by a Registrar who had taken his details and advised him to wait for a nurse or an orderly to take him up to the ward. That had been hours ago.

The frustration simmered within him. He tried to distract himself by observing the other people in the room. There was an old man flipping through a newspaper, a young woman scrolling on her phone, and a mother trying to soothe her restless child. They all seemed resigned to the wait, a resignation Matt found hard to accept.

'Excuse me,' he finally approached the receptionist, his voice edged with impatience. 'I've

Seeking a Cure

been here since 1pm. When can I expect to see someone?'

The receptionist offered a placating smile. 'I'm sorry for the delay, sir. I'll check with the nurses' station right away.'

Matt returned to his seat, feeling slightly appeased but still unsettled. The minutes dragged on. Just as he was contemplating leaving, a nurse finally appeared. She was a middle-aged woman with a kind face, looking slightly flustered.

'Matthew O'Reilly?' she called out.

'That's me,' Matt stood up, relief washing over him.

'My apologies for the delay. We've been swamped today. Follow me, please,' she said, leading him to the elevator. The ride to the third floor was quiet, the nurse checking her clipboard occasionally. Matt looked at the ascending numbers above the elevator's entrance, each ding marking a move closer to an unknown future. As the doors opened onto the third floor, he stepped out into a corridor that looked much like the waiting room below – functional, unremarkable, yet somehow promising a start to the journey for which he had braced himself.

The ward was a vast, open room, each corner awash with the unforgiving glow of fluorescent lights. Beds, lined along the walls, were each cordoned off by nothing more than sheer nylon curtains. These flimsy dividers fluttered gently, giving a pretence of privacy that was, at best, an illusion. The subtle sounds of life – conversations, the rustle of movement, even the

137

Frank Fahy

quiet swish of curtains – melded into a continuous soundtrack.

He was directed to the second bed on the left, a neatly made cot with crisp sheets. The nurse pulled the curtain around with a swoosh, offering a momentary illusion of seclusion. She asked him if he had any sharp objects in his bag. Matt reluctantly handed over his razor, spare blades, and nail clippers.

'We'll take care of these for you,' the nurse declared brightly, before stepping out. Matt sat on the edge of his bed, the mattress firm beneath him. The ambient noises of the ward crept into his consciousness – the distant coughs, the muffled footsteps, the soft beeps of medical machinery. It was an orchestra of institutional life, unfiltered and unceasing.

Having surveyed his scant personal area and put away his toiletries, he decided to investigate his new environment. Pulling back the curtain, he realised that his bed was positioned directly opposite the nurse's station. Three white uniforms were busily watching computer screens and typing on keyboards. Occasionally, bursts of conversation and laughter echoed from the room. Matt turned towards his left and saw a sign for the canteen at the end of the corridor. He walked slowly, trying to familiarise himself with his new surroundings.

As he progressed along the corridor he noticed that there was an entire row of rooms marked 'Private' along the right-hand side. *Why wasn't I offered a private room?* Men and women in dressing gowns and slippers appeared from time to time. Some headed in the direction of the

Seeking a Cure

canteen. Others disappeared out through what looked like an emergency door. Each time this door opened, the scent of nicotine snaked its way onto the corridor. As Matt drew closer he could read the hand-printed sign, *Smoker's Balcony*. Obviously, a lifetime of habits and indulgences did not cease at the front door but persisted even within the confines of these pristine surroundings.

Just then, a woman in a faded dressing gown appeared, her hair a tangle of grey and white.

'First time in this paradise?' she asked with a wry smile that didn't quite reach her tired eyes.

Matthew nodded, still taking in the surroundings. 'It's... different than I expected,' he admitted.

She chuckled. 'I'm Maeve,' she said, 'but everyone calls me Queeny.'

'Hello,' was all that Matt could muster.

'You'll get used to it here. You don't get your privileges yet. You can't leave the ward without permission. Up here, they don't offer much in terms of coffee, but I can sneak you a real cup from the shop downstairs.'

Matt flinched. He hadn't been told that his freedom was curtailed in this manner. Recovering his composure he said, 'That would be nice, thank you.'

The offer of kindness came as a surprise, but it served to anchor him to the new reality he was facing. As she shuffled away, Matt couldn't shake the feeling that he had become a prisoner. This restriction to his movements chafed against his desire for freedom, but a further frustration

139

Frank Fahy

gnawed at him. Why do I have to find out the rules from a patient?

It wasn't long before another presence made itself known. An elf-like figure emerged from the Private Room to his right just as he was passing. The tilt of her head exuded confidence; her posture relaxed despite the confines of the hospital.

'You're Matt, right? The new guy?'

A playful smirk danced on her lips. She was youthful and vibrant. She gave off an air of insouciance and defiance. Matt noticed that she was barefooted. Her long blonde hair, the loose-fitting green polo sweater and her white tennis shorts reminded him of Twiggy from the 60s. She let her back slide down along the wall until she landed cross-legged on the floor, her movements fluid and assured. Matt watched as she curled her legs beneath her with an effortless grace that drew the eye. *How does she know my name?*

'That's me,' he replied, feeling the age difference between them like a chasm. Yet, the chasm seemed to narrow as she reached out her hand towards him. Matt bent down, her perfume enveloping him, a scent that spoke of life beyond these walls. She leaned in, close enough for him to feel the warmth of her breath.

'I'm Lucy,' she said softly. 'If you need a tour guide, or just someone to talk to, I'm here.'

Her offer was generous, laced with an allure that was both inviting and alarming. Matt could feel the pull, the instinctive urge to lean into her space, to accept the comfort she offered. Were all patients as open as this?

Seeking a Cure

'Thanks, Lucy. Maybe I'll take you up on that chat,' he said, his voice steady, betraying none of the internal struggle her proximity provoked.

As he walked away, her laughter trailed behind him like a promise or a warning. Matt was left to grapple with the reality of his situation. The ward was a microcosm where the usual rules didn't apply, and every interaction was fraught with potential meaning. Before he could explore any further, a nurse's shrill voice called out his name. The nurse, with her clipboard, indicated that he should return to his bed. She was ready to discuss the procedural aspects of his stay.

Matt hurried back, passing Lucy on the way.

'Have fun,' she whispered playfully.

'Be careful of Lucy,' the nurse said as she settled herself on the edge of Matt's bed. 'She's a regular here. She comes in to see us every three months or so. She likes men – especially older men.'

Matt turned away in embarrassment. The nurse's preamble had barely begun when the man in the adjacent bed, divided from Matt's only by the same thin curtain, began to shout. His shrieks became louder as he gasped for air, a panic attack seizing him in its unforgiving grip. The nurse whisked back the thin curtain and immediately began to tend to the man. Other white uniforms converged, their trained calm a counterpoint to the man's distress. Matt couldn't help but overhear the conversation taking place beside him.

'Now Joseph, there, there. Breathe slowly, deep breaths. That's it.'

141

Frank Fahy

Another voice. 'What was it that brought this on, Joe? Can you tell me?'

'I went for a walk on the corridor,' the man gasped.

'Take your time, Joseph. Tell us slowly what happened.'

'Everyone was looking at me. They were all staring at me. I couldn't take it.'

'It's okay now, Joe,' the nurse's soothing voice again. 'You're safe here now with us. We'll give you something to help you relax.'

Matt was reminded that other people in this ward suffered from mental anguish and distress which manifested itself in a more external, physical way. By comparison, the stress in his own body or mind was invisible.

***

The next morning, Matt entered a sparsely decorated room, its barrenness echoing the unease that knotted in his stomach. He anticipated a discussion with the team about his fibromyalgia. Things did not go as planned. Instead, he was greeted by a solitary figure – a young psychiatrist with a neatly groomed beard.

'Hello, Mr O'Reilly. Could you please fill out this test booklet?' Dr Sharif handed him some papers, bypassing any preamble.

A flicker of annoyance stirred in Matt. 'A test? What for?' His voice was tinged with disbelief, – edged with a growing sense of affront.

'It's our usual process for newcomers,' Dr Sharif said, his attempt at reassurance only amplifying Matt's irritation. 'Before you start, could you tell me what day it is today?' Dr Sharif asked without a glimmer of a smile.

Seeking a Cure

Matt's frown etched deeper. The query, absurdly basic, would have been comical if not for Dr Sharif's earnestness. 'I believe it's Wednesday...?' Matt said, his answer sounding odd to himself.

'It's Thursday, actually, Mr O'Reilly. And the date?' Dr Sharif corrected gently.

Matt's response was sharp. 'Dates don't matter much to a retired man,' he said, his voice laced with frustration.

The doctor pointed to the first page of the test. 'Please draw a circle in that space. Then put in the numbers of a clock.'

This task, trivial in its nature, felt like an affront to his pride. He completed it, each stroke of the pen silently affirming his indignation.

'Good. Now show the time as ten minutes past eleven.'

These questions, these child-like tasks, belittled him. The doctor's mobile phone sounded. Without apology, he answered and hurriedly left the room. Matt used the moment to regain his composure. He took some deep breaths and resolved to keep his temper long enough to complete the ridiculous exercise. He skimmed through the booklet. Each question seemed a veiled insult to his intelligence. He answered them, not out of cooperation, but defiance, a quiet demonstration of his undiminished mental acuity.

When Dr Sharif's returned, his surprise at Matt's quick work was more hurtful than heartening. 'You've solved number seven faster than anyone I've seen, since I came here,' Dr Sharif remarked, admiration in his tone.

143

Frank Fahy

Matt was secretly pleased. Finally, they would realise that they were dealing with a sane intellect.

'And how long ago was that?' Matt's reply was laced with bitterness, not the satisfaction such praise should have warranted.

'Two weeks,' replied Dr Sharif, his warmth fading into professional detachment.

Matt, his annoyance palpable, shifted the conversation.

'When do I see Dr Murray?'

His eagerness was to address his real concern – his fibromyalgia – not his cognitive abilities. Dr Sharif arranged the meeting for the next day. As Matt left, his victory felt empty, overshadowed by the demeaning nature of this first encounter.

***

After a sleepless night, Matt requested his razor and was guided towards the shower room. He realised that he had forgotten to pack shaving foam, but a helpful lady from the housekeeping staff provided him with a soap-filled sponge which substituted nicely. He was determined to be freshly groomed, alert and ready to challenge any simplistic judgments. He would meet the chief psychiatrist as an equal, with all the might of his intellect and experience.

Upon entering the consultation room, Matt was greeted by the familiar starkness: white walls that seemed to leech warmth from the space. He settled into his chair, facing his 'team' – Sharif, a familiar face now, and Dr Murray, whose formidable reputation loomed large in the room.

'Good morning, Mr O'Reilly,' Dr Murray's voice cut through the silence, clinical and distant. 'I

Seeking a Cure

understand your rheumatologist referred you to us. Could you elaborate on that?'

Matt shifted in the unyielding chair, the discomfort mirroring his inner turmoil. 'Dr Murray,' he started, his voice strained, 'my rheumatologist believes that stress, perhaps linked to unresolved past issues, might be exacerbating my fibromyalgia.'

Dr Murray, unblinking, dissected Matt's words with a clinical detachment. 'Your rheumatologist's theories on fibromyalgia are quite intriguing. Let's delve deeper into that, shall we?'

What followed was an intense session of probing questions, each of Matt's painful episodes laid bare and analysed. Relief washed over him as the interrogation ended, but it was short-lived. Dr Murray peered over his glasses, a wave of his hand dismissing Matt's concerns.

'Stress, unresolved issues – these aren't your problems, Mr O'Reilly. You are obviously very well educated. More importantly, you are intelligent. Your personality seems outgoing, vibrant, aligning with your creative pursuits.'

Unused to hearing such blunt compliments, Matt couldn't stop a flush of embarrassment colouring his cheeks. Dr Murray continued to talk about fibromyalgia, its theoretical root causes, and particularly a tendency to assign the label to conditions that seemed to have no other explanation. As far as Matt could ascertain, Dr Murray's views were in sharp contrast to Dr Keogh's perspectives. Concluding with a disdainful shrug of his shoulders, he declared,

145

Frank Fahy

'Inform Dr Keogh that stress or depression aren't your afflictions. You appear quite well-adjusted.'

Those words seemed to compress the room around Matt, his breath caught in a vice of confusion. 'Does this mean that I am not imagining the pain?'

'I've no doubt that your pain is real. But as you are aware, steroids haven't worked in the long term. How long are you on steroids now? Twelve years? Far too long. You should never have been put on steroids in the first place. Steroids only cure symptoms, not causes.'

'But what can I do about the pain?'

'The bald fact of the matter is that you have to put up with your pain. There is no cure for fibromyalgia. Sure, you can manage for a while on over-the-counter painkillers, but long term, there is no medical cure that we can offer.'

'Does this mean I can leave?'

'A few more assessments,' Dr Murray replied, his voice as cold as the room. 'Once we've finalised everything, including discussions with your partner, for collateral, you should be back in Galway by midweek.'

A mixture of hope and scepticism swirled in Matt's mind. 'So, after these tests, I can go home?'

'There are formalities to attend to,' Dr Murray answered, devoid of empathy. 'You're not confined here, Mr O'Reilly. Use the library, take walks. We'll liaise with Jenny, and you can expect to return to Galway shortly.'

As Matt stood, a wave of disappointment washed over him. He remembered Nurse Helen telling him about the extensive team that would

146

Seeking a Cure

be caring for him in hospital. The absence of a psychologist, pharmacist, and occupational therapist felt glaring.

'I take it that I am not confined to this ward. I can come and go as I please?'

'Just let the nurses know where they can find you. Use your time here to rest and relax,' Dr Murray said, before turning back to his file to scribble some notes.

Matt departed the room enveloped in a cloud of confusion. The intense meeting left him adrift, a solitary figure navigating the complex maze of conflicting medical opinions. He sought a few moments of solitude to gather his thoughts. After resting on his bed briefly, he rang Jenny.

'What's the news, Mattie?' Jenny asked with a hint of eagerness in her voice.

'Hi Jen. Any news from home?' Matt responded, his tone casual yet interested.

Jenny sighed lightly, 'I miss you, Mattie. Con and Kathleen were asking for you. Poor Con has a touch of the flu. He's taken to the bed.'

Matt chuckled softly. 'Ah, Con's hardy. Preserved by the salt air. It'll take more than a cold or a flu to keep him down. He'll be up and about in no time.'

Jenny enquired carefully: 'But what about you? How did your meeting go? What did the chief psychiatrist say?'

Matt's voice was relaxed, almost nonchalant. 'He says I'm fine, Jen. No stress, no depression, nothing to worry about. I don't really need to be here.'

'And when are you coming home?' Jenny's voice held a hint of urgency.

Frank Fahy

Matt hesitated, choosing his words with care. 'Well, love, it's not as straightforward as we hoped.' A sigh at the other end of the phone told Matt all he needed to know about Jen's reaction.

'So, you're not coming home?'

'Not immediately,' he said. 'Before he's happy for me to leave he wants to ring you. They're planning to call you on Monday to confirm a few things. 'A collateral phone call' is the official name for it. They want to check with you if the stories I've told them here are true.'

'Why would you lie, Mattie?'

'Maybe the odd exaggeration or two, Jen. I've been known to take artistic licence with a few of my tales!' he laughed.

'Oh! I'll set the record straight when they ring me. Why do they have to wait until Monday? Have they planned any medical interventions over the weekend?'

'Strangely enough, they haven't mentioned any interventions at all. I honestly don't know, Jen. Maybe they want to run more tests, but they're all just formalities.'

Jenny's frustration was palpable. 'And have you still got the pains and aches?'

'Oh, the Fibro flare is as active as ever. My fingers are the worst. I can hardly make a fist anymore. Neck, shoulders, back, arms, legs... you name it! You know what I'm like after being in a new bed!'

'Oh, Mattie. I was hoping you'd be coming home to your own bed sooner.'

Matt sensed her disappointment. 'I know, Jen. It's out of my hands, love. For now, I'll just relax,

148

Seeking a Cure

maybe work on my novel in the library. A bit of quiet time, you know?'

Jenny's tone softened. 'I understand, Mattie. Just... take care of yourself, okay? And call me if you need anything.'

'I will, Jen.'

'Okay, Matt. Don't forget I'm here waiting for you. Since Con's been under the weather, I haven't seen much of Kathleen. The days are hard enough to fill around here when you don't have company.'

'Don't worry about Con. He's tougher than he looks,' Matt reassured her, his voice carrying a comforting warmth. 'Tell Kathleen to pickle him with plenty of hot whiskey. I'll talk to you later.'

Matt decided to investigate the floors below. He meandered through the corridors of St Jude's, his steps becoming lighter with each new discovery. On the ground floor there was a shop with newspapers, books and snacks, a separate coffee shop and a public restaurant where visitors and relatives could dine with the patients. Matt experienced the relief of a man who had just shed the mantle of prisoner.

The hospital's garden was a burst of colour, a refreshing change from the white and beige of the wards. He wandered aimlessly, a sense of newfound freedom guiding his path. The library was difficult to find. He had to ask twice at Reception for directions. He eventually located it tucked neatly in a corner of the corridor near the Oratory. For all the world, with the exception of a small handwritten sign that stated *Library Room 47*, this could have been just another patient's room. It was small but compact.

Frank Fahy

Matt found solace among the shelves lined with an eclectic mix of literature and medical texts. Here he met a man who introduced himself as Mike. He had a curious fascination for maps and a light-hearted perspective on life. Without introduction Mike launched straight into a conversation as if Matt was an old friend whom he knew for decades.

'Did you know, in an upside-down world, Ireland could high-five Scotland?' he chuckled. Mike had sketched a pencil drawing of Ireland over which he was tracing the shoreline of Scotland down over Carlingford Lough. 'Almost a perfect fit!' he declared. His humorous approach to linking land masses brought a smile to Matt's face.

As Matt opened his laptop, ready to dive into his writing, Mike continued his banter about rearranging the globe.

'I'll leave you to solve the mysteries of the world,' Matt quipped. 'I have my own work to get on with now.'

The morning passed in this unlikely camaraderie, a blend of storytelling and laughter. Matt appreciated the gentle normality of this interaction, a welcome respite from the rigidity of his recent days in the ward.

***

In the restless corridors of the hospital, a sense of urgency buzzed like a hive of bees disturbed. Doors slammed, urgent voices echoed, and the scurry of footsteps resonated with a disquieting rhythm. Matt lay in his bed, his attempts at sleep thwarted by the rising commotion. A nurse, slight and ghostlike, materialised at the foot of his bed,

Seeking a Cure

offering a page from a stack of A4 sheets that she was distributing.

'What's this about?' Matt asked, his voice quivering with a blend of confusion and nascent fear as his eyes skittered over the chilling message.

'It's an alert, Mr O'Reilly,' the nurse responded, her calm voice stark against the storm in his mind. 'There's a Covid outbreak in the hospital.'

Those words struck Matt like a hammer blow.

'But I can't get Covid,' he shouted. 'It would kill me.'

The hospital, a supposed sanctuary, was now a trap. Panic surged in his throat, prompting a frantic call to Jenny. Her words were a clarion call: 'Get out now, Matt!'

He surged towards the nurses' station, finding the head nurse, a bastion of rules and red tape, preparing for her departure.

'Nurse, I have to leave,' Matt implored, his voice slicing through the tense air.

'You can't,' she replied tersely, her face an impassive mask of bureaucratic indifference.

'I have to. Give me my belongings or I'll leave without them,' Matt insisted, his demand slicing through the charged atmosphere like a knife.

The nurse's gaze turned steely. 'You lost that right when you were admitted. Only a doctor can discharge you.'

'I'm leaving, with or without a doctor's approval!' Matt's voice boomed, emphasising his irrevocable decision.

The standoff intensified, the head nurse clinging to protocol as if it were a lifebuoy in a stormy sea. But Matt, fortified by his previous

151

Frank Fahy

brush with death, stood immovable, his defiance a bulwark against their regulations. The other patients stirred, their whispers of anxiety and fear causing a flurry of tension at Matt's bold declaration. The mention of Covid sent shivers through the ward.

'Mr O'Reilly, please,' the nurse's voice wavered, her grip on control slipping. 'We're getting the doctor.'

'How many doctors do you have for this crisis?' Matt pressed, his disbelief ringing through the ward.

'Just one,' she admitted, her voice tinged with embarrassment.

'One? In a hospital during an outbreak?' Matt's outrage reverberated, his accusation of negligence hanging in the air like a dark cloud.

Instructed to return to his bed, Matt instead began to pack, each item he stuffed into his suitcase a step closer to freedom.

'You're causing a disturbance,' the nurse hissed, her voice laced with desperation.

'I'm saving lives,' Matt retorted sharply, 'starting with my own.'

At the height of the tension, the nurse acquiesced, offering to help with his suitcase – a tacit admission of defeat. Matt didn't linger. If it weren't for the sudden arrival of a Registrar, he would have been gone. As the young doctor faced Matt, his youthful face stark in the clinical light, his professional concern battling academic curiosity, he was met by Matt's wall of desperation and resolve.

Seeking a Cure

'Just in time, Doctor,' Matt began, his voice trailing off, his gaze piercing. 'You seem unprepared for a pandemic.'

Caught off-guard, the doctor hastily asked the nearest nurse to provide him with a face mask, a flustered apology escaping his lips. He turned back to Matt, attempting to regain composure.

'Mr O'Reilly, I understand your concerns, but...'

'I'm not just "concerned," I'm leaving!' Matt interjected, his voice shaking. 'Covid is snaking its way through these wards, and I refuse to be a sitting duck!'

The doctor, struggling to assert authority, countered, 'I can't discharge you without proper procedure. It's against hospital policy.'

'To hell with policies,' Matt spat out, his hands balling into fists. 'My taxi's on its way, and so am I.'

'Mr O'Reilly, let's be rational,' the doctor tried to soothe. 'Would you sign a release form?'

'Sign away my rights after being promised safety here?' Matt scoffed, a hollow laugh escaping him. 'Not a chance. I'll hold you accountable if need be.'

The tension peaked as the doctor uttered, 'Then, I can't let you leave.'

Matt's eyes blazed with determination. 'Call security, but they won't stop me.'

And with that, Matt charged out of the ward, and into the lift, his suitcase trailing him. He approached the front door unchallenged. With suitcase in hand and a jumble of bags haphazardly slung over his shoulder, he dashed down the hospital steps just as the taxi pulled

Frank Fahy

up, headlights cutting through the night. Matt flung his possessions into the boot which had opened automatically and settled himself in the passenger seat.

'Where to, boss?' the taxi driver asked, a hint of a Dublin lilt colouring his words. The interior of the cab was warm, a welcome contrast to the chill outside.

'The airport,' Matt panted, slumping into the seat, his voice steady with resolve.

'On to catch a flight or just the bus?' the driver inquired, pulling away from the curb, his accent thickening with curiosity.

'Bus to Galway,' Matt admitted, watching the city blur past.

The driver nodded. 'Ah, the night bus. You'll be there in no time. Dublin's a small oul' spot at this hour.'

The journey to the airport was a swift one, the roads nearly empty, the city asleep. Matt's mind wandered, but the driver was keen to chat, filling the silence with tales of Dublin life, his voice a melody of the city's heart and humour. Once at the airport, Matt exchanged a brief farewell with the driver and stepped out into the night. He found the bus easily, its engine humming in the dark, ready to embark on the long journey west.

The bus ride was tedious, the landscape a monochromatic blur as they sliced through the night. Passengers were few, some dozing, others lost in thought. Matt was alone with his anticipation, the rhythm of the road lulling him into a state of introspection. Hours slipped by until finally, the first light of dawn began to edge over the horizon. Galway approached, the city

Seeking a Cure

wrapped in a soft mist, streets quiet and expectant.

Jenny was there at the bus station, the anxiety on her face yielding to a tentative smile. With a weary grin, Matt embraced her, the stress of the journey dissolving in her arms. Home. The word filled him with warmth as he stepped through the door. The familiar scent of books and lavender greeted him, a sensory promise of peace. He was back in his own bed at last, the comfort of the familiar lulling him into a deep, restorative sleep.

Two days after his return, the ominous scratch in Matt's throat burgeoned into a relentless assault. His eyes, red and itchy, waged their own war against comfort, and his nose, a traitorous faucet, offered no respite. Reality itself seemed to fray at the edges, his every muscle screaming mutiny, his throat a barren desert of discomfort. Jenny, ever the vigilant sentinel, cast a worried glance his way.

'Matt, love, you might have to take a Covid test,' she urged, the gravity in her voice anchoring him to an unwelcome possibility.

With a grim nod, Matt agreed. They retrieved a test kit from the medicine cabinet, the starkness of its plastic a cold foreboding against his fingers. Administering the test was a small act, yet each second that ticked by as he awaited the result was a lifetime of anxiety.

Positive.

The black line glared up at him from the test like a final verdict. A visceral cocktail of disgust and fear churned within him. It was inconceivable, a cruel jest of fate. The hospital,

155

Frank Fahy

his supposed sanctuary, had become his unwitting betrayer.

With shaking hands, he dialled St Jude's, the numbers a blur of rage and trepidation. 'What the hell is going on there?' Matt's voice crackled through the phone, tinged with the sharpness of betrayal. 'I trusted ye, stayed in your clean rooms, followed every rule! And now? Covid? This is how you repay that trust?'

The nurses on the other end faced the brunt of Matt's ire, his words filled with accusation and disbelief. Beside him, Jenny's presence was a quiet comfort, her touch a wordless vow of solidarity. Matt's ordeal within the hospital's walls had reached a denouement, not with the solace of healing, but with the very affliction he had been vigilant against. The irony gnawed at him, a bitter reminder during the long days of sickness and convalescence that followed. Instead of clarity and recovery, the hospital had delivered a virus to his doorstep – a grim and unwanted guest.

A week passed, and Matt got no relief. Hot and cold sweats at night, thumping headaches, and a constant feeling of nausea from the large doses of steroids fogged his already clouded brain. On the Sunday night after his return, while Jenny was attending her choir practice in the city, Matt's silhouette could be seen pacing slowly towards the very edge of the pier. His feet, leaden with the weight of seventy years and the relentless gnawing of fibromyalgia, carried him inexorably towards the embrace of the ocean. The briny tang of sea air was a slap, a call to the raw nerves that

Seeking a Cure

screamed through his being, the endless agony of long Covid that haunted his every breath.

Matt stood at the edge, wind whispering around him. Time seemed to stretch as memories flooded his mind – moments of joy, dreams lost and found, love that had endured despite his struggles. *Is there still hope?* The question lingered in the darkness. His heart raced as he peered into the abyss below, feeling the weight of his years and his illnesses. The night air was thick with salt and unanswered questions.

But then, a gentle touch broke through the haze of despair. A hand, worn by time and sea, rested on Matt's shoulder. He turned to find Con, the old fisherman, his eyes carrying stories of storms weathered and calm seas cherished.

'Matt, my old friend,' Con's voice was a comforting whisper, imbued with the wisdom of the waves. 'The sea's not the answer tonight.'

A flicker of something unspoken passed between them, an understanding born from years of shared silence and simple nods. Matt felt the pull of the abyss lessen, the grip of despair loosening as Con's presence anchored him to the present.

'Come,' Con urged, leading Matt to his boat, anchored at the pier. 'Let's celebrate life, battered and all as it is.'

Con helped Matt descend the wooden steps and together, they boarded the small vessel, its wooden frame creaking gently under their weight. Both men disappeared into the candlelit warmth of the small cabin. The boat rocked softly, cradling them in its embrace as Con uncapped a bottle of whiskey. The amber gold liquid, a distilled essence of time and care, splashed and swirled invitingly into two coffee mugs. The first sip was warmth, a fire reigniting in their aged hearts. They sat, side by side, the boat swaying with the rhythm of the sea. Con poured more whiskey, its aroma mingling with the salty air, a toast to their shared journey.

As they drank, the night transformed around them. The stars seemed to shine a little brighter, the ocean's melody a little softer. They spoke of life, of its trials and triumphs, each word bearing witness to their resilience.

'Here's to us, Matt,' Con said, raising his glass. 'To the storms we've weathered and the calm seas we've sailed.'

Matt echoed the sentiment, his heart lighter, the shadows of his thoughts dispersed by the camaraderie and the gentle sway of the boat. They sat there, two old friends, adrift on the sea of life, finding solace in the simple joy of being alive, together in their seventies, defying the odds with each shared laugh and each sip of whiskey.

***

Matt's depressive behaviour since his Covid diagnosis was a source of constant worry to Jenny. She harboured serious concerns about his mental state, and unknown to Matt, had written a letter to his GP expressing her fears. There wasn't much more she could do. She resolved to attend her choir practice, upholding a semblance of normality. As she approached the Band Room, she dialled Matt's number on her mobile phone. It rang persistently, unanswered.

Seeking a Cure

'Must have gone for a walk,' she murmured, envisioning his phone abandoned on the kitchen table.

Upon entering the room, Jenny hung up her coat and her handbag and sorted through her folder of music. The choir master instructed everyone to take their places. Jenny noticed with some surprise that Kathleen was absent. Typically the first to arrive, Kathleen had always been her steadfast companion in the soprano section.

'I have a sad announcement,' the choir master declared. 'We will be without Kathleen McDonagh tonight. Her husband, Con, passed away suddenly this afternoon. Please, let's observe a minute of silence in his memory. May he rest in peace.'

Overwhelmed, Jenny leapt from her seat and hurried to the back of the room. She fumbled through her handbag in a state of agitation before finally seizing her mobile phone. She pressed the redial button once more. Back at the house, Matt's phone on the kitchen table vibrated slightly, buzzing insistently. Still there was no response.

159

TV Junkie
Josephine McCann

Grey snowflakes flutter, landing,
softening the clink of cold hard clods
sprinkled on the recently lowered
coffin. Memories and emotions interred
or does closure belong elsewhere?

Not my story to write
But a tale that ought to be told.
An only daughter married to an only son
As per the marriage agreement, no offspring.
Ex British Major, of Irish parents, to be
obeyed.

She would be buried with him, he had
decreed,
Far from her birthplace and the culture
In which she had been reared and
Which to her heart she held dear,
Where she once modelled for Dior.

Given to me a treasure trove of her paperwork,
Now homeless and without owner.
The inventory, alone, comes to eight pages.

With documents, photos, letters dating
from 1803 to current times, the colonisation
of Tasmania is contained therein. Memories
of a lady whose origins were both Irish and

TV Junkie

English
and who saw herself as of high social standing
retained evidence of the many exciting
decades of her life.

Her late husband had introduced us as
'His wife, a TV Junkie.' It was only after
He had passed we got to know her for herself.
We do not share his description.

The Good Old Days
Elizabeth Hannon

I 'm not sure when we got our first black and white television, probably before some All-Ireland Football Final in the late fifties. I know that we could only get the BBC for years before RTE broadcasts were received in Donegal. One of my favourite memories from our early television viewing days is 'The Good Old Days' – an old-time music hall variety show presented by Leonard Sachs. It recreated the atmosphere of the Victorian music halls with songs and sketches performed in the style of the original artistes. The audience dressed in period costume and joined in the singing, especially 'Down at the old Bull and Bush' which closed the show each week. The programme ran on BBC television for 30 years (1953 to 1983).

Leonard Sachs, in white tie and tails, introduced the acts for the show from a table permanently situated at the side of the stage. He was a hero of mine. He used such a collection of juicy, mouth-watering frothy word concoctions to introduce the artists. I would watch the show just to hear his authentic but totally over the top introductions. Intoxicated with the exuberance of his own verbosity, his gavel raised he would utter such a stream of hyperbole and onomatopoeic, alliterative salvos that guessing what act or feat the artists were going to perform, was part of the

The Good Old Days

fun. When my husband, Michael, was asked to act as Master of Ceremonies for the Amateur Irish Musical Society (AIMS) regional concert, it was decided to produce it '*a la* Leonard Sachs' and 'The Good Old Days'. Local talented soloists, duets, choirs and musicians were invited to perform. The programme was decided. Rehearsals progressed. The costume department had a field day decking out the participants. Michael was told to don evening dress, white tie and tails, with cufflinks, cummerbund and top hat. A side table was discretely positioned on the stage side apron, complete with a single rose, brandy flagon and snifter, extra-large white, handkerchief and the all-important gavel.

Michael asked me to help with writing the script for his introductions. I was thrilled and delighted. I ransacked dictionaries, thesaurus, lexicons, and what have you, to satisfy my appetite for appropriate words. The concert was a resounding success. Recently I reviewed the script and enjoyed musing to whom, among the Write-on community, I would assign, the over-the-top descriptions. So for one occasion only I ask you to mute your mics as I invite Michael to raise his gavel and introduce –

In a triumph of piquant perspicuity and convivial, cordial, cheerful connoisseurship, the ladies and gentlemen of the Write-on Society invite *Ms Mary Hodson* to don her glasses, raise her gavel and open tonight's show.

In a jubilant gem of joyous jovial jocund jocularity, this dashing devastatingly debonair dreamboat and blasé bachelor baritone bon vivant, will give his rendition of 'Some Enchanted

Elizabeth Hannon

Evening', for your delicious gratification and enjoyment, please welcome, *Mr Frank Fahy*.

Now for your divertissement delectation and delight, we present two divine divas who will give an exegesis, an éclaircissement, an exemplification of soprano sublime sententiousness, our own comely coloratura Cantatrices, singing for your pleasure, the 'Letter Duet' from Mozart's 'The Marriage of Figaro' please welcome the charming, *Ms Anne McManus* and *Ms Mary Rose Tobin*.

With magnanimity and munificence of monitorial skills, master of le bon mot, in sartorial elegance, expansive evaluator par excellence, this urbane avuncular bon vivant, connoisseur of poetry and sheer know-how, a writer for all seasons reading from his latest opus. I give you *Mr James Conway*.

On her cherished guitar, in a gracefully gifted glissando of gloriously golden grace notes garnished with genuinely great versatility on our heartstrings, from that garden of gentility, Germany and Westport, I give you, the glorious, *Ms Grit Metsch*.

Winningly winsome and whimsically well-adjusted our next writer is the epitome of efficiency and efficaciousness, a delectable damsel of daunting dexterity with both paintbrush and pen, single-minded in her pursuit of perfection on piano, stalwart in support of her hubby's environmental objectives, please welcome *Ms Nollaig O'Donnell*.

On a tree by a willow, wallowing in warbling wetness, the tomtit tells of his traumatic turbulent tendentious love affair. Here to sing the

The Good Old Days

Tit Willow song from the Mikado is *Mr Seamus Keogh.*

Next we have a colligation and contesseration (harmonious assemblage) of choristers in soporiferous resonant scintillation, singing for your gratification and edification, I give you the Write-on choral society – The Chatting Canaries! Please welcome on stage: *Kathleen, Alice, Ann, Josephine, Molly, Judith, Jutta, Joanne, Geraldine, Thomas, Brian, et al.*

Gracefully gifted in gentle grand eloquence with great versatility in vocalisation confabulation and communication, energetically enthusiastic and effervescently animated, Dynamos of developmental democratic diplomacy, provocatively unrestrained in sophisticate sophistry, unfailingly supportive of loquacious self-indulgent posers like myself this time I give you –

Chiefly yourselves!

My Earthly Ties
Mary Hawkshaw

The setting sun is closing the day,
Gliding silently across the skies,
Trailing her golden plumes of light
In hues of red, yellow, blue, and grey.

The colours blend, becoming a crimson glow,
Sweeping over the light of day.
The earth dons a cloak of red and gold,
In concert with the blazing sky.

Swaddled in this heavenly dance,
With invisible hands holding mine,
I drift beyond the bounds of time,
Enraptured in surrounding glory.

In this kaleidoscope of lights, eternity unfolds.
I taste the deep joy of serenity.
But, I'm pulled away by my earthly ties,
The fallen leaf, and the human soul,
Woven into the fabric of our being.

'What majestic power creates this heavenly
mosaic?'
Inspiring and enchanting all of us to partake.
That power from our eyes is heavily veiled.
Maybe to some, this revelation is told.
But for me, the mystery remains
While I grow old.

Daisies and Strawberries
Mary Hodson

'He loves me, he loves me not...' The chant, almost melodic, accompanied the gentle plucking of wild daisies' petals – a ritual of hope and anticipation. Each petal floated to the ground, a soft whisper against the backdrop of our leisurely walk home from the national school. The final petal's verdict, 'he loves me,' was a harbinger of joy, igniting youthful hearts with the warmth of potential affection from the boys we admired in sixth class.

The national school, a stoic edifice erected in 1840, five years before the Great Famine, stood as a sentinel at the village outskirts. Its foundation in the aftermath of the Penal Laws signified a new era of enlightenment, transitioning from the covert Hedge Schools that secretly educated children of 'non-conforming' faiths. These illegal classrooms, nestled in nature's embrace, were vibrant with the clandestine exchange of knowledge, underpinning the indomitable spirit of education against the odds.

With the advent of government-paid national school education in the 1830s, the echoes of children reciting lessons in hushed tones among the hedges faded into history. Our parents, whose education journey ended in sixth class, were nonetheless versed in the art of reading and

Mary Hodson

writing – highlighting the resilience and value placed on knowledge despite the constraints of their time. They championed the cause of education as a key to unlock the shackles of poverty, embedding in us the belief that knowledge was not just power but liberation.

'Study your books,' my father would often say, his voice imbued with the weight of unfulfilled dreams and the fervour for ours to be realised.

The poignant tale of our mother, who, despite passing the scholarship exam for secondary school, had to forego this opportunity as her contribution was indispensable at home, unfolds a narrative of sacrifice and resilience. Her journey from the confines of a demanding job, where her roles blurred between shopkeeper and caretaker, to finding solace and success in the warm embrace of the Ritz Café in Sligo, was marked by silent battles and unspoken dreams.

Our daily pilgrimage to school, through rain or shine, demonstrated our endurance. I recall my initiation into this rite of passage in 1961, my heart buoyed by a mixture of excitement and trepidation. The journey was an adventure, punctuated by the camaraderie of neighbours and the protective shadow of older students. The school itself, with its austere classrooms, ink-stained desks, and the comforting warmth of morning fires, was a crucible of character and intellect.

Each day unfurled with the rigidity of chores, the simplicity of porridge and whipped eggs for breakfast, and the anticipation of stories shared along the road home. This road, lined with the treasures of nature – wild strawberries hidden

Daisies and Strawberries

like jewels in the underbrush, the tart sweetness of sloes, and the unexpected generosity of neighbours – created a rich array of experiences that enriched our simple lives. Those were days of laughter and tears, of lessons learned in and out of the classroom, and of dreams nurtured in the fertile soil of imagination.

As we navigated through the rigours of school, with its stern discipline and the looming threat of the rod, we also discovered the resilience of the human spirit. The humiliation of punishments, the solidarity in shared adversities, and the triumphs in small victories shaped not just our memories but our very beings.

The echo of the school bell, signalling the end of another day, was a clarion call to freedom – the freedom to explore, to dream, and to simply be children revelling in the fleeting moments of childhood. Reflecting on those days, with the wisdom of years, I see not just the challenges we faced but the beauty interwoven with those challenges.

The daisies and strawberries, symbols of our innocent quests for love and delight in nature's bounty, were also emblems of our journey – a journey marked by the steadfast belief in the promise of tomorrow, nurtured by the sacrifices of yesterday.

Piecing It All Together
Kathleen Phelan

Ideas flutter around my brain
One trying to bond with the other.
Like a murmuration of starlings.

Words, elusive as wind
in the desert,
hover in the silence
between a full stop and
the next capital letter.

Slowly they descend
into my pen.
Then land on the page
Where we wrestle
Into the night.

The verbal storm abates.
We find common ground.
Following a difficult labour.
A poem is born.

Discrimination
Seamus Keogh

Train whistles piercing
Shunting busy, busy
Factory sirens blasting out
Machines busy busy
Store window signs say
Apply for vacancy inside
Foreigners stay outside.
The glass ceiling is no myth
Social prejudice does exist.
I am abandoned, cast aside
Ethnicity and colour decried

My brain tries to escape
From a cranium skull shell
This cage that is my Hell
I want to fly beyond me
Turn back and to be free
Renounce this human body
That is not me. I am a Soul
A wretched Soul in dismay
I am lost on God's pathway.
I didn't choose my colour
Or place of birth. I, a being,
Am entitled on this Earth.
Hear my cry. I am like you
Albeit of perceptible hue.

Echoes of Friendship

Mary Rose Tobin

I stood at Veronica's grave, the cold wind whispering through barren branches. The grey sky loomed, heavy with unshed tears. Six years after Clara's funeral, I was reading at her mother's grave, surrounded once more by grieving faces. Memories of shared laughter and silent screams haunted me. The rawness of the moment clung to me, heavy with the scent of moist earth and decaying leaves.

***

One chilly November evening, during my first year of college, I found myself restless and irritable. The house was unusually quiet, the kind of silence that made my boredom feel even more oppressive. My mother, noticing, suggested, 'Why don't you phone Clara Long?'

'Clara? She wouldn't want to go out with me.'

'Give her a call. You might be surprised,' said my mother.

Clara and I had attended the same secondary school, but she moved in a circle I envied. I was in the studious class, while the girls in the other class seemed to have much more fun. I craved their stylish clothes, boyfriends, and social lives. Clara had remained in school to repeat her Leaving Certificate, while I had moved on to

Echoes of Friendship

college and found myself now with very few friends.

My hand trembled as I picked up the phone, my pulse quickening with each ring.

'Hello?' Clara's voice came through the line, warm and familiar.

I took a deep breath. 'Hi, Clara, it's me. I was wondering if you'd like to go out this evening?'

A moment of silence hung in the air, and I braced myself for rejection.

'Oh, absolutely!' she exclaimed, her tone brightening instantly. 'I'm thrilled to you rang!'

I let out a breath I hadn't realised I was holding, feeling a wave of relief.

That's how it all began. Every Saturday night, full of excitement, we got dressed up and headed off for O'Grady's or the Dew Drop or whichever watering hole held the most allure for us. We would get ready for the outings in Clara's house, and it was there I became acquainted with her mother, Veronica.

Meeting Veronica for the first time was intimidating. Tall and handsome, with a booming voice and an unwavering Cork accent, she took everything in with her discerning gaze. Her relationship with her daughter fascinated me. As the oldest of nine, I didn't get any private time with my own mother. Observing Clara borrow her mother's clothes, debate her opinions, and share her friends was a revelation for me. She even called her by her first name, Ronnie.

I loved going to Clara's house. Because her mother was in the interior design business, it had a touch of sophisticated style that I'd only seen in magazines. It was also peaceful, which for me

Mary Rose Tobin

was a dream, coming from a home in constant chaos. Infants, toddlers, dogs, cats, tin whistles, guitars, the TV, the radio – the background noise was constant. By contrast, Clara's home was an island of tranquillity.

From Veronica's stories I gradually gleaned a picture of her past. One rainy afternoon, over a cup of tea, I asked her how she ended up in Galway.

She smiled as she remembered. 'I left home to study medicine in my early twenties. Can you believe it?'

'Really? But you didn't finish... What happened?' I asked, genuinely curious.

'Ah, it was Peter,' she said, her voice softening. 'A rugby player. His energy swept me off my feet. We got married not long after we met, and I left college.'

Her face clouded over as she continued. 'But then, life has its ways, doesn't it? I'm sure Clara has told you that Peter died suddenly when she was only two. I still remember that day clearly. The phone rang, and I knew something was wrong before I even picked it up.'

Suddenly uncomfortable, I blurted out. 'I'm so sorry, Mrs Long. That must have been incredibly hard.'

She nodded, her grip tightening around her cup. 'It was like a storm hit us, turning everything upside down. But I had Clara to think about, and Peter's business to manage. There was no time to fall apart.'

'How did you cope with it all?' I asked, in awe of her strength.

Echoes of Friendship

'One step at a time,' she said, a determined tone in her voice. 'I went to trade shows, attended business meetings, and learned on the go. People doubted me, a single mother trying to run a business in the 1960s, but I couldn't afford to listen to them.'

Her words were powerful, revealing the steel that carried her through those challenging times.

Veronica worked hard, yet she still found time for bridge, golf, fashionable clothes, and socialising. Young and vibrant, she had many opportunities to meet new people. Now and then, she met someone she thought Clara might take to.

On one occasion, she invited a charming man, Roger, to the house. He was tall, well-dressed, and seemed genuinely interested in both Veronica and her daughter. They sat together in the living room, with Clara perched on the edge of the sofa, her eyes narrowing as she observed Roger.

'So, Clara,' Roger said, offering her a warm smile, 'your mother tells me you enjoy painting. I'd love to see some of your work sometime.'

Clara's lips pressed into a thin line. 'I don't show my paintings to strangers,' she replied coolly, crossing her arms.

Veronica shot her daughter a reproachful glance. 'Clara, that's not very polite.'

'It's all right, Ronnie,' Roger interjected, trying to ease the tension. 'I understand.'

But Clara wasn't finished. 'Ronnie, can we leave now? We're going to be late for the pictures.'

Mary Rose Tobin

Veronica sighed, recognising the familiar resistance. 'Excuse us, Roger,' she said, standing up. 'It seems we have plans we can't change.'

As they left, Clara clung to Veronica's arm. 'We don't need anyone else, Ronnie,' she insisted, her voice resolute.

Veronica could only nod, realising once more that Clara was opposed to anyone new entering their lives.

***

The first noticeable thing about Clara was her laughter, which made everyone around her smile. Whenever she walked into a room, there was an undeniable spark—her eyes always seemed to hint at the next adventure, dancing with mischief and excitement. When Clara told a story, her animated gestures and confident delivery captivated everyone. Her long, shiny chestnut hair caught the light, shimmering as she moved.

I always felt so good when she was around. Her small acts of kindness – like slipping an encouraging note into my bag when she knew I was having a tough day or tearing me away from my studies for a picnic by the river – were constant reminders of her unwavering support. She made me feel valued with her attentive nods and warm smiles. She was always there for me.

Our friendship blossomed, and soon we, along with three fellow students, embarked on a working summer in London. The Kensington hotel where we had secured jobs as chambermaids provided us with a large apartment in White City. It was filled with a constant buzz of activity and the scent of new possibilities.

Echoes of Friendship

Each morning, the hum of the daily tube journey greeted us, a harbinger of the drudgery we faced at work. But the evenings and weekends brought freedom. The streets of London were alive with the sounds of buskers, the aromas of street food, and the vibrant energy of a city teeming with life. White City became an extension of UCG, and it seemed that every Galway student who passed through London found their way to our apartment. That summer, we forged connections with people we wouldn't have come across in Galway, forming lifelong friendships that would withstand the test of time.

For Clara and me, the change was tremendous. Accustomed to living at home, the excitement of having our own apartment, jobs, and money was exhilarating. Back then, Galway was just a small town in the west of Ireland. Here in London we could go to West End shows and see hit movies that wouldn't arrive in Ireland for another eighteen months. We could go shopping in Portobello Road or Kensington High Street and deck ourselves out in fashionable embroidered jeans, high-heeled wooden-soled clogs, and Afghan sweaters. There were scores of tourist attractions that we had never seen before, and hundreds of opportunities. We just loved our new life.

'This city is ours for the summer,' Clara declared, her eyes sparkling with excitement.

One night in London, Clara and I decided to hit a new club in Soho. The music was loud, the lights were dizzying, and the energy was electric. We danced until our feet hurt, losing ourselves in the crowd. At some point, Clara dared me to get

Mary Rose Tobin

up on stage with the band, and to my own surprise, I did. The crowd cheered as I sang a few off-key lines, Clara laughing and cheering me on from below. We stumbled back to the apartment as the first light of dawn broke over the city, giggling like schoolgirls and vowing to never grow up.

Sharing a bedroom, our bond deepened during our late-night talks. We'd often return from nights out, tipsy and laughing, collapsing onto our beds exhausted and exhilarated. One evening, after an impromptu adventure in Camden where we danced until dawn, Clara's voice lowered to a whisper, betraying an inner turmoil.

'Ronnie's getting married,' she confided, her voice barely a whisper as if speaking it aloud made it real. 'His name's Gerry. He's a bank manager, a widower with three kids. Ronnie says he's kind and patient, and always has time to listen to her.' She paused, her fingers nervously twisting the edge of the blanket. 'I told her I'm not going to the wedding. I can't imagine someone else in our lives, in our home. It's always been just the two of us. What if this changes everything?'

The topic began to dominate our late-night talks. There were moments when I had to remind her, 'Clara, it's late, let's pick this up tomorrow.' As she confided her fears about Veronica's remarriage, she revealed a vulnerability that changed my understanding of their dynamic.

'I just don't know how to feel,' she admitted another night, her emotions raw and unfiltered. 'And Ronnie doesn't see my point.' We were on the roof of our apartment, sharing a bottle of cheap wine, the city lights sprawling beneath us. In moments like these, amidst our wild college escapades, her fears felt all the more poignant.

Her anxiety about the changes consumed her. But gradually, through our endless conversations, she began to see things differently. One evening, with a sigh, she said, 'I suppose I can't spoil Ronnie's chance of happiness. I'll contact her and tell her I feel okay about it now. And I'll go to the wedding.'

Returning to Ireland, our lives shifted back to their usual rhythms. I immersed myself in college again. Once the wedding was over, Clara moved to Limerick for a course in European Studies. Her life opened up, with opportunities to learn new languages and travel across Europe. Her days were filled with friends and activities that kept her busy. Between her travels and studies, our time together dwindled. Occasionally, she would mention in passing how Gerry and Veronica were getting on, sharing little anecdotes about their life together.

'Gerry made a fantastic roast last Sunday,' she'd say, her voice tinged with a mix of acceptance and lingering curiosity about this new family dynamic.

Clara was a constant source of encouragement as I navigated the challenges of college. I remember struggling with the decision to switch courses. Clara spent hours on the phone with me, discussing my options and helping me see the bigger picture.

Mary Rose Tobin

'You've got to follow what you're passionate about,' she would say, her enthusiasm infectious. Her belief in me bolstered my courage.

I often visited her at home, particularly when she was going back to college, to help her pack. Inevitably, Veronica would rifle through her suitcase, uncovering a pilfered joint of meat from the freezer or a brand-new jacket earmarked for the next trade show. Veronica's eyes would pierce into mine as she said,

'I know you can't tell a lie! Which of my belongings has she taken this time?'

I was so terrified of giving Clara away that I almost stopped visiting!

I often think about the day that we decided to skip college for a spontaneous trip to the beach. We borrowed a friend's car and drove for hours, singing loudly to the radio with the windows down. When we finally arrived, we ran straight into the freezing water, fully clothed, and splashed around like kids. We built a bonfire as the sun set, sharing secrets and dreams as we watched the flames dance. My parents were not amused, but the adventure was worth every scolding look.

As our college years drew to a close, life began to shift gears. The carefree days of student life were giving way to new responsibilities and opportunities. Clara and I spent two further summers together, working in the States, before graduating. During this time, I went through a rough patch with a boyfriend. It was Clara who sensed my distress before anyone else. One evening, she took me aside and said,

180

Echoes of Friendship

'You know, you deserve someone who makes you smile, not someone who leaves you doubting yourself.' Her words were a turning point, helping me gather the strength to end an unhealthy relationship.

After graduation, life took us to Dublin. The city became our playground, filled with late-night pubs, spontaneous road trips, and the occasional wild party that ended with us watching the sun rise over the Liffey. But soon, our paths began to diverge. Clara met Dan, a quiet, dependable solicitor. He had a gentle presence that contrasted with Clara's vivacity. His steady blue eyes and reassuring smile quickly became her rock, offering stability and support through all her spirited ventures. They married and soon had three beautiful children.

My job was incredibly stressful. The late nights and high demands were taking a toll on me. One evening, as I was drowning in paperwork, Clara showed up unexpectedly with a bottle of wine.

'You look like you need a break,' she said, her eyes full of concern.

I sighed, feeling the weight of my workload. 'I don't know how much longer I can keep this up,' I admitted. Clara sat me down and we talked it through, her practical advice and calming presence helping me see a way forward.

'Remember, you can't pour from an empty cup,' she reminded me. She threw me a lifeline, offering a much-needed respite from the chaos of my work.

We saw less and less of each other. I was focused on my career, while Clara was looking after her children and running a small,

181

Mary Rose Tobin

successful interior design shop. Our friendship, though solid, was at arm's length. We talked often on the phone and, from time to time, had dinner in each other's houses or went out for an evening. Our attempts to reconnect were always marked with regret.

'Maybe next month?' Clara would suggest, the reality of our separate lives echoing in her tone. But happily, whenever we did meet, it felt as if no time had passed.

One evening, as we sat in her living room, Clara mentioned, 'Veronica and Gerry are coming up for a visit next weekend. It'll be nice to see them and have a family dinner together.' The mention of her mother and stepfather brought a warm smile to her face. They were such a great couple.

***

Not long afterwards I was sipping my morning coffee when the phone rang, the early call from Clara immediately filling me with a sense of foreboding.

'It's Gerry,' she said, her voice a mix of sorrow and disbelief.

My heart sank. 'No, what happened?'

'He passed away suddenly last night,' Clara explained, her words heavy with grief. 'A heart attack. No warning.'

The news hit hard. Gerry had become a steady presence in Veronica's life, bringing her much happiness. I felt a deep pang of sadness, not just for the loss of Gerry, but for Veronica, now facing the spectre of solitude again.

Months passed, and life resumed its usual pace, though the shadow of Gerry's absence

Echoes of Friendship

lingered. Clara and I continued our routines, our conversations still frequent but tinged with a new understanding of life's fragility.

I'll never forget the afternoon, when her son was about seventeen, that Clara called again. Her voice was unusually tense.

'I have an appointment at the hospital tomorrow,' she said. 'I'm a bit concerned.'

'Do you want me to come with you?' I offered, feeling a knot of worry tighten in my chest.

'No, it's all right,' she replied, trying to sound reassuring. 'Let's see what they say first.'

A few days later, she called me again, her tone now serious.

'I'm being admitted for surgery,' she said. That evening, as I walked into the hospital ward, the sterile smell and beeping machines amplified my anxiety. Clara lay in bed, looking pale but determined. When she saw me, she managed a weak smile.

'Just a bump in the road,' she said, her voice hoarse but defiant. Seeing her so frail, yet so resolute, my heart ached for her.

The smell of antiseptic filled the air, mixed with the distant murmur of nurses and patients. I only stayed for a short while before leaving her to rest.

Days turned into weeks and Clara remained upbeat about her illness. But each visit to the hospital, each phone call, brought us closer in a way that reminded me of our younger years. The tempo of our lives had changed again, and all we could do was move forward, one step at a time.

A couple of weeks into her illness, at a medical conference, I bumped into Clara's cousin. We found ourselves talking. The hum of the

Mary Rose Tobin

delegates' chatter surrounded us as we sipped our tea.

'It's a tough situation,' he said, shaking his head. 'Especially knowing how little time Clara has left.'

I nearly dropped my cup. 'What did you just say?'

He looked at me, puzzled. 'You didn't know? I thought you were aware. Clara's cancer is terminal. Her doctors only give her about a year.'

My world spun, and everything felt distant. Clara, with her infectious laugh and unstoppable spirit, was facing an unimaginable future. The air felt thin, and I struggled to breathe.

'I... I didn't know,' I stammered, my voice barely a whisper.

'I'm so sorry,' he said, seeing the shock his words had caused. 'I assumed she had told you.'

I nodded, the weight of the revelation settling heavily on my shoulders. Clara, my vibrant, spirited friend, was going to die. I took a deep breath, trying to steady myself. I needed to figure out how best to support her.

The rest of the day felt unreal. That evening, I called Clara. She answered on the second ring, her voice as cheerful as ever.

'Hey, what's up?'

After some chit-chat I swallowed hard, trying to keep my voice steady. 'Clara, I met your cousin Jim at that conference today.'

There was a brief silence on the other end. 'Oh,' she said quietly.

'Why didn't you tell me how ill you really are?' I asked, my voice breaking.

'I didn't want to upset you,' she admitted.

Echoes of Friendship

Tears welled up in my eyes, but I blinked them away. 'Don't ever worry about upsetting me. I'm here for you, Clara. Whatever you need, whenever you need it.'

'I know,' she replied softly. 'Thank you.'

Clara was in great spirits most of the time. She insisted that everyone who visited was cheerful and positive. One thing she could not tolerate was to see anyone cry about her illness. I never cried in her presence. But many times, on the way home from visiting her, I had to pull the car into the side of the road to wipe the tears from my eyes and take some deep breaths before I could continue.

She maintained the bravest face possible and was determined that she would see her kids grown up before she died. I have a photo of Clara seeing her son off to his graduation ball, and it upsets me to this day.

She passed away shortly before her fiftieth birthday. The morning was unusually quiet when my phone rang, the screen showing Veronica's name. A sinking feeling gripped my heart as I answered.

'Hello?'

There was a pause, then a shaky breath. 'She's gone... Clara's gone,' Veronica's voice trembled, each word soaked in disbelief and sorrow.

I felt as if the ground had been pulled from under me. 'No... it can't be,' I whispered, my throat tightening.

'Last night,' Veronica continued, her voice cracking. 'We were all with her. She just... slipped away.'

185

Mary Rose Tobin

Tears streamed down my face as I listened, the weight of her words pressing heavily on my chest. 'Veronica, I'm so, so sorry,' I managed to say, my voice barely holding together.

'She was so courageous,' Veronica said, her sobs breaking through. 'Right until the end. But now she's gone, and I... I don't know what to do. She was everything to me, my only child.'

My heart shattered for her. Veronica had already endured so much loss, and now this. 'I wish I could take away your pain,' I said, between sobs. 'Clara was... she was extraordinary.'

'I know,' Veronica whispered. 'I know.'

We stayed on the phone for a while, sharing our grief in the silence, the enormity of Clara's absence sinking in. As I hung up, the reality of the loss hit me with full force. Clara was gone, and nothing would ever be the same again.

Clara's husband and children took charge of the funeral arrangements, supported by her close-knit circle of friends. As the arrangements were being made, Veronica wondered why I wasn't included in the ceremonies. She called me, insisting:

'You need to be a part of this. I want you to read at Clara's grave.'

I couldn't deny her this request.

'You were a true friend to her,' Veronica insisted, her sincerity evident even in her sorrow.

The cemetery was in a picture-perfect setting, the Corrib in the background, the grave adorned with floral tributes, and the Galway countryside stretching out beyond. As we assembled at the graveside, the murmur of the gathering was muted by the gentle rustling of leaves. I took a

186

Echoes of Friendship

deep breath, feeling the rough texture of the paper in my hands, and stepped forward. My own words seemed inadequate to do Clara justice, so I chose instead to read a poem for her:

'Do not stand at my grave and weep,
I am not there; I do not sleep.
I am a thousand winds that blow,
I am the diamond glints on snow.
I am the sunlight on ripened grain,
I am the gentle autumn rain.
When you awaken in the morning's hush,
I am the swift uplifting rush
Of quiet birds in circled flight.
I am the soft stars that shine at night.
Do not stand at my grave and cry,
I am not there; I did not die.'

I finished and glanced at Veronica, who nodded encouragingly, tears glistening in her eyes. The poem's words resonated deeply.

Later, as we all prepared to leave, Veronica came to my side.

'Thank you,' she whispered. 'You honoured her perfectly.'

I nodded, unable to speak, the lump in my throat too large.

***

For weeks and months after the funeral, I was desolate. The weight of Clara's absence hung over me like a shadow, and I struggled to stay afloat. One day, a couple of friends mentioned that Veronica was constantly asking about me.

'She wants you to visit her,' they said. I couldn't understand why she singled me out from

Clara's other friends for special attention, but the persistent requests nudged me into action.

I decided to go and see her. She had downsized after Gerry died and now lived alone in a beautiful little bungalow in Oughterard. The house had a stunning view of Lough Corrib and was charmingly decorated. When I arrived, Veronica greeted me warmly, ushering me inside.

'It's so nice to see you,' she said, taking out the good china for tea. As she poured, her hands steady but her eyes betraying her sadness, she made it clear that she wasn't ready to talk about Clara.

'The garden looks lovely, Mrs Long,' I ventured, trying to fill the silence.

'Oh please, call me Ronnie! And thank you,' she replied, a faint smile touching her lips. 'The garden's been my saviour.'

We made small talk for an hour or so, skirting around the topic of Clara. The conversation felt like a delicate dance, each of us careful not to step on painful memories. It was all a bit awkward.

A month later, I visited again. This time, Veronica seemed more at ease, her movements less hesitant. We spoke about the changing seasons, the view of the lake, and the small joys that punctuated her days. After that I went to see her often. The visits, though marked by an unspoken grief, slowly began to feel like a step towards healing.

On one visit, as we sat by the window watching the sun set over the lake, Veronica turned to me, her eyes reflective.

Echoes of Friendship

'It's okay for us to talk about Clara now,' she said softly.

I took a deep breath, feeling the lump in my throat. 'Oh yes, well, whatever you think...'

She looked down at her hands, then back at me. 'There's something I wanted to say to you.'

I leaned in, sensing the gravity of the words to come. 'What is it, Ronnie?'

'I never told you, but that letter Clara wrote... I knew it had your support behind it,' she said, her eyes meeting mine with a mixture of gratitude and sadness. 'I have you to thank for my marriage with Gerry working out.'

Her words hit me like a wave, leaving me momentarily breathless.

'Letter? What letter? I stammered.

Memories of the late-night London talks with Clara flooded back, and the impact of those hours began to dawn on me.

Veronica's gaze softened. 'You helped her accept it, didn't you? She told me it was your advice that gave her the strength to write that letter.'

Tears welled up in my eyes. 'I hadn't even remembered ... I didn't know it had made such a difference,' I whispered, my voice breaking.

Veronica reached across the table, her hand covering mine. 'It did. More than you realise.'

We sat in silence for a moment, the weight of unspoken words hanging between us. The sun dipped below the horizon, casting a warm, golden glow over the lake. In that shared silence we found a fragile peace.

From then on, our conversations flowed more freely. We talked about Clara, shared our

Mary Rose Tobin

memories, and allowed ourselves to laugh and cry. The visits became a source of consolation for both of us, a way to honour Clara's memory and find comfort in each other's company. The garden, vibrant with hydrangeas and fuchsias, became a backdrop for our healing process.

***

Clara's husband Dan remarried in due course. His new wife, Evelyn, showed remarkable humanity in building a blended family that seamlessly included Veronica. Evelyn's kindness and organisational skills were evident as she made a point of keeping Veronica close to her grandchildren. When it was needed, she found the perfect sheltered accommodation, ensuring it met Veronica's exacting standards. During a visit, I noticed how Evelyn had gone out of her way to decorate the place with Veronica's favourite pieces.

'She always loved this vase,' Evelyn mentioned, her voice soft. Her efforts brought a sense of warmth and familiarity to this strange place.

Like all of her previous homes, this little house could have featured in *Homes and Gardens*. I enjoyed visiting her there. Veronica had a magic touch, and surrounded herself, even in later life, with style and glamour. I was moved when she introduced me to people not, as heretofore, 'Clara's friend,' but as 'my friend.'

Veronica died in her late eighties after a short illness. I was touched by the family's request that I read at her grave. As I stood there, reflecting on her life, I felt a profound sense of gratitude for having known both her and Clara. I was mindful

Echoes of Friendship

of how intertwined our lives had become, and of how even the smallest actions can have a lasting impact.

After the funeral, I drove to Veronica's garden and sat quietly there. It was now overgrown, but still hinted at the elegance she had once brought to it. I thought back to the countless nights Clara and I had spent talking, the dreams we shared, and the fears we faced together. Veronica's words echoed in my mind:

'I know I have you to thank for my happy marriage with Gerry.'

Encouraging Clara to accept her mother's remarriage had been, to me, a small insignificant display of solidarity. But its ripple effect had changed lives.

As I left the garden, I felt a sense of closure. Clara and Veronica were gone, but the echoes of their friendship, courage, and acceptance were all around me.

The Watcher
Mary Hawkshaw

I am a beacon of hope
Flickering across this war-torn land,
Where children's cries can't fade away.
They lie buried beneath the rubble and decay.

In Gaza.
I am their light, their truth, with my arms open
wide.
In this endless night, I'll be their guide.
In the turmoil of storms and endless fears,
I'll wipe away each falling tear.

Israel,
You have turned away from all my words and
me.
Your sword of death flies in the skies,
And plunges deep to pierce their sunrise.
War has claimed each precious child.
Wisdom will forever ask you why,
You choose a path where thousands would die

In homes where children laughter filled their
dreams,
Now horror leaps and terror screams.
Your
War has cleft my heart in twain.
In realms of peace, where I abide,
I have chosen the innocent to be by my side.

The Watcher

In the horror of war, in the day's fading light,
I am their voice, their truth, I feel their plight.
In the heart of despair, where innocence weeps,
I am the guardian, the watcher, who never
sleeps.

One Field Once More
James Conway

And out of a white, stone cottage
she came above the smoke of whisper
with bog and cold fields rising and lonely
days of missing laughter, bent beside a fireside

listening to the walls of rumour... that's all they
could say 'she's been crowned queen of the
orphans'

surrounded by the haunt of hymns, one pitch
higher
than another, yes the girl who is a neighbour's
adopted

daughter, the one with the silent tongue... let
her so,
steer her boat of wisdom, each testy wave
embracing
her in the wood of a thousand ribs, where
episodes are
forever, where her heart is all horizon to the
core...

let silence be her oars of observation, she of a
stone
white cottage above the smoke of whisper...
resting now on the shoulders of forever, scooped
up at the gates of one field, once more.

A Mother's Dilemma

Kathleen Phelan

I had given up on pleading with my daughter Yvonne to tidy her room. My pleas were as useless as a kite without wind. The floor was buried under a mountain of wrinkled shirts, dog-eared novels, damp towels, and broken gadgets. It looked like a half-finished jigsaw puzzle that no one wanted to complete. The smell of stale pizza and dirty socks lingered in the air, making me gag. The only sound was the buzzing of a fly, trapped in the window.

Next week was her 16th birthday, and she was out with her friends on a shopping spree. I decided to do a bit of organising to surprise her. I was hoping she wouldn't come home for hours. And thankfully, I managed to fit the puzzle together just in time.

The bedroom had plenty of shelving, a decent-sized dressing table, and a nice-sized wardrobe. You could say everything that had a home had been evicted. I got to work putting each item back in its proper place. By the time I was finished, it looked as organised as an upmarket boutique. The clothes were neatly folded, stacked, or hung. The dressing table was clear of clutter, and the shelves displayed her favourite books and photos.

She arrived home to see me standing in her bedroom, proud as a college graduate. She

Kathleen Phelan

entered and squealed like a piglet finding a truffle. She put her arms around me and kissed me.

'Oh, you are the best mammy in the world. But now I won't be able to find anything. So don't EVER enter my bedroom again. And where's my diary? I left it under the pillow.'

I felt a pang of guilt. I had found her diary and read a few pages. I couldn't help myself. I wanted to know what was going on in her life. And what I read shocked me. She had a boyfriend. A secret boyfriend. And they were planning to run away together. I swallowed hard and tried to act casual.

'Oh, your diary? I put it in the top drawer of your dressing table.'

She narrowed her eyes at me, opened the drawer and took out her diary, then gasped. She turned to me with a look of horror and anger.

'Mum, how could you? Why did you read my diary? How could you invade my privacy like this? How could you lie to me? How could you ruin my birthday?'

'Yvonne, love, I only moved it to the drawer. I didn't read it,' I lied.

'I know you read it because the bookmark is on a completely different page to the one I left it on,' she said.

My heart pounded in my chest, my throat tightened, and my eyes stung with tears. I had messed up. I had pushed her away. I had lost her.

'Yvonne,' I said, 'we need to talk.'

She ran out of the room, slamming the door behind her. I heard her footsteps on the stairs, then the front door slamming. She was gone. I

A Mother's Dilemma

collapsed on the bed, feeling the softness of the sheets and the warmth of the sun on my face. I had solved the puzzle, but at what cost?

St Bridget
Nollaig O'Donnell

Stories we are told of Bridget of the Gael;
Founder of monasteries and brewer of ale!
From a slave, like St. Patrick, to a saint of our
isle;
To your wells we have flocked during many a
trial.
Pal of the powerless, the meek and the mild;
Healer of sick and saint for the child.
Friend of the Earth – finding God in creation;
Your green cross of Christ – symbol for our
nation.
Now, drawing near the end of the cold winter-
time,
And the long, dark days we leave behind;
To the light, once again, we look in hope,
As it spreads o'er the land like your holy cloak.

Bheith Gheal
Póilín Brennan

When dear Beith beckoned in golden russles
a call so clear in welcomed bough.
A knowing of knowings – an emotion so great
of love, tenderness – a euphoric joy.

In warmth I felt a oneness – imaginings and
transfigurations.
No separation – an element of elements,
of kin and kind and swirling energies.
Knowing someday I will be you, and you will
visit me, sharing sighs and russled whispers
on the breeze.

A chara Bheith Gheal – a sage of now.
A nature Bandia of pure abandon.
Ó talamh 'is spéir, akasha of wisdom,
a divinity of áilleacht – dlúthchara mo chroí.

Smelling of Roses
Frances Dermody

On her walk to work every morning, Kate stopped to admire the roses. Until last Monday, the sight and smell of pink roses had been enough to brighten her day. On her way home on Monday, she stole a single rose and gave it pride of place on her kitchen table. That rose was proof that she could still feel the thrill of something forbidden and fight back against the woman who hadn't felt excited about anything in a very long time. Stealing that one rose on Monday was enough to make her feel her heart pounding in her ears. By Wednesday, one rose was no longer enough to keep up that feeling.

Yesterday, she had taken every last one of the roses, for the feeling only. Pink roses themselves had lost their appeal through their everyday presence in her kitchen. Upping the crime level had come with a feeling of being watched from a distance, yet there was no evidence anywhere of the person who had nurtured the roses for years.

This morning, police cars and cordons surrounded the rose garden. A dark-haired woman in a white plastic suit was taking soil samples close to the rose bush. Kate felt her heart pound in her ears all over again. Was she in trouble? Was she a suspect in some terrible crime? This was way better than stealing roses.

The Discovery of the Death of a Goose

James Conway

Stumbling he falls
on a shadow of life
knees and head first
with elbows and torso
landing behind.

At first, then second
the silk of feathers
of neck hot and broken
sends the devil running
laughing screaming
up and down his spine.

Tingling in a sea named
'red hot cerebral'
he wretches, then stretches
forward, hugging his wound
of borrowed misfortune,
his goose dead and grey
in a womb called boghole,
stricken down by some rat
shaped jet ferrying loafers
to a week or two of sunburnt
gluttony and apartmental lust.

'Scream please geese, I'm crying!'

Perfect Passings
Deirdre Anne Gialamas

My siblings and I returned from school one day to an eerily silent house; no bubbling, boiling sounds came from the kitchen, no welcoming clang of cutlery being set hurriedly on the dining room table. We glanced at each other for clues for this odd state of affairs. There was a brief note: 'Do not disturb!' 'Serve yourselves.' We discovered her ensconced in the sitting room pouring over an oversized volume, *The Complete Works of Shaw*, lost to the world. Later times it would be Ibsen or her old friend G.B. again or some biography of someone we'd never heard of. Though she did deserve them, my mother only rarely allowed herself those beautiful breaks from bedlam. They were also breaks for us from homework and good behaviour.

Occasionally there were other absences from the kitchen sink and those were not good. We'd find her bent over, glasses halfway down her nose, at the knitting machine, housed in the same sitting room.

'Oh, God,' we'd moan, 'Mammy's knitting!'

She would draw the handle over and back, over and back, stopping often to make readjustments and to check the results.

'Don't speak to me, please,' she'd demand. Although anxious to complete whatever

Perfect Passings

garment she was working on, often a jumper or cardigan for one of us, she would always have food left ready in the oven.

Born in the midlands of Ireland, her only sibling volunteered to work on the farm so my mother could continue her secondary education. Graduating with top marks, she taught school for two years, then worked for a period as a solicitor's personal assistant. When I was around eleven or twelve, she unwittingly discovered to her dismay that I knew nothing about Geometry. My school taught subjects through the medium of Irish and at times it was challenging to keep up.

Clad in black, with starched white relief near her mouth which droned on about angles and theorems, my Maths teacher tried hard, but I was writing fairytales in my head and pondering all the great ones I had read. Soon after, a blackboard was purchased. Having first established that indeed my knowledge was nil, my mother tutored me first in English, then translated it into Gaeilge until I fully grasped everything and even began to see the beauty in it all. In class I thrived for a short while. Soon the lack-lustre nasal intonations coming at me, invading my ears, deftly delivered me once again into the embrace of the Brothers Grimm and Hans Christian Andersen and their wonderful world of words. However, I shall never forget the divine patience and empathy my mother showed me during our blackboard sessions, and my learning went way beyond Pythagoras and his corners.

Deirdre Anne Gialamas

The saddest I ever saw my mother was when we were marched up, one by one, to see her on a large iron bed in her cold high-ceilinged room. Propped up with several pillows by my father, her pale face merged with the sea of white linen on which she lay. This is one of my earliest memories of my mother, shortly after her newborn died. I kissed her on the forehead. Grief, grey coloured, shadowy, was in the air vying with the stillness. Following her first brood of five robustly healthy babies, my mother had given birth to two girls who both died in their first weeks of life. When pregnant with the eighth, she refused to buy any baby necessities or prepare in any way for the birth.

'I was so certain this one would die too,' she told me years later. Though four weeks premature, 'this one,' Paul, came out roaring, now a strapping six-foot four charmer.

My mother's heart swelled with abundant love for all of us. That she had a favourite, Fintan, did not diminish in any way her deep feelings for the rest of us. In my teens, she would tease me by saying,

'Deirdre, you ought to make a cup of tea for your brother, poor Fintan,' and I would spit fire. Often her great-grandmother was quoted in a half-serious, half-mocking manner: 'The men, the men, look after the men!'

In bygone days, the men worked long hours in the fields and the women kept house. My mother could understand this arrangement since if the men were not clothed and fed, there would be no hay made, harvests collected, cows milked or food to cook.

Perfect Passings

My mother was a worrier. Did she worry for her children's welfare, relatives, friends, the poor and hungry? Surely all of these. On my visits home as an adult, we would usually sit across from each other in the dining room on the comfy armchairs by the fireplace and chat until nightfall. After hours of talk and laughter, content that all was said, we would lapse into a delicious, trance-like silence, loath to break the spell by switching on the lights. It was on those occasions I would see a tension taking over my mother's smiling face, barely discernible in the near darkness.

'Mammy, stop worrying,' I would reprimand, 'You'll get cancer, I see you stewing' and then she'd shuffle and ask, 'What will we have for supper?'

'Tis the musha.'

None of us ever knew what 'the musha' was. It often punctuated the end of a conversation, a task completed. It sometimes served as an answer to a perplexing question. She did continue to stew, and she did get cancer five years before her death.

'You know, you were so right, Deirdre,' she would later admit. I reassured her that studies now showed no direct link between worry and cancer. She could not abide the punchy slogans used by fundraisers for cancer research, so pointedly chose not to donate to them. She was not 'battling' cancer nor was she a cancer 'survivor,' she had cancer, that was it. Not for her the whispered 'I have the big C' as it was often referred to by many.

Deirdre Anne Gialamas

It seemed cruelly ironic that a woman so ahead of her time, with a keen interest in health and nutrition, should get this disease. On my mother's shelves sat books on food additives, the infamous 'Es' being of greatest interest and concern. In the early seventies, she took up a modified version of macrobiotic cooking. Hoping for a long life for all of us, we dined on mushy mounds with unfamiliar smells.

'It's an acquired taste,' she'd retort if we complained. Millet, bulgur, buckwheat, black-eyed peas, black rice and lentils of every colour filled a large wooden box on the kitchen counter with 'B R E A D embossed on its lid.

A close friend once said to me, 'What's that? Sure you have only birdseed in there. Where's the bread? Oh, God help you!'

She owned two pressure cookers when they were virtually unheard of. She learned Transcendental Meditation and some of us called her a hippie. Paul showed great curiosity about this strange new practice, which had his mother disappear upstairs for twenty minutes morning and evening. He would wait until a short time had elapsed then burst suddenly into her bedroom, certain that this time, he'd find her suspended in mid-air. He was always too late. She would be resting quietly, eyes closed, stuck fast to the bed.

My daughter Fiona was born seven weeks premature on the first of January 1998 in Athens, where I live. An epidemic of European Flu, which inflicted dangerously high fevers on its victims, was in the news. My husband and three-year-old son were ill with it the very week

Perfect Passings

I took my infant home. Clinic staff had warned me it was critical she not contract any infections, so I had in-laws help me stock up on disposable gloves and gallons of rubbing alcohol. By isolating my daughter, as well as scrubbing down handles and my hands repeatedly, she escaped unscathed.

Meanwhile, back home in Dublin, my mother had undergone yet another operation, her final one. She was weakening by the day and knew she would not recover. Some weeks before she died, I said to her,

'Mammy, listen, I know I won't see you again, since you're going to die, so I'll say goodbye on the phone. Can you do me a favour, though? Will you promise to come back and haunt me?'

I immediately felt remorse for the words that came out of my mouth, even though we had always spoken with ease on the subject of death. A pregnant silence ensued. I waited; sure I'd killed her. I waited more. Then a small, thin voice said,

'Oh, it hurts, I thought I burst my stitches'.

My mother paused and said in a more audible tone;

'In all my puff I've never heard of such a request!'

She was laughing, I was laughing relieved I hadn't hastened her demise.

Hearing of my decision not to travel and fearing I'd greatly regret it later, my sisters urged me to reconsider. By then Fiona had achieved a respectable weight and had reached her original expected date of delivery.

Deirdre Anne Gialamas

'Take that baby home to Mammy', my sister Mary begged. We both arrived on 22nd March, Mother's Day in Ireland, without any notice. As I stood in the open doorway holding my child, my mother looked right across the room at us and perked up a little as she recognised me and exclaimed in a soft tone,

'Well... Deirdre Mooney!'

My name never sounded so sweet. I knew by the joy in her voice I'd made the right decision for the three of us. Fiona was carefully placed in her arms for a few seconds and only two words were uttered,

'She's exquisite!'

'Does Deirdre know she has all the wealth in the world?' she would later ask my sister Irene, referring to the two children I'd had so late in life.

Irene simply replied, 'Yes, She does.'

Soon all my siblings had converged in Dublin from various corners of the world. We nursed our mother, spoke to her, laughed with her, lay beside her quietly in turns. We ensured she had effective pain relief, prepared an outfit of her choosing and followed her guidance on assembling items needed for the priest's visit to anoint her. One day she polished off a whole barmbrack, an Irish sweetened fruit bread, with a dear friend and neighbour over a pot of tea.

'Well, it's not going to do me much harm now,' she had said, the entirety of the afternoon visit conducted in their native tongue, Gaelic.

As my mother began to fade, we kept vigil outside her room sitting on the last few steps of

208

Perfect Passings

the stairs, taking turns to spend time with her. On one of those occasions, she confided in me that she was spiritually quite ready to die, at peace with herself, and her family and friends though one niggling concern about the actual mechanics of dying remained, preventing her from being totally at ease.

'Will I be coughing and spluttering?' she asked me. This both chilled and warmed my heart at once. Chilled it as I thought of my mother being pained by such dread, warmed it with gratitude for this incredible opportunity to reassure her and assuage her fears. Having worked in France for several years as a freelance nurse, I had many terminally ill clients and so my experience with death was considerable. Happily, all my clients had had smooth transitions. My mother trusted this and felt greatly relieved.

Aunt Margaret, my mother's only sibling, flew in from New York City the morning of 28th March 1998, the day her sister passed away. Many hospice staff around the world have observed that the dying can choose, to a certain degree, when to die, delaying their time of departure to say farewell to loved ones coming from afar. This was evident in my mother's case. She knew her sister would have been distraught if she had not been able to bid farewell to her. The priest was called the same morning to give her the last rites. We all stood around her bed, three tall sons, three daughters, our father and Aunt Margaret. When the priest remarked that it must have taken an awful lot of porridge 'to feed this lot' a

Deirdre Anne Gialamas

tiny, proud smile crossed my mother's lips. She looked content, satisfied, and slipped further away throughout the day.

With her husband of fifty years lying by her side, my mother took leave of us that same evening at ten minutes before eleven. The clock in my father's ham radio shack, which had kept perfect time for over twenty years, stopped short at 22.50 never to go again like in the old song *My Grandfather's Clock*. One of my brothers opened the window to let her spirit float freely. Later, the undertakers carried her remains out of the house. Just as her body was carried under the hall lamp, the bulb blew with a little puff, and someone remarked that the light had gone out of the house.

As fate would have it, there was a gravediggers' strike in full swing in Dublin, resulting in my mother not being buried until April 2nd. So, my father said goodbye to her fifty years to the day after he first set eyes on her; April 2nd , 1946. Police bikes and cars escorted the funeral hearse to Shanganagh, where my mother was laid to rest.

After the funeral, we came back to the house, where kind neighbours and friends had refreshments in waiting, delicious homemade pies, cakes, tarts, madeira buns and sandwiches. I wanted to tell you, Mammy, how wonderful the sitting room looked with the double doors opened onto the dining room, all the best chinaware in use and some borrowed for the day. I overindulged, chatting and laughing giddily through the whole send-off, intoxicated with the sugar. The day was all

Perfect Passings

about you. I knew that later that night I would come up to your bedroom and you would pull back the duvet on Daddy's side as he'd be in his shack and I'd know you meant 'Hop in, keep warm' and we'd chat happily about the long day. And your soft eyes would smile at me gently.

We didn't have our little tete-a-tete; I just cried in my room next to yours.

Returning some days later to Athens, I was comforted somewhat by the bitter-sweet balance of nature, of life itself. I had lost you, my mother, yet gained a daughter. While you were still alive, I had withdrawn my request for return visits, and you never did come back except in the sweetest and most comforting of dreams. You have gone yet still remain so intimately with me in my way of mothering my children, my gestures, my efforts to impart wisdom to them. Oftentimes I feel it is you, not I, standing here.

The Scottish poet, Robert W. Service wrote in the last verse of his poem *The Mother*:

'There will come a glory in your eyes,
There will come a peace within your heart;
Sitting 'neath the quiet evening skies,
Time will dry the tear and dull the smart.
You will know that you have played your part;
Yours shall be the love that never dies:
You, with Heaven's peace within your heart,
You, with God's own glory in your eyes.'

Bamboo Wings
James Conway

The dreams were like small
jingles, little coins, round
faced, bronzed maybe, if I
could decipher their thoughts

in clouds, all the while down
darkened lanes where light
sought out, twinkling, its
breath climbing where no

dream was meant to be... in birth
and they were alive again, warm
with every calibre of tingle

waiting with seconds and rumour,
packing themselves, invisible into
the yawn of the morning falling

with Bamboo Wings holding me up

Love is – 'Chips'
Thomas MacMahon

Primary school – a good leveller for the social
classes.
Doctors, engineers and block layers mix with all.
A good education to play with the masses.
Nobody made to feel different or small.

Adventures to a different suburb.
Football matches were seven-a-side.
Greens surrounded by the urban.
All the boys and girls play with pride.

Snap, flap, whirl, extractor fans come alive.
And then the beautiful smell of chips comes
across the green.
The chorus of mothers calling for tea has
arrived.
'Macker, come in for your tea,' straight from Mrs
Geareaty's lips –
And I was accepted.

Piano Man
Mary Rose Tobin

The invitation to the reunion sat at the edge of Chris's cluttered piano, a nagging presence against the backdrop of scattered sheet music and lesson plans. It seemed out of tune with the rhythm of his days, which now marched to the steady beat of piano lessons, the adrenalin of weekend gigs, and the song writing that filled his rare free nights.

He had no intention of going to the reunion. That part of his past was long behind him. But the memories began to flood back anyway.

Twenty-five years had passed since the day Chris, alongside his classmates in the medical faculty, had donned the cap and gown. He could still remember the faces of his classmates, bright with the promise of healing others. Chris had walked the same stage and grasped the same diploma. But there the similarities ended. While his peers successfully navigated their internships and hospital placements, he had foundered under the pressures of clinical rotations. In particular, the ugly rages of consultants proved more than his spirit could bear.

Today, he was working on a song, his entry for the *Galway New Music Festival* competition. The prize money would come in useful, and he had some promising ideas. The song would be

Piano Man

a reflection on his own life, written in the style of a Bob Dylan ballad.

His eyes moved to the framed photograph over the bookcase. A small boy with blonde curls and piercing blue eyes sitting at a piano, his little fingers effortlessly coaxing out intricate tunes. Despite his tender age, everyone said his musical talent was unmistakable. Yet, Chris was aware that the image did not reveal the full story. A restless energy flickered behind the youthful gaze. His younger self was racked with tension and anxiety.

The photograph nudged him towards some lines for his song:

In a room filled with silence, a tiny boy plays,
Curious fingers finding each phrase,
Blue eyes piercing as golden curls shine
In a whole world of dreams each note he'd define.

Next in the song he could mention his schooldays. In the classrooms and playgrounds, Chris remembered being adrift in a sea of faces, his talent overshadowed by his struggles to connect. He grappled with the weight of his own solitude, yearning for companionship amidst the bustling hallways. More words for the song flowed from his memories.

In school, classes chatter, his spirit won't lift.
A wandering mind is a curse or a gift.
Alone in a crowd, he's there but he's gone

Mary Rose Tobin

The songs of the mind, they just flow on and on.

Now well into his memory trip, Chris thought about how, in medical school, he found himself torn between two worlds: the promise of a successful career as a doctor and the siren call of his true passion, music. Each year brought with it renewed desires to abandon the path laid out before him, to forsake the safety of academia for the uncertainty of a life devoted to melody and rhythm. Yet, time and again, he succumbed to the persuasive voices of his parents, urging him to stay, to follow the rational course set forth by others.

Chris shuddered as he relived the home tensions that simmered beneath the surface; the heated dialogues that unfolded about Chris's path in life. It was not until he completed his internship, standing on the precipice of a future forged in medicine, that he finally found the courage to defy expectations. He would never forget the day he told his parents.

At the family dinner, emotions were high, simmering just beneath the surface.

'Chris, your father and I have been talking. We really think you should reconsider your decision to leave ...

'Mum,' Chris interrupted before she could even finish, 'I've heard this speech before. Yes, I know medicine is a great career and all, but...'

'But nothing,' she cut in, her voice a mix of exasperation and worry. 'We're just thinking of your future.'

216

Piano Man

'Yeah, well, my future's not in a hospital,' Chris shot back, barely containing his frustration.

His dad, not one to beat around the bush, jumped in. 'Music is a hobby, Chris. You need to think about your future. A career in medicine is stable, respectable,' Be realistic...'

'Realistic?' Chris's voice climbed. 'Because following what you want is unrealistic?'

Mum's response was tinged with concern. 'We just want what's best for you. We don't want you to struggle, chasing a dream that might never come true.'

Chris's reply was firm. 'I know, and I understand your concerns. But I'd rather struggle doing something I love than feel trapped in a life that doesn't fit me.'

Dad's frustration was evident. 'You're being naïve and immature. Life isn't about doing whatever you feel like. It's about making smart choices.'

Chris stood his ground. 'Isn't it smarter to follow a path that makes me happy? I don't want to wake up one day, realising I lived my life according to someone else's idea of success.'

Chris, please,' his mum tried again, softer this time, but Chris was already steamrolling ahead.

'No, I get it, okay? I get it. You're worried. But I'm not you. This... this is me trying to be me.'

Dad's patience had run out, and his next words were cold and final. 'Fine. Ruin your life. But don't expect us to watch and applaud.'

His voice was devoid of the warmth Chris had hoped for, and he recoiled as if struck.

217

Mary Rose Tobin

'Chris,' his mum started, but her husband's stern look cut her off.

'No. He's made his choice. Let him live with it.'

The conversation ended there, but the echo of their words hung heavy in the room, a chasm growing between them.

Chris' mind returned to the song.

Oh Chris, Oh Chris, with your heart on the keys,
Fighting the tide, always trying to please.
Caught in the storm of what you should be,
The song of your soul sets you free.

Chris embarked on a new chapter of his life. He traded his stethoscope for the piano keys, his white coat for a battered leather jacket. And after years of struggle, he carved out a niche for himself as a piano teacher and a gigging musician. He found solace in music, but the echoes of a career unfulfilled lingered, a haunting melody that sometimes played in the back of his mind. Now how to put that into the song? Maybe...

Christopher, Christopher, heart on your sleeve,
You'll find your place if you just believe.
In the power of music to heal and to mend,
Your journey's not over, it's just around the bend.

As his fingers hesitated over the words, his phone broke the afternoon's silence. It was

Piano Man

Michael, always more scalpel-sharp than the rest.

'Chris, you've been ghosting us, dude. Are you coming to the reunion?' Michael's voice was insistent.

'I don't know, Mike... I'm afraid I won't fit in... I don't belong...,' Chris's words trailed, heavy with a sense of inadequacy he couldn't shake.

'Don't be daft, Chris. You think any of us have it all figured out? We're all just winging it, man.'

'It's not that simple. I just feel... so out of place with you lot. We live in different worlds.'

'Chris, that's rubbish, and you know it.'

The sincerity in Michael's voice, his genuine wish to see him on the night, was the nudge Chris needed, a lifeline thrown across the chasm of years and doubts. He picked up the invitation again, the paper softened from the weeks of indecision. With a deep breath he decided it was time to face the music of his past.

'All right, you win, I'll come.'

***

An earlier gig meant Chris was late arriving. As he followed the signage for the reunion, he almost had a change of heart. The ornate doors of the grand ballroom seemed to scream at him that he was in the wrong place. 'This isn't for me,' he muttered, and he turned abruptly on his heel to leave.

Just then, he felt an arm slung around his shoulder. 'Great to see you, dude. Come on, let's liven up this party. We're sitting at the same table.'

Mary Rose Tobin

They took their seats. The group at the table were already at the coffee stage, clearly engrossed in a serious discussion. Michael interrupted to begin a round of introductions. Chris saw faces that flickered with familiarity. They looked up and greeted him – one with a smile that didn't quite reach her eyes, another with a boisterous slap to his shoulder that felt too loud in the soft elegance of the room. He was placed across from Sarah, her hair still as fiery as her ambition had once been. Next to her was Joe, the high-flyer of the class, whose laughter exuded confidence and affluence. His hair had begun to grey at the temples and his smile, once quick and confident, now seemed to hold a hint of reserve.

'So, Chris, you're a full-time musician now?' Joe asked with a half-mocking smile, swirling a glass of red wine.

Chris matched his gaze, unfazed. 'Yeah, that's me. And how's the consulting gig going?'

'Paediatric surgery,' Joe replied. 'Rewarding, yet...' he trailed off, the weight of unspoken struggles heavy in his pause.

Before Joe could elaborate, Sarah, with dark circles under her eyes hinting at countless sleepless nights, jumped in. 'And ER – relentless is putting it mildly. You end up carrying the weight of the world.' Her voice cracked a bit. 'Some... you can't save. Their faces haunt you.

At the table's end was David, an endocrinologist. His frame had filled out over the years, signalling a life of comfort. Laugh lines crinkled at the corners of his eyes. He

Piano Man

interjected with a scoff. 'Oh, come on now, it's not all gloom. We've had our days in the sun, haven't we?' But his attempt at levity fell flat.

Grace, her elegance tinged with the weariness of experience, countered softly, touching David's arm. 'Sure, but at a steep price. Just look at my personal life...' Her hair, once dark and lustrous, now sported streaks of silver.

The conversation veered into introspection. Michael, paused, a fork hallway to his lips, his expression contemplative. 'Thought surgery was my calling. Turns out, it was more about learning who I am.'

Sarah's voice softened, a shadow of her earlier vitality. 'Losing my first patient changed me, not just as a doctor, but at a fundamental level.'

Joe, swirling his wine again, shared a bittersweet smile. 'Those marathon shifts, they teach you more about yourself than any textbook.'

David adjusted his glasses with a resigned chuckle. 'I dreamed of revolutionising healthcare. Reality check – bureaucracy is the real beast.'

Grace leaned in, her voice heavy with the wisdom of hard-earned experience. 'I thought I knew what I was signing up for in public health. Then came the pandemic. It taught me resilience in ways I never imagined.'

The conversation ebbed and flowed, as they shared anecdotes. They spoke of decisions that altered lives, bureaucracy that strangled passion, personal sacrifices made at the altar of

Mary Rose Tobin

their profession. Marriage problems, troubled teenagers, career-damaging mistakes – it seemed nobody's life was perfect.

'And you, Chris?' Sarah asked, turning the focus back to him. 'Do you miss it? The medicine?'

Chris's hands folded in his lap, feeling the ghostly weight of a stethoscope that no longer hung around his neck. 'I don't,' he confessed. 'I'm happier now. I earn a decent living doing what I love, and we have two great kids.'

The table's chatter dwindled to a murmur, a collective introspection descending upon the group.

Sarah's voice was soft, almost to herself, 'It's strange, isn't it? How we measure success. I used to think success was all about the white coat, the title.'

Joe's laugh was a quiet echo of his former confidence. 'And now?'

Grace looked up, her eyes reflecting the wisdom of hard choices. 'It's just not what we all expected.'

David nodded; his demeanour softened. 'Maybe that's the real success, finding your own way, even if it's not what you thought it would be.'

***

A lull in the festivities, an expectant pause. Everyone moved out to the piano bar. Chris gravitated instinctively to the piano stool, recalling the many times he had gigged here. He loved this piano. How would Walking on Memphis sound?' he found himself wondering. His fingers found their home upon the keys.

222

Piano Man

One of the women, Elena, her eyes glistening, laid her hand on Chris' shoulder.

'Would you play *Piano Man*?' she asked, her voice a mixture of hope and nostalgia.

'Why not?' said Chris.

Into the expectant hush he played the opening notes of Billy Joel's song. The room fell silent, captivated by the feeling and passion that flowed from his fingertips. The conversations ceased, and all eyes turned to him.

As Chris's fingers worked the piano, the melody, with its familiar patterns, began to weave its magic. His mind drifted. The words of the song could not have been better suited to the occasion.

Son, can you play me a memory,

I'm not really sure how it goes,

but it's sad and sweet, and I knew it complete.

when I wore a younger man's clothes.

As the song moved on, each line reminded Chris of a different friend, lives and aspirations reflected in the characters of the song.

He's quick with a joke or to light up your smoke.

But there's somewhere that he'd rather be.

Chris pictured Michael, whose laughter hid a longing for adventure beyond his familiar surroundings.

Well, I'm sure that I could be a movie star,

Chris continued, his thoughts drifting to Grace, her acting a distant memory, scripts gathering dust as practicality took precedence over passion.

Mary Rose Tobin

And Paul is a real estate novelist.

Chris' voice was soft with empathy as he thought of Joe, whose dreams of literary fame had been overshadowed by the demands of everyday life.

And the waitress is practicing politics.

This was for Sarah, her restless spirit always seeking meaning in the mundane.

As the businessmen slowly get stoned

Yes, they're sharing a drink that's called loneliness.

But it's better than drinking alone.

Chris' eyes rested on the faces around him, the shared laughter a temporary balm for the solitude that their chosen paths had brought about.

One by one the medics joined in, their voices rising in song, a chorus of lives lived, of battles fought, both in hospitals and beyond. They were doctors no longer; they were humans, alive and vibrant, united by a musician whose path had diverged from theirs in a hospital ward years ago.

As the night wore on, the party continued in a whirlwind of laughter and music, with Chris at the heart of it. All the old favourites were requested and played, people sang along whether they knew the words or not, and dance moves were energetically improvised. Surrounded by friends old and new, Chris revelled in the joy of the moment. And as he played the final, final request, *You Saw the Whole of the Moon*, a sense of fulfilment and recognition enveloped him. The reunion, a gathering he had almost shunned, had become

Piano Man

a symphony of acceptance and the stage for his quiet triumph.

***

Next morning, the group WhatsApp lit up with messages that sparkled with the energy of the previous night.

Michael kicked things off, his message buzzing with energy: 'What a blast last night, folks. Big shoutout to Chris for turning the hotel foyer into our personal concert hall. And yeah, we might not win any awards for our backing vocals, but who cares? It was epic. Let's keep the good times rolling and make sure we're all up for the next round.'

Sarah quickly followed, her words filled with warmth: 'Chris, you're a wizard, I swear. Last night was transformed the moment you started playing. It went from routine to extraordinary in a heartbeat. Your talent for bringing people together is just... wow. Thanks for giving us a piece of that magic.'

Joe couldn't resist chiming in: 'Dude, you killed it! Honestly, I thought we were in for another run-of-the-mill reunion, but then you took it to a whole other level. Your music isn't just about the notes; it's about the moments you create with them. Absolutely brilliant.'

Grace joined in, her message like a hug through the screen: 'Chris, you never disappoint, do you? Classics, laughter, and some pretty questionable dance moves – what more could we ask for? Here's to more unforgettable nights like this one. Stay safe, everyone, and see you at the next one!'

225

Mary Rose Tobin

And then came David, ever the reflective one: 'Chris, it's David. Your performance last night was a turning point. What started as a subdued evening became something spectacular. You have this incredible ability to transform the energy of a room. Major respect for lighting up our reunion like that!'

Nobody seemed to realise that for Chris, too, the reunion had been transformative. No longer the dropout who couldn't cope, he was the heart of the party, the one who had found a different way to touch lives. His self-esteem soared with the realisation that success is not a one-size-fits-all, and happiness is not a direct result of career achievements.

Sitting at the piano the words for his chorus came spontaneously:

Christopher, Christopher, where did you roam?
Your heart hears a song and it's guiding you home.
Through the twists and the turns, the highs and the lows,
You'll find your peace where a melody flows.

Burdened Bog
Deirdre Anne Gialamas

O burdened bog
What lies beneath
Your sodden store of history
Whisper in your windswept tones
Speak to me of spirits starved
Under your purple furze
Drowning in your acidic drink
Final quenching of human thirsts.
No Phidian beauties trod their hungry way
Down deep into your darkest bowels
But slips of girls, hollow-eyed
With arms that pulled groping mouths
To arid breasts.
My back can feel the labour
Of long-lost turf gatherers
I taste the rough unbuttered bread
They shared just after twelve when
Distant bells rang out the Angelus
I dare not walk your wet wilds
Alone or neath Irish moon
Your spongy mass of brown
Could bounce me up
Draw me down
For they call to me
Your voices through the heather

And wonder whether anyone had come
To offer morsels from their larders.

The Poet who Sat beside me on the Train
Anne O'Callaghan

(In memory of Anne, who sadly passed away before seeing this publication. May her spirit find peace and her memory live on through these words.)

He sits beside me
on the train
as my baby nestles
sleeping in my arms:
warm bright clothes
new baby boots.
In the cold dawn
of a windy autumn day
I think of what lies ahead:
what I've left behind
I'm torn.

I can ring them every day
I can ring them every day
I can ring them every day.

He asks my baby's name
and where I'm going.
Though I'm tired, I tell him.
He is kind, unobtrusive
and buys me a cup of tea.
As the train rushes through
the grey landscape

The Poet who Sat beside me on the Train

houses wake up to a new day:
figures move in kitchens,
bedroom lights switch on,
cars leave driveways.
The dreaded day has come.

'Are you interested in poetry?'
'Yes' – I say – and this is true.
He takes out his book
of newly published poems;
reads to me as my baby sleeps,
his face animated, expressive
his voice in turn humorous, sad
angry, sardonic: embracing his life.
I am honoured, fascinated.
At the station the cold air wakens my child.
He helps me with my bags,
opens the taxi door
'Would you bring this woman
to Crumlin Children's Hospital please?'
He thanks me for listening to him
and wishes me well.

I do ring them every day,
and after three weeks
we come home, my baby weak
but recovering, back
in the real world again.
We all know his face,
recognise his voice:
politician, philosopher,
man of conviction, but to me
he will always be
the poet who sat beside me
on the train.

Nora's Journey

Mary Hawkshaw

The rising sun began to warm the earth, freeing it from its long, cold winter days. A warm mist hovered over the ground. The tall hedges on each side of the lane came alive with chatter and movement as hundreds of birds danced from branch to branch, staking out their territories. They paid no attention to the older couple walking past in silence. After years of togetherness, their thoughts were in communion. Their vegetable allotment waited at the end of the laneway.

Nora and her husband Tommy, in their late sixties, were on a mission today: to rescue themselves from the misery haunting them. They had become shadows of their former selves, fading into life's background – there, yet not quite there; present, yet devoid of action. Now, in the core of their souls, a tiny flicker of hope had begun to light slowly. They had a dream, and with hope in their hearts, they pursued it with renewed vigour. Nora looked older than her years; the burden of worry she carried grew heavier with each passing year. Her once vibrant red hair retained only a few strands of its original colour. Her freckled face, now drawn and tired, struggled to keep pace with Tommy's long strides, often turning her steps into a trot.

Nora's Journey

Tommy, often lost in thought, had to be reminded with a tug on his jacket to slow down. He walked with his head bowed under his old tweed cap, his appearance and demeanour showing the effect of his regular escape to alcohol. Gaunt and tired, with deep crevices that once bore the bloom of vigour and pride, he still, despite their differences, blended harmoniously with Nora into a united couple against the world.

Nora and Tommy, like most villagers in their community, had been swept up in what was dubbed a miracle. The arrival of Global B&B brought unforeseen prosperity to their small village. Nearly every house was on board. Those who didn't have space to rent wondered about the amount of money the others were making. The lace curtains were pulled back and forth on the cleanest windows in the village. The sole shopkeeper basked in his newfound happiness, diligently restocking his shelves while whistling a merry tune, wishing for more hours in the day. The streets overflowed with tourists speaking various languages; the villagers, having given up trying to ask where they were from – most didn't understand them anyway – sat on the walls with folded arms, observing the endless parade of all shapes and sizes and colours of clothing they had never seen before, meandering on their only paved road.

Upon reaching the allotment, Tommy asked, 'Now, Nora, what do you need?'

'A large cabbage and a cauliflower will do,' Nora replied.

'Righto,' he responded, leaning on his shovel. He took his time examining each vegetable ridge,

231

Mary Hawkshaw

enjoying the lush growth. Time pressed on Nora, but for Tommy, it was an opportunity for contemplation. Selecting what he considered the most abundant cabbage, he asked with a broad smile, 'Nora, is this cabbage too big?'

'Ah, it's fine. Just bring it up,' she responded.

He placed the cabbage in her plastic bag and then paused again, searching for the best cauliflower. Losing patience, Nora urged, 'Tommy, for God's sake, just pick any one of them. I've got a mountain of work ahead.'

'Right, Nora,' he quickly complied, adding the cauliflower to her bag. He offered to accompany her, but she refused.

'No, you go to the pub. I'll be fine. See ya later,' she said, tucking her French loaf under her arm and picking up her plastic bag of vegetables.

When she reached her house, her guests' car was still in the driveway. Not wishing to meet them, she walked past and into her neighbour's garden, standing well-hidden under their weeping willow tree. Keeping her eyes on her front door, she reflected.

'Tommy means well, but when it comes to cleaning, he's more of a hindrance than a help. He deserves a few pints though, I won't begrudge him that – after all, he is willing to sleep in the car while all this is happening.'

Eventually, the door opened, and her guests departed. Meanwhile, as Tommy neared the pub, the sound of lively chatter reached his ears. Anticipating the warmth inside, he briskly rubbed his hands together and swung the doors open with a bang. He was instantly met with a

Nora's Journey

chorus of cheerful voices and a welcoming wave of smiling faces.

'Hiya, Tommy, hiding from the cleaning, are we?' called out a voice.

'You know me, Ritchie, I wouldn't know a mop from a bucket,' Tommy joked.

The pub's regulars joined in a harmonious chorus, 'And that's the truth!' they sang, their laughter filling the room.

'What's it today, Tommy? The usual?'

'A pint of Guinness would hit the spot, Ritchie,' Tommy replied with a grin.

'Right, another Guinness, Sean!' Ritchie called to the bartender.

Around him, the patrons cradled their drinks like treasures, each sip followed by a contented sigh. They raised their glasses in unison to each gaping mouth. The creamy froth stayed on their lips before releasing collective, hearty belches. This ritual of camaraderie was punctuated only by the occasional need to refill their glasses or the casual jostle for a vacant stool.

Back at the house, Nora tossed her cauliflower and cabbage onto the grass and unlocked her door. A thick, damp odour hit her in the face. 'A good airing out will fix that,' she began, removing the sheets from the beds and giving them a thorough shaking through the open window before replacing them back on the beds. The pillowcases were next and received the same treatment. The physical gyrations needed to get the heavy duvets back on the beds played havoc with her arthritic knees. Draping herself over the bed, exhausted, she closed her eyes. Then she remembered Tommy's reassuring words: 'Nora,

Mary Hawkshaw

we are in the land of gentry, landlords of our own destiny. Free at last. A lord and lady in the making.'

These words had a powerful impact on Nora. She sprang back to her work with renewed happiness and finished the bedrooms in record time. Descending the stairs with a plastic bag of dirty towels, Nora spotted her neighbours through the window, Gloria and Assumpta, deep in conversation. Suddenly, a loud bang startled both. Standing up for a better view, they spotted Bridget, another neighbour, directing two tall gentlemen with large suitcases away from her house and shouting, 'It's Nora Kelly's house you're looking for, not mine!'

Bridget clambered over the garden wall and joined them. 'There I was, doing my dishes,' she told them. 'I felt an uneasy feeling in my bones. I turned around, and two large strangers stood before me like two statues. Jesus, I couldn't understand what was happening. I thought my legs would go from under me. I knew I was shouting, but I couldn't hear my own words. After getting them out of the house, I nearly took the door off its hinges with a bang.' Gloria and Assumpta listened, transfixed, and shocked, unable to offer any consolation as they watched the big men head towards Nora's house.

Nora had only half-finished the cleaning job when there was a knock at her door. Her pounding heart echoed in her ears. Could they be here already? She didn't move a muscle and waited. Suddenly, the knock came again, only this time much louder, followed by a strong American accent saying, *'Hello in there?'*

Nora's Journey

'God, they're here!' The plastic bag slipped from her hands and rolled down the remaining stairs. Peeping through the open window, she saw two very tall and broad American gentlemen smiling up at her.

'Hiya, you're early, just a minute, I'm coming down.' Breathless, she tried to regain her composure before opening her door. Haunted by memories of her very first guests, she took some deep breaths. 'Hello, come in,' she said gingerly, turning the latch. She tossed the black plastic bag of towels into the garden, narrowly missing their large suitcases, and closed the door.

'My name is Clive; this is my friend, Peter,' the man said shaking hands with Nora. Looking up at the height and breadth of the two men standing before her, she worried about her beds collapsing. Returning to the kitchen, she hastily washed the dishes. Then, after wiping her hands on her apron, she proudly placed her French loaf on the kitchen table. Avoiding eye contact with her guests, they stood staring at her, not knowing whether to sit or stand. In her hurried state, asking her any question was impossible.

'Well, everything is ready for you now,' she muttered, brushing past them with her pillow and blanket under her arm. She picked up her bag of towels, and walked around their suitcases. Turning around, 'Clive,' she shouted, 'when you're leaving, throw the key in the letterbox.'

'The letterbox?' Clive repeated, coming into the garden. 'Where is it?'

'In the door,' Nora replied. Looking at the cabbage and cauliflower on the grass, Clive called, 'Nora, I think you've forgotten something.'

235

Mary Hawkshaw

'No, that's a little present for your dinner,' she replied.

Picking them up, Clive asked, 'Do they have to be cooked?' But there was no reply; Nora was gone, making her way back to her car.

Nora had never left her village. Her world was small, and as far as Nora was concerned, the outside world had nothing to do with her. She was familiar with the English accent from the radio and had an idea of the American accent, but she never thought about how she sounded to others herself. Her first American guests brought this home to her with a bang. They couldn't understand a word she said. Her nervousness just added to the problem; it made her stutter for the first time in her life. While giving them a tour, she had to repeat everything.

'The hot tap is on the right,' she informed them.

'You mean the faucet, Nora.'

'The couch pulls out into a bed for some extra space for you.'

'You mean the Chesterfield, Nora,' they corrected her.

'Yes,' Nora repeated. 'And the range is here.'

'You mean the stove, Nora.'

That evening, Nora tried to explain the trauma she was experiencing to Tommy. 'It's like speaking a different language. The letterbox is a mailbox, the footpath is a sidewalk, biscuits are cookies, presses are cupboards, a petrol station is a gas station in America. What do they call places with real gas, not petrol? A bucket is a pail, and Tommy, a brush is a broom.'

'Could they fly away on it, Nora?'

236

Nora's Journey

'I almost wish they could,' she replied. 'And Tommy, rubbish is trash.'

'Nora, you need to be firm with them and tell them it may be trash to them, but it's still rubbish to you. Nora, we are landlords now, part of the aristocracy; we must learn to communicate like them. Just try listening; it's the way it is in the land of gentry.'

'But Tommy, they even asked me if I was Dutch! What would I be doing in an Irish village if I was Dutch? Did they know where they were at all?'

As Clive placed the cauliflower and cabbage on the kitchen table, he asked, 'Are we in the right house?'

'Well, it sure as hell isn't the one across the road, Clive.'

'It's very basic and dreary; what do you think, Peter?'

'That's an understatement. Clive, what we have here is a non-starter.'

Pots and pans were haphazardly piled near the range. They searched for a cooker but found none, just a large black kettle sitting in the middle of the range.

'This is where we'll have to cook, Peter. No switch to turn it on; it must work by direct heat,' Clive observed, a bag of coal and turf beside it.

'Do you have any idea how to start a fire?'

'No,' Peter replied, 'but it's probably similar to a campfire.'

Clive opened the range door, crammed in some coal, turf, and newspaper, and struck a match, tossing it into the range. Jumping back, he shut

Mary Hawkshaw

the door with a bang. Black smoke swirled, engulfing the window in the range.

'Does that look right to you, Peter?'

'Well, where there's smoke, there must be fire,' Peter responded, half-joking. Suddenly, Peter leapt up, shouting, 'Fire! Fire!' as thick black smoke billowed into the kitchen.

Nora, lost in thought in the car while waiting for Tommy, jolted upright when he burst through the pub doors, looking like he was fleeing the gates of hell. 'NORA! NORA! THE HOUSE IS ON FIRE!'

Starting the car, Nora watched Tommy run and dive into the front seat. They screeched to a halt outside the house. Black smoke was billowing through the front door. Her terrified guests, standing in disbelief, looked on helplessly.

'Oh, Lord! Tommy, we've lost everything.' Tommy darted through the black smoke into the kitchen, and opened the damper in the range. Instantly, the smoke began to flow through the chimney. After throwing open the back door, he wiped his eyes with a wet cloth.

'Thank God, it's just smoke damage, and it's contained to the downstairs.'

Outside, Nora's guests and neighbours clustered anxiously, their eyes fixed on the door. Nora joined them just as Tommy emerged, coated head to toe in black soot, his blue eyes the only recognisable feature. Nora collapsed to her knees on the grass, sobbing. Tommy hurried to her side.

'Nora, the damper was closed; that's all. Once the smoke clears, we'll clean it up.'

Nora's Journey

Assumpta and Bridget soon arrived, bringing tea and sandwiches.

'I must be in shock; I can't get up from the grass,' Nora cried out. 'Dear Jesus, while I'm on my knees, please help me. I'm responsible for all this chaos,' she prayed.

'Tommy warned me months ago, "Nora," he said, "look at the Royal Family; they'd be out on the street by now if they didn't change their attitude and talk to people." But did I listen? Oh no, not me. Dear Jesus, you see everything; can you help?'

Her prayer was interrupted by the sound of vomiting. Nora saw Clive hanging over the wall, ghostly as if the life was drained from him. She quickly resumed her prayers.

'God, what have I done? I could have killed them,' she wailed uncontrollably. Her cries echoed throughout the neighbourhood, startling her remaining neighbours who rushed to her garden to help. They thought she was losing her mind. Assumpta helped her to her feet, while Clive and Peter came over to reassure her. Tommy, standing on the wall, shouted, 'All clear!'

The exhausted guests dragged their suitcases upstairs and collapsed onto their bed, instantly sinking as the mattress springs stretched to capacity.

'God damn it,' Clive muttered, 'we're in the land... of the Lilliputians.'

Tommy fetched a mop and bucket and began scrubbing the walls and floors, while Nora cleaned the windows and furniture.

'We came so close, Nora; it's a good lesson for us. Has the scare cured you?' Tommy asked.

239

Mary Hawkshaw

'I can honestly say I'm completely cured,' she replied.

The guests thought they were dreaming when Nora and Tommy appeared at the end of their beds. Nora's fears were confirmed when she saw the beds resembling hammocks more than beds.

'Make it quick, Tommy,' she whispered, edging towards the bedroom door.

'We have everything ready for you now,' Tommy announced. 'Would you like to sleep or come down and have a look?'

'We'll take your word for it, Tommy,' they muttered, exhausted.

'Okay then, goodnight to you,' Nora said, then dashed down the stairs and through the front door at breakneck speed.

'Nora, what's the rush?' Tommy called out.

'RUN, TOMMY, RUN!' she shouted

Big Hair
Deirdre Anne Gialamas

Big hair
Was her thing
Until the rot
Charged in taking
No prisoners
The plughole boasting
A weave of yellow strands.

Not one to bemoan
Life's hand,
A meeting was set
Up with the High Street
Man at number 37.

Three weeks later to
The day
A bag of loosely clad bones
Atop spindly legs
Strutted triumphantly
Out of 'Warren's Wigs'
Bold blonde curls
Cascading down the shoulders
Of the young woman,
Almost hiding her
Thin, translucent face.

Oxford Dictionary
Kathleen Phelan

'This isn't what it looks like,' said Ben, holding up a thumb-blackened copy of the Oxford dictionary.

'And no doubt but you're going to tell me exactly what it looks like,' said Kathy, his sister.

'This book contains all the books that have ever been written in the English-speaking world,' he went on. 'All the words are in alphabetical order, of course. But all they need is a bit of juggling and teasing out. You get them in the correct order and hey presto you have a blockbuster.'

'Okay, you keep juggling while I do my homework, but keep your mouth shut. I'm studying for my leaving cert, you know. What an idiot you are, Ben.'

'Can't you be kind to Ben?' her mother, Sarah, said to Kathy when they were alone.

'Mam, for heaven's sake, it was only last week he called me out to Daddy's workshop and showed me a block of wood. "Look, Kathy," he said, "inside this block of wood is a masterpiece of Madonna. All I have to do is chip away the parts that aren't Madonna." For God's sake, Mammy, one day he's Stephen King, the next day he's Michelangelo. I'm sick listening to him.'

'Kathy, he's only twelve years old, and you have to admit he has a good imagination.'

Oxford Dictionary

Sarah went out to the workshop. Everything was just the same as it was when Tim left. There was a pile of sawdust on the floor just below the lathe that held an unfinished chair leg. The block of wood that Ben dreamed of turning into Madonna. Chisels, vice grips, cramps, rasps... all neatly hanging from nails above the workbench.

Later that day, she met her childhood friend Patricia for coffee. 'Tim's workshop is filled to capacity with everything a cabinet maker could need yet it feels empty as moorland in winter,' she said to Patricia.

'Ah, Sarah, come on now. I don't know where you got that idea. Moorland is teeming with life all year round. All you have to do is look more closely. Moorland is home to grouse, owls, snipe, skylarks, and much, much more. The skylark is my favourite, though.' Then she closed her eyes and, as if in a trance, and gave a spiel.

'You know, Sarah the skylark is a symbol of the joyous spirit of the divine; it cannot be understood by ordinary empirical methods. The poet, longing to be a skylark, muses that the bird has never experienced the disappointments and disillusionments of human life, including the diminishment of passion.'

Sarah abruptly interrupted her, 'Stay away from Wikipedia, Patricia, I'm not in the mood for sermons.'

Sarah's mother, who had been widowed at fifty, used to say that it was easier to cope with the idea of her husband being dead than having left her for another woman. It was a horrible idea, and, although Sarah would be ashamed to admit it, that's exactly how she felt.

Kathleen Phelan

From the beginning, she should have seen the signs. His staying out late. Working until all hours. Convincing her to give up the job that she loved, in the library. He often made her doubt her sanity by convincing her certain things hadn't happened.

'That's called gaslighting,' said Patricia.

'Look, Patricia,' said Sarah, 'he's very generous with money. He's great with the kids, and unlike some fellows, he isn't violent.'

'Sarah, you don't thank someone for not hitting you. As for being kind to the children and being financially supportive, that's what a parent is expected to do.'

As Sarah reflected on her situation, she realised life wasn't a tidy dictionary with neat solutions. Much like Ben's thumb-blackened Oxford dictionary, it required some juggling and teasing out. In this puzzle of existence, she aimed to rearrange her story with resilience, wit, and an intellectual twist, mirroring the skylark's dance above the moorland of possibilities. The pages of her life were ready for a blockbuster, not confined by alphabetical order but enriched by the artful arrangement of her own choosing.

244

Hearth
Póilín Brennan

In times of cloth to measure,
summer bog days drawing down winter teas
on a rickety buggy, over broken planks to
deter the gougers.
Flasks, sandwiches, a cafe noir, should work
testify.

At the heart of the house stood proud Tirolia
whistled kettles, aired clothes, bathed bones
and bums.
And woe betide the apprentice who shifted the
damper and let it go to ember.
Dall ar an draíocht and ritual of the hearth.

Oh, and the curse of the forbidden immersion!
A last resort for the bedraggled breadwinner
should maidens fail at tending Tessie
muttered through gritted incantations of 'the
switch'.

Over warm tea came his seanchaí tale of
bikeshop craic.
Of kilted Páidy and the sinking bike only a
ladder could save.
Bedads, there were those who paid and those
who ducked and dived,
As the doorbell halted his teatime scéal.

Huggles – A Love Story
Mary Hodson

They embarked on the Sligo train to Dublin, at the break of dawn on a bright summer's morning. The engine hummed, warming the carriages for the passengers about to leave on the three-hour journey.

Among them was a boy filled with anticipation for the adventure ahead. Trains were his world, brought to life by endless episodes of *Thomas the Tank Engine and Friends*. His excitement was shared with his Nana Mary, Granda Kieran, and his inseparable companion, Huggles.

Their bags were packed with favourite treats: Jaffa Cakes, Jammy Dodgers, and Kieran's iced buns.

'Look,' Thomas said to Huggles, adopting the role of both friend and protector, 'we're on Thomas the Tank. We're going to Dublin! Are you excited?'

His eyes sparkled at the thought of meeting his cousins, Emma and Connor, envisioning the hours they would spend building Lego and re-enacting scenes with *Thomas the Tank Engine and Friends*.

Huggles, his bright yellow companion, slightly brown-stained from countless adventures and reluctant washes, was more than ready. Huggles had been his constant

246

Huggles – A Love Story

friend since he was two and a half years old, a faithful companion introduced when he moved from a small cot into a big bed to make room for his baby brother, Alex. Huggles, with his big toothy smile and floppy ears perfect for twirling during times of distress or sleepiness, was a source of endless comfort.

The day in Dublin was a whirlwind of joy – games where Huggles was the star, laughter filling the room, and chicken nuggets and chips for tea. They ended the day curled up together, watching *Thomas the Tank Engine and Friends*, content and tired.

The return journey was bittersweet. As the train left the city's hustle, the countryside rolling by, Thomas, with Huggles on his lap, drifted to sleep. Nana Mary and Granda Kieran watched over them, their hearts full of love for the boy and his beloved Huggles.

Arriving back in Sligo, the rush off the train was frantic. Amid the hustle, Nana Mary's voice cut through, laced with panic.

'Where's Huggles?'

In the chaos, Huggles had been left behind, taking off on an unintended adventure back to Dublin. The search for Huggles was desperate, inquiries made at lost luggage and with the station master yielding no sign of the beloved Huggles. To soothe Thomas's distress, they offered hope, suggesting Huggles was on an adventure and would return soon.

But the night was long and sleepless for Thomas, the absence of Huggles a gaping void. Then, in the soft light of dawn, an excited call

Mary Hodson

from his parents, Angela and Victor, beckoned Thomas to the gate.

There sat Huggles, returned from his adventure, a Kinder Surprise in tow, a thoughtful gesture that only Huggles could conceive. Tears and laughter filled the reunion, a promise made under whispered breaths: 'Now, no more adventures apart'.

Settled together, watching their favourite show, Thomas's words to Huggles were a vow of undying friendship, 'Please don't go on an adventure again without me. I missed you... I love you, Huggles.'

Nobody Told Me
Geraldine Warren

Nobody told me
My face would fall,
not off my head or anything
Just descend onto my chin
Which has moved precariously
Onto my chest
Which is touching my waist
Waist? That thing flapping
Against the tops of my thighs
Why didn't somebody warn me?

What Words Can Do
Mary Hawkshaw

Peer through our window and see the beauty
of what words can do.

Screens flicker to life, showing eager, joyous
faces. A symphony of souls, each with their
words fresh and bright.

Poems, stories, songs, and plays emerge in a
burst of splendid light.

Our tapestry of memories, ideas, dreams, and
hopes is intricately woven, revealing our
innermost thoughts. Words from the depths of
our hearts and minds, once quietly sealed, are
now revealed.

Our words become wildflowers, dancing with
glee, bursting with colour, vibrant and free.
They dance in vivid splendour, a reflection of
you and me, showing the intricate patterns of
our shared humanity.

United, we weave our words into glittering
stars, a mosaic of light in a darkened world.

We find tranquillity.

Keeping the Piece
Frances Dermody

It's the last case of the day in Galway District Court. The sticky heat of mid-July is an extra cause of discomfort, even in the shade of the courtroom. Rumour has it that being the last case of the day is an advantage with Judge McIntyre, that indifference and leniency go hand in hand by the time the last case comes before him.

Michael Kelly is in court for the second time in only four weeks. He is drunk and unsteady but making a big effort to control his wayward body movements. A respectable appearance is always a priority for Michael on these occasions, but the heavy suit has created a dripping sweat problem and a balance problem whenever he needs to dry his forehead with his sleeve.

The charge against him is a vicious assault on Tom Fahy outside Paddy's bar, only two days after his last appearance in court. Tom is standing on the other side of the judge. As an innocent victim, he hasn't taken respectability as far as wearing a suit, but the heat has made his low-key efforts pointless. Even the longer strands of hair dragged across his bald patch have been soaked and give him the appearance of a man who has not washed in a very long time. Sober and upright, Tom is ready to stand

Frances Dermody

up for the rights of innocents. His face is bandaged, with bruising and stitches peeping out for extra pity. Fake tears are close as he tells the court that it's a miracle that the Kelly lad hadn't killed him.

The judge is not moved by Tom's whining.

'Both of ye were here four weeks ago, Tom Fahy, and you were the one in trouble that day. Don't try to pull the wool over my eyes. What happened to the big promise ye made to keep the peace?'

Michael is the one jumping in to answer, waving his hand high, like a child in school begging to show off that he knows the right answer.

'I swear to God, Judge, I couldn't keep the piece because I couldn't find it. It wasn't my fault it was pitch black up there after the lightning on the Friday. I know I did wrong to bite Tom's nose off, but I did look everywhere for it later on. Anyway, wasn't it the luck of God that one of the taxi lads found it and handed it in to the Gardai? I was thinking, Judge, seeing as Tom got his nose back and it all ended well, maybe we could shake on that promise and start again?'

Judge McIntyre's indifference has got lost in the proceedings; he has the look of a man wanting to commit another act of violence.

'I've heard enough now. Listen to me and listen well. This is the last time I'm putting up with this carry-on. If I ever see either of ye in front of me again, ye won't be heading home to enjoy the sunshine like ye are today. Next time

Keeping the Piece

it will be the full force of the law, a full ten-year sentence. Am I making myself clear?'

Michael's punishment is read to the court without giving either man a chance to answer. He will pay all of Tom's medical expenses and work under a community service order for one hundred hours. Tom has been sulking, head down and arms folded in silence since the judge had the cheek to include an innocent man in an official reprimand. Michael is happy to take centre stage again; relief, alcohol and exaggerated gratitude are all combined in the shouting from his corner of the courtroom.

'I will to be sure, Judge. Thanks. You're a top man, Judge. I always knew you were a top man. I promise I'll work my backside off for the community service crowd. I won't let you down, Judge. Thanks again.'

The grovelling is a waste of time, Judge McIntyre has already walked out of the courtroom. Michael and Tom leave together, with Michael leaning on Tom for support by the time they reach the steps and the blinding sunshine outside. Paddy's bar is just around the corner, the perfect place to forgive and start again.

A Bouquet of Words for Mary
Elizabeth Hannon

(I was once advised that flowers should be given not at funerals but while the person is able to enjoy smelling them. I am gifting these few words to a dear friend on a very significant birthday so she can enjoy what her friends think about her. Happy Birthday!)

A Ballyliffin girl, with deep Donegal roots transplanted to Galway by her wonderful late husband, John.
Painter, musician and trumpeter extraordinaire.
Together they produced three handsome offspring,
who have given them seven grandchildren to cherish.
Mary is thrilled with her delightful great granddaughter.
And can't wait to welcome number two.

Mary adores and is adored by her three stalwart brothers.
She has no sister but some true female friends
– their friendships forged over many years,
through happy, sad and fraught times.
She has her own very definite sense of fashion and style,
never showy, always timeless and elegant.
Her direct straightforward talk sometimes

254

A Bouquet of Words for Mary

surprises
but her sympathetic manner reveals a heart of
gold.
Her rulebook for living a careful Christian life
is 'Work hard, clean up and get on with it'.
A water baby from childhood, she thrives on
physical exercise.
Self-reliant in most things, she is willing to try
new ways
especially in mastering her iPhone capabilities.

Gifted in the arts of knitting, cooking, baking,
Mary is ultra-generous in sharing what she
produces
with family, neighbours, and friends.
She always gives time and unstinting support
to those needing backup and care.
In her own quiet way Mary is a lynchpin
In the local community, unaware, I believe,
of how highly she is held in their esteem.

Tobernalt

Mary Hodson

My earliest memory of journeying to the Holy Well at Tobernalt dates to when I was around seven years old, in the early 1960s. Our father, may he rest in peace, took my sister Kathleen and me – as the eldest children in the family – on his bicycle to Dawn Mass at 6am. For us, this was an extraordinary adventure. The anticipation began weeks in advance, with the announcement that Garland Sunday was on the horizon. We were promised a visit to the Holy Well as a reward if we were well-behaved, helped with chores around the house, and took care of our younger siblings.

The history of Tobernalt predates the advent of Christianity to Ireland in the fifth century. It was the main area where the pagan festival of Lughanasa was celebrated alongside the festival of St Patrick. The festival of Lughanasa was eventually Christianised and became Garland Sunday. Garland Sunday takes place every year on the last weekend of July. It is an opportunity to unite in prayer and thanksgiving, handed down through the generations.

The meaning of Tobernalt or the Irish version Tobar nAlt is most likely to mean the well in the cliff. Alt refers to a body part or joint. Therefore, Tobernalt is the curative well for body pain.

256

Tobernalt

Tobernalt is also associated with penal times in Ireland; it became a sacred place for the celebration of mass, which was forbidden under the penal laws. The mass rock is still in use at Garland Sunday and at other religious events.

There are many holy wells all over Ireland – 2,996 in the Republic and 187 in Northern Ireland – many of which were sacred places long before they were credited with the Christian saints' names that some bear today. Indeed, it is argued that the relationship between well water and spirituality could be as old as humanity itself.

'Tobar' is the Irish word for well. So anywhere with a name beginning with 'tobar' indicates that a holy well is featured nearby. Nearly all holy wells are in stunning locations, high up in the mountains, isolated islands, or in wild and remote places. These wells certainly lend themselves to peaceful prayer, contemplation, and appreciation of nature and their surroundings.

The well at Tobernalt is very important to the local community. There is a very fine line between protecting the wells and interfering with them – some communities would not want their wells to be nationally recognised – they want to keep them private.

Attending Dawn Mass as a young child remains a treasured memory. On the eve, we fasted from bedtime, usually at 8pm, until receiving Holy Communion at 6:30am. This lengthy fast was a significant challenge for us as children, but we were expected to honour these church traditions. We embarked from our

Mary Hodson

home in Carnaugh, Ballintogher, awakened by our mother at 4:30am and dressed in our Sunday best. We set off for the Holy Well at 5am, navigating the Long Stretch, past Slishwood, Dooney Wood, the Two Lovers' Knot, Aughamore, and around Lough Gill. Along the way, our father regaled us with reminders to behave during Mass and to remember our ancestors who had made the same eight-mile pilgrimage from Carnaugh in their day.

Arriving in time to secure a spot to the left of the main altar, just below the steps leading down to St. Anne's Shrine, we were enveloped by a sense of belonging as Mass commenced and our community gathered. The presence of neighbours, aunts, and uncles added to the joy and the profound sense of connection to something larger than ourselves.

One year, post-communion, I nearly fainted, but my father swiftly came to my aid, supported by a kind lady who offered me a drink until I could eat something more substantial. The midges were an inevitable nuisance, yet we entertained ourselves with the neighbourly advice of catching one and 'tickling it under the wing' to avoid further bother – a belief we held dear.

After Mass, we lit candles and visited the shrines with reverence, then made our way home, looking forward to the family's afternoon visit to the Holy Well. The afternoon brought its own delights with stalls offering everything from religious items to sweets and the especially prized dillisk. The joy of spending our pocket money on what seemed like exotic treasures, the community spirit felt during these gatherings, and the simple pleasure of a family picnic on the grass are memories I cherish deeply.

The Holy Well, for me, represents a sacred and tranquil refuge, echoing the resilience and faith of our ancestors during trying times. My visits there, walking in the footsteps of generations past, fill me with a profound sense of privilege and continuity. My husband and I have shared these stories and this sacred place with our children during summer visits from England, instilling in them the same reverence for our heritage. Our youngest daughter even chose the Holy Well as the backdrop for her wedding photographs. Now, I bring our grandchildren there, teaching them the same rituals my father taught me, in the hope of passing on this rich legacy.

In loving memory of our dear sister Kathleen, whom we lost suddenly on 28 March, 2021.

Kathleen's absence is deeply felt by her loving family, children, and grandchildren.

As you pass by the Holy Well, think of Kathleen and kindly light a candle in her memory.

The Niedermayers
James Conway

Broom out those memories
those caught up in leaves
and shades all of a haunting
where a family picture stands
immortal, happiness in
a new land, as laid down
by life and hope, sweet
beings like those swimming
in a surge of rapture.

Later with their chip of bargain
kidnap's terror steals her
fleecing breath, no news steers
her into darkness, smothered
by the curse of loss she will
go with her daughters
into a watching where
they will meet him
in a field beyond
the rill and rhyme of light,
rosy even in evening's
calling where her nightmare
burns crisp, curling into terror
damp now in all its horror.

Circles

Deirdre Anne Gialamas

Early in the morning, before the first shoppers began to trudge in, a lone figure occupied a spot next to the tiny Kapnikarea Church on one of Athens' main shopping thoroughfares; Ermou Street. His clothes were skimpy, his trousers falling just short of sockless feet. With hands cupping a metal container, raised in a silent plea for help, he was a study in still life; a statue that had escaped plunder, yet found no home on Acropolis Hill. He had cleared a small circle in the deep snow. 'Funny,' he thought, 'how no one ever believes it snows in Athens.'

Dimitris, strangely suspended halfway between a sitting and standing position, slowly cast his eyes around the now dwindling crowds then up to the rapidly darkening sky. He resigned himself to the probability that he'd made his takings for the day. Every blink of his snow-sodden lashes tortured his eyes. His nostrils, iced together, forced his mouth to gape open. It began to snow even heavier than before.

'What use is this horrid white stuff to humans, it freezes us! I fail to see its purpose. Freezes us, causes traffic jams... then it's reduced to sludge, ugly grey sludge.'

Deirdre Anne Gialamas

Was it really only last December he was headed for the Alps, on one of his many impromptu skiing trips with his fiancée, Antonia? She was not enamoured with the endless sea of white, or the biting cold. 'It dries my skin. The glare makes me frown, you know. I couldn't bear those terrible lines between my eyes, Dimitris darling.' She did, however, bask in the après-ski activities, always dressed to the nines for the fine dining and champagne-sodden evenings. Often, on those getaways, Dimitris would ski for hours during the mornings following the soirées. He didn't mind a tumble or two before returning frozen, but alive, to the sleeping Antonia.

Now he was frozen again, but not by choice. He felt his cup was heavy with coins, though maybe not quite as heavy as he'd expected. After all, it was Christmas Eve. Then he remembered his trousers. As he was drinking his second coffee in mid-afternoon, he had heard a worrying sound of cloth ripping, 'Pffffh,' immediately feeling even colder in his nether regions. Standing up stiffly to full height, he soon realised, to his mortification, that the seat of his pants had suffered such damage they could no longer stay up on his thin frame. How would he make it home to his spot under the bridge? 'I'll be arrested. That will really be the swan song of Dimitris Papadopoulos. What if, what if it makes the papers?' he fretted, 'Former CEO of Megalinks found with his pants down in the city centre, to face charges of, charges of...' His thoughts scrambled furiously at the gravity of it all.

Circles

Gingerly, he sat down on the low wall surrounding the church, slowly gathering the remnants of cloth about him, in a vain effort to retain what little dignity remained to him, following ten months or so on the street. A gaggle of hardy Greek grannies, black from crown to toe, stumbled out from the place of worship just behind him. They wound their shadowy way into the night, the more beady eyed of them crossing themselves feverishly as they came upon him. He knew the sweet aroma of incense would have drifted out with them, but could not smell it.

Looking past the dishevelment, one would not be blamed for considering that here was a man who once was a pianist or a surgeon. Perhaps he was an artist whose work was no longer fashionable. His long slender fingers suggested good breeding, his well-angled forehead a keen intelligence. 'Have to catch the last trolley bus tonight, I must, I must.' He tried to pass unnoticed on those trips to and from his new home near Ano Patissia train station in the north of Athens.

Not all passengers on the Number 5 trolley were concerned about Dimitris' need for anonymity, openly pinching their noses, affronted by Athens' 'New Poor' as the press called them. Antonia had always preferred to be picked up in the Mercedes. She would tell Dimitris public transport was for the poor or those bores ranting on about carbon footprints and such silly things. When the activity of her beloved's company plummeted due to the relentless recession, and Dimitris couldn't

Deirdre Anne Gialamas

afford to keep his car, she thought it a brilliant idea for him to chauffeur her around in taxis.

***

As he went home at night from his spot on Ermou Street, Dimitris could fight shy of hostile eyes by travelling back to his earlier life as a child growing up in the quaint village of Levidi, in the Peloponnese peninsula southwest of Athens.

The lush, fertile plains of his birthplace soothed him. He could see his mother cutting the homemade feta cheese with precision and adding it to cucumbers, onions, and the rosiest of tomatoes in a round enamel dish, then drenching the mix in Kalamata olive oil and oregano. Breaking off chunks of the crispy yellow Horiatiko bread, she would place several in the middle of an old basket. They would eat together with his father, Nikos, sitting at the long wooden table covered with a blue chequered oilcloth. Often joined by uninvited bees and mosquitoes from the green oasis in front of the veranda, each place setting would have an old cloth to wave off the noisy gate crashers. Waiting for his parents to start first, Dimitris would watch in wonder at the almost sacred manner in which they lifted their hands steadily to their mouths, chewed slowly, and continued reverently until their plates were emptied.

Although a man of few words, Nikos Papadopoulos' love for his only child was lauded by the village. He and his wife had sacrificed more than was really known to offer their only offspring a gentler life. The morning

Circles

his son left for University in Athens, Dimitris' father was up since dawn sitting in the kitchen, teasing a string of beads round and round his fingers, waiting. 'Agori mou,' (my son), he said to Dimitris, his gaze fixed on the boy about to fly the nest, 'We are not alone in this world; we need each other. What goes round, comes round. Do only good!'

Mrs Papadopoulos busied herself trying to close the suitcase she'd stuffed with dripping feta cheese in waxed paper, jars of olives, koulouria (rusks) covered in sesame, and honey her neighbour had brought the evening before. A change of clothing wrapped tightly around two large spanakotiropita, (spinach-cheese pies), her specialty, lay on top. As she kissed him goodbye, something unknown to Dimitris flitted through his mother's eyes mingling with the pride and love he knew she felt for him.

As CEO of Megalinks, Dimitris had an excellent salary and the de rigueur lifestyle alongside it. The latter took an immediate hit as he could not find any employment, despite being prepared to accept lower positions.

'You're overqualified,' rang in his ears as he doggedly continued his futile search for work.

His skis were the first to go, some furniture, artwork, followed by each of the twenty-seven bespoke Saville Row suits ordered on his myriad weekends in London. He held on dearly to his powerful, remodelled Sunbeam S7 motorbike, even though he had rarely driven it, but let it go the very same day his gym membership expired.

The last straw was the foreclosure on his spacious city pad near the American Embassy on Vasilissis Sophia Street. Antonia had asked Dimitris if she could use his place as her postal address and had often boasted to her friends about where she lived. Shortly after moving out of his apartment, his fiancée became busy, indeed way too busy to meet her beloved.

***

Ermou Street, finally abandoned by its desperate, last-minute bargain hunters, was now still, the pervasive white fluff further adding to the deafening silence. Many of the streetlights near him had been vandalised so Dimitris knew he would not be spotted easily. He reached into the inner pocket of his light denim jacket where he had emptied his stack of 5, 10, and 20 cent coins and placed them on his lap. The 50 cents and the few talira, or five-euro notes were secreted just inside his last pair of silk boxer shorts in a tiny pocket. Having long stopped puzzling over the mystery of pockets sewn into undergarments, he was grateful for the renowned Italian's forethought, evident in their functional design. He began the count. His total for the day revealed that he and the others would tonight dine like kings.

'Kameel will surely have the vegetables ready, and not too salted,' he thought hopefully, as grim hunger grabbed his guts. 'I'll get a few wines on the way home in the AB supermarket just before the bridge, and a small box of melomakarona, (Festive walnut-filled treats) 'Oh yes, and some AB juice for Christmas morning would be wonderful with the

Circles

croissants Nikos collared from the bakery on Patissia Avenue.'

Nikos and Kameel had been homeless for several months. Kameel had privileges to shower every now and again in a shelter but never had a bed. Kostas had been dismissed some months before by an employer who could no longer pay him. He had fallen foul of the law on several occasions when found stealing his dinner. Kameel worked in a tiny, cramped grill house for ten hours a day, six days a week. He was allowed to take whatever meat was due to expire in a day or two at the end of his shift, his boss often adding fruits and fresh yoghurts to his employee's plastic carry bag. 'Kameel does know how to turn a bit of meat into a meal. Maybe there'll be sausages tonight, but those will need cooking, until black. Yes, yes, quite black. And the wine, the wine should smooth our palates.'

Dimitris had first met Kameel in the tiny takeaway called 'Souvlaki Corner' when he'd gone in there reluctantly, to eat something hot after a particularly good haul of €14. Nine of those had already paid for hot coffees and two koulouria and his trolley ticket home.

'Hello, my friend,' greeted the good-looking man behind the counter. 'What would you like?'

Dimitris had instantly felt irritated by this overly familiar, yet common way of speaking in Athens.

'Yes, well, give me two chicken sticks and some fries.'

Five minutes later, his hunger the only sauce, he was digging into the mediocre meat

267

Deirdre Anne Gialamas

and starchy chips. 'That will be €5.50 please,' said the smiler, offering another napkin to Dimitris who blurted out that he only had €5.

'Don't worry, my friend, here's a drink to wash it down.'

On learning that his customer was living on the streets, Kameel invited him back to his place under the train station at Ano Patissia. Dimitris, to his own surprise, joined him at closing time. There he met Kostas, and Nikos, both from Kypseli, central Athens. Nikos quickly assembled a bed and Kostas wrapped a newspaper around his own lumpy pillow and held it out to Dimitris.

'Sleep, welcome my friend.'

For the first few weeks, Dimitris kept his distance in the little home under the railway bridge and made sure his area was as tidy as the others. Most nights the four men supplemented what Kameel brought home with whatever they had stolen, bought or found in bins, and ate together.

Dimitris learned that five million people had left Kameel's country, Syria, a million or two coming to Turkey. Many had continued on to Greece with hopes of pushing further into Western Europe. Kameel cried softly for his siblings left behind and his dead parents. Dimitris remembered Sabbarah, the young girl from Aleppo who had cleaned his home for some time and proved very reliable and honest though he had never bothered to speak much to her and called her Theodora. Kameel dreamed of owning a brand-new mobile with clear reception, packed with data. The cheap

268

Circles

battered model he carried was his only thread, a thin thread, stretching precariously back to his former life.

The new member of the group spoke of his childhood in Levidi and how he never set eyes on his mother again after leaving for Athens. 'She'd had cancer before I left but didn't want to trouble me as I had long studies ahead of me. My father followed her one year later.' Dimitris recounted how he had no one to share his loss with at the time and had become obsessed with financial security and amassing material goods. Embittered with life's nasty turns, he thought only of upward mobility, forgetting his parents' philosophy of embracing the art of giving. He had few friends. Hordes of women eagerly chased him, greatly admiring his ambition and lifestyle. Then Antonia appeared and put a halt to this.

Nikos spoke of giving up drinking and finding his feet again. It was close to two years since he had separated from his wife and then infant son. His gait was sometimes unsteady. Although his cavernous eyes unsettled Dimitris, he sensed that Nikos' thin frame housed a stout heart and knew he'd easily be overlooked in a crowd as the cloak of poverty engulfed one's identity in one's own land, let alone in a new land.

Kostas, the youngest of the trio, shared his longing to return to college to complete his studies. He was forced to drop out when his father lost his position in retail and his mother's hours were drastically cut. He had supported them as best he could with his

Deirdre Anne Gialamas

meagre wage, for a time. His first stint in prison, though short, made him more defiant and found him incarcerated for two more visits as a guest of the nation.

No one was circulating now. A few mangy-looking mutts roamed by, sniffing diligently around where Dimitris sat, frozen, then sauntered off on their quest for food. He was not intimidated by the hungry ramblers as he'd often shared bits of leftover pizza and burgers gathered from the bins outside the local fast-food shops with them. It seemed like the snow had no mercy, on and on it fell.

'This was no manna,' he mused angrily. 'It's killing me. I'm only 33. That's when Jesus died. I'm too young to die.'

Looking back at the white-capped little church he panicked that he hadn't prayed more. Just as he knew he must throw decency to the wind and try to make it home in his sad rags, a silver Mercedes drew up out of nowhere, parking illegally right by the church entrance. The driver hopped out promptly and rushed to the passenger side to open the door for a young woman. She wore dark glasses and a large-brimmed hat. She regally accepted the man's outstretched hand, and both proceeded into the church.

This strange and pleasant diversion relieved Dimitris from his worries momentarily as he gazed admiringly at the fine vehicle, fondly remembering his own model from another era. His eyes ran along the streamlined curves of the roof down to the robust wheels anchored squarely on the ground. To the side of the front

270

Circles

wheel Dimitris saw what looked like a small dog or cat lying inert on the road. The cold had reached Dimitris' soul, his breath a cotton cloud in front of him. 'I'm hallucinating,' he thought, making an almighty effort to stand up and hold his pants on all at once.

The stiffness got the better of him and he fell back down. The forlorn little bundle of fur pulled at his heartstrings, and he made another gallant attempt to stand. This time he stayed upright. 'The police could swing by, and I won't be home for Christmas. Got to be home for Christmas.' Ignoring his short-lived saviour instincts all he could think of was to get home. 'If I take baby steps and stay close to the shop walls no one will notice me.' He started towards home, 'Must get back to the others, have to make it before my trousers fall apart altogether.'

His joints creaked with every forward thrust of his legs, exquisite pain shooting up through his tired, thirty-three-year-old body. Antonia had always urged him to use the gym in any free time he had as she liked her fiancé to look buff. Dimitris wondered how she'd admonish him now if she were to spot his frail, gaunt body and sunken eyes. Or would she just look past him, not see?

Dimitris stopped. Turning round, making sure to grab his clothes tightly, he went back to find the poor creature under the car. The Merc was no longer there, but thankfully it seemed like the little animal had not been run over. 'It must be so cold, poor unfortunate creature.' It was heavier than he expected, and Dimitris found the perfect shelter for it in his front pocket. He could keep his hand there to warm the stray and at the same time deftly hold up his pants and draw little attention. 'We must get home for the others... the last bus...'

Even before he had struggled all the way down the grass embankment just under the railway bridge, Dimitris imagined the feast he was about to partake in; he was home. Four hungry men broke bread together and filled their cups over and over under the shelter of Ano Patissia bridge, then slept in the bosom of their new family on Christmas Eve.

Kostas was the first to wake on Christmas morning and went round to wake the members of the snoring orchestra.

'Happy Christmas, Happy Christmas, Kronia Polla, Kronia Polla.'

'Long Life, Long Life,' he sang to the others.

With a jolt, Dimitris remembered last night's rescue. He hoped it was safe and would be warmly accepted into the family's embrace.

'Listen, listen, I have a present for us all, a new pet!'

Dimitris reached into his empty pocket. 'Must have crawled out when I was sleeping.' He had begun drinking enthusiastically on arrival and had no recollection of placing the little animal between the covers and cardboard of his sleeping section. Pulling back the old blankets with mounting worry that it might have died in the night, Dimitris and his family gaped in awe at the Christmas present spread before them. The whole bottom half of Dimitris' makeshift bed was strewn with a treasury

Circles

densely packed with stacks of €500 notes. At the edge of the bed was a black furry ladies' dress-bag.

In early January, as the men shopped for new wardrobes, a 'Breaking News' item appeared on the large TV screen in the stylish shopping mall in Marousi, an upmarket suburb.

'*A Greek couple were arrested today in connection with the robbery of a top Government leader's private house safe. It is thought that the haul could be in the millions. According to the police, the said politician adamantly disputes those generous estimates. It is rumoured in Syntagma's corridors that he is haunted by the taxman. Mr Stavros Kokkino, 32, together with his accomplice, Ms Antonia Peridis, are this afternoon being moved to Korydallos Prison to await a date for trial.*'

Hysterectomy
Kathleen Phelan

You are redundant like an old sock
slipping inside a worn-out shoe,
or unsteady as an upside-down pear.
A warrior, now without a soul.
You have succumbed to gravity.
I am fragile as a delicate glass sculpture,
easily shattered by the slightest touch.

I have begun to speak in clichés.
I have no depth.
I use phrases like: 'What doesn't kill you makes
you strong.'
Or 'The darkest hour is just before the dawn.'

Yet I have proof of your existence.
You have served me well.
The progeny alternate.
One drives me to the doctor.
The other to collect my prescription.
Or vice versa.

Remember Humanae Vitae?
And how we didn't dance to its tune?
We danced to nobody's tune but our own.

Farewell, my trusted friend.
It's now time for us to part.
And thanks for everything.

Imagination Unleashed
Mary Hodson

I maginative Mary, my English teacher had written in red in my copybook, a response to my tale about a penny's journey. I cherished crafting that story, my imagination soaring. The penny, adorned with a hen and chickens on one side and a harp on the other, had lain on the lane leading home. Picking it up, I pondered, 'Who owned you? Where have you been?' That penny's adventures intrigued me, so when tasked with a story in class, it inspired my pen.

My teacher awarded a B+ and praised my creativity in vibrant red. I was ecstatic. At home, I eagerly shared my story and the teacher's words. But reality struck with dismissive remarks. 'Imagination won't land you a decent job... This daydreaming nonsense... You should focus on your maths instead.' These words stung, shattering my confidence in imagination.

Consequently, I suppressed my creative spirit. No longer did I wonder about Heathcliff's turmoil in *Wuthering Heights* or the plight of Judah's family in *Ben-Hur*. Even my dreams of waltzing in Vienna, sparked by the Strauss series on TV, faded. 'Imaginative Mary' became a label of mockery within my family, leading me to shut away my creativity, deemed harmful and devilish.

Choosing nursing, a field ruled by science, I tried to confine myself. Yet, my innate

Mary Hodson

imagination occasionally surfaced, guiding me to make unconventional decisions for my patients facing harsh realities.

Then, in 1975, John entered my life. A passionate artist, he reignited my imaginative spark. Together, we explored London's art world, Beethoven's symphonies, and the city's lush parks. My imagination, once dormant, now blossomed.

Years later, a chance encounter with an ad for a creative writing group marked a turning point. I joined, finding a sanctuary for my creativity. Here, I realised that both John and I were artists in our own right – he with his paintings and I with my words. Slowly, I began embracing my imaginative side, sharing my writings within the group's safety.

One day, I might even share them with my family. My recent publication about 'The Holy Well' filled me with pride. It reawakened me to the value of creativity, no longer stifled or unappreciated.

In today's world, artistic and imaginative skills are not just encouraged but seen as vital across careers. As Leigh Hunt wisely said:

'There are two worlds, the world that we can measure with a line and a rule, and the world that we feel with our hearts and imagination.'

276

I Long to Hide
Geraldine Warren

I long to hide
in a sliver of your heart
where no one else has been
That I may steal your first breath
before you wake.

No Regrets
Anne McManus

A leafless tree is framed in the window; it stands close to the glass like someone peering in to catch a glimpse of the occupants. Frost glistens on the lower branches where the brief sunlight failed to reach. Dim evening light slants into the small sparsely furnished bedroom, creating a surreal atmosphere. A man lies motionless on the bed; he appears to be quite old, and possibly unconscious. Another figure is seated on a chair at the window, eyes closed, hands folded on her lap. Everything is shades of white. There is absolute stillness inside and outside. The scene has the appearance of a tableau in a waxworks. Time has no place here. The man stirs. Barbara moves to the bedside, lowers her head for a few seconds and then quietly moves back to the chair.

She is there for a particular reason, to honour a promise made many years ago to her former husband. But it is not just that which has kept her here – for how long now? She has lost count of the days; they have simply melted into each other. In that time her thoughts have vacillated between pity, loyalty, guilt, and gratitude. Above all, she hates to think it might be good old-fashioned Irish guilt; surely, she had shaken all that stuff off years ago.

No Regrets

Definitely not love, not now, not after all that has happened. Gratitude, yes it must be, gratitude for release from the prison of predictability, and a future of incalculable boredom. He had swept her out from behind the counter of her parents' shop in the flat Irish Midlands to a world of writers, poets, and television personalities. She had taken to it in style, even adapting to a new language with the zeal of a convert. Her new life in Lyons was hectic, exhilarating. She, being outgoing, became so popular among his friends and work colleagues that he became jealous; it had caused many a row between them.

Their divorce came about because he resented her ambition to become a doctor, something she had always wanted to do. She came to the belief that it was because he regarded her as less intelligent than himself and felt threatened by her. Having her as a stay-at-home wife suited him, and his lifestyle. But she also knew that without him she had been destined to a life of unbearable monotony without any prospect of escape.

She shudders to think about what her life would have been like if he hadn't come into the shop all those years ago to buy a packet of cigarettes. Winter it was too, and scarcely a customer all day except the regulars who believed they were doing you a favour when they asked you to put it on the book. Four years she had spent at her parents' beck and call, ever since she had fallen foul of the nuns in the local school. Worse still she was the youngest of three sisters who progressed from school, to

Anne McManus

college and to well-paid jobs. So no Leaving Cert for Barbara, no career, nothing but the prospect of a dull life in the navel of Ireland until her dying day – even in desperation she would never have married one of the local farmers to endure the slavery of the farmyard, and a life of making do in a cramped damp house with one or both of his parents. Behind the counter she had some status even if the highlight of her day was deciding what colour she would paint her nails

Barbara had scarcely looked up the day the man came into the shop. She was too absorbed in flicking through a magazine while listening to loud music on the radio. His polite cough made her look up.

'Perdón, cigarillos por favor.'

'Yes, yes, of course.'

'You live aquí.'

'All my life, yes.'

'You know about the pantanos – perdón – bogs?'

'Bogs? You mean that wet land that's all around us here?'

'Yes. Saber the 'istory.'

'All I know is that there are too many in Ireland.'

'But that is why I come here. We have no bogs in Spain.'

'None at all?'

'Not one. I am come hacer una película.'

'About bogs?'

That was the start of their relationship. He came to Ireland, she went to Barcelona. Her parents were outraged when she left for good.

280

No Regrets

Barbara made several attempts to contact them by phone only to be cut off. Then she tried writing but to no avail. She did stay in touch with her younger sister in a haphazard way and she visited Barcelona many times. Barbara never regretted leaving, never went back to Ireland.

Her former husband was not a generous man; a veneer of boyish charm had camouflaged his self-absorption. It had taken her years to admit it to herself as she had wanted him to be perfect. In spite of that they had several good years together before they divorced. He was successful in his world, and she had followed her ambition to become a doctor.

These last few weeks have given her time for reflection; she regrets nothing, is proud of her success of becoming a doctor in a foreign country. It had taken years of study, firstly to learn the language, to take the necessary state exams, to get a place in medical school as a mature student, and to finally graduate with an Honours degree. She got a job immediately in the national health service, mostly dealing with older patients. In fact, she went on to make a special study of geriatric patients and their needs, both medical and psychological, eventually earning herself a reputation in that field of geriatric medicine.

Meanwhile, her ex-husband advanced his career in the world of entertainment, had numerous affairs but never remarried. Neither had Barbara remarried, despite a number of serious relationships. She had no regrets about

281

Anne McManus

that, being so absorbed in her research and medical duties in a number of hospitals.

They met from time to time never by arrangement but rather by chance. Two years ago he was diagnosed with terminal cancer. He took the news very badly, incredulous that he could be struck down out of the blue, he who prided himself on his fitness. Within a week of his diagnosis he had contacted Barbara to remind her of her promise.

The door opens quietly; Barbara does not need to turn her head to see who it is; she knows it is Michael, her only child. He comes up behind her and gently massages her shoulders. Neither of them speak for a few moments. The man sighs gently. Barbara makes to move but Michael goes to the bedside. He whispers so softly that Barbara cannot hear; then he bends his ear to the man's mouth.

'It's time,' he says to his mother.

Although Barbara knows this moment is inevitable, nevertheless she feels a tremor run through her body. She stands up, hesitates, then moves to the bedside. She takes the syringe from the dish on the bedside table then plunges it without hesitation into the emaciated arm. They hold the man's hands as his life fades away.

Neither Barbara, nor Michael utter a word. She has kept her promise.

What Lies Ahead

Anne Murray

I travelled with the bull man,
Windows open in the van,
No satnav then to guide the way.
We navigate by bales of hay.
Listening for direction from the cow.
The only way that we know how to find the
shed.
At one end he inserts A. I.
At the other end I hold her head.

All is changed from before
Now online is ChatGPT4
mobile phone and Google map
Alice Irvine has her own app.
A.I. now means something different
Human brains could be redundant.
Be on your guard, change is near.
What is A.I.? Something to fear?

No one knows what lies ahead,
Is it for good or should we dread
The works of a computer's mind –
A mind that may be hard to find.
Nothing lasts forever,
Life moves on, it's very clever.
Progress can't be stopped, my dear,
Relax, enjoy, and never fear.

What if?
Deirdre Anne Gialamas

What if, like topsy
I never was born
Mary jimmy blank fintan irene paul
Would be our family's rollcall
To sidle sleepily to the breakfast table
Warm milk and wisdom
Dished out by father
As mother stirred the porridge
Testing the four-times-tables
Before we five stepped out to school
Yawning on too early, frosted mornings?

What if I were born
And growed up rich
An only child
And never had to wait my turn
With everything called mine
The presents neath the tree
At end of year named just for me
My every whim and fickle need
Fulfilled with speed

What if?

What if pigs could fly
And little people
Did not call for war
But shared lush fields
From their own lots
On which to sow
Fresh thoughts and crops
And sought to learn
The stranger's wont
What if...?

A Normal Couple (extract)
Olga Peters

28–30 August 1940: The First Air Raids

Emma was awake immediately. She looked at her luminous alarm clock: twenty-five minutes past midnight. At first she thought it was Jo crying, but then remembered that he'd just been fed. No: the steady wailing tone – rising and falling, rising and falling, impersonal and relentless, for two interminable minutes, a frequency which penetrated her whole being. She must have missed the earlier 'aircraft approaching' signal – this was the full alarm: they had ten minutes to reach a shelter.

Leo was up. This time they'd gone to bed fully dressed, as recommended by the authorities. In the first three alarms two weeks earlier, they'd gone to bed as usual. But no raids followed, and this had given them a false reassurance. On the fourth night the full alarm had barely ceased and they were still in the flat when they could make out the rumble of aircraft. But they passed over them to offload their cargo on some other less fortunate part of the city. After that they decided it would be safer to be better prepared.

Emma grasped the baby and wrapped him in a blanket, Leo snapped up their two

A Normal Couple

emergency suitcases at the hall door, and they were out of the flat just as the signal wailed itself to silence.

'Cellar or Post Office?' called Emma.

'Post Office.'

As they rushed downstairs they were joined by Frau Sonntag. The other inhabitants of the apartment house must already have left or fled into the cellar.

'We're going to the Post Office, Frau Sonntag,' gasped Emma, changing Jo to her other arm so that she could grasp the handrail. They didn't dare use the lift. 'Is your husband in the Ministry?'

Frau Sonntag just nodded.

Five minutes later they had reached the modern building on Konstanzer Strasse. It had extensive cellars with several exits, which, as was common knowledge, had been built five years earlier for just such a purpose, long before there was even talk of a war. People had joked about it. 'Good for growing mushrooms!'

Emma almost panicked when she saw the crowd, mainly women and children and older people, trying to elbow their way in, but the wide entrance doors admitted them all quickly, and the broad stairs down into the cellars allowed them to scramble into the shelter in less than a minute. The vast area was furnished with rows upon rows of benches and some wooden tables, and streams of people were milling about settling themselves in small groups. Together with Frau Sonntag, they pushed their way as far into the centre as possible, away from the heavy metal doors

Olga Peters

which would close off the room. Emma and Leo immediately began to unpack their gas masks and the gas tent for Jo and to pull them on. It was still an awkward struggle, despite having practised it several times. She was familiar by now with the correct sequence for adjusting straps, goggles and mouthpiece. Jo whimpered as Emma pulled the rubber tent over him, and she hoped he'd go back to sleep quickly. How fortunate that his next feed wasn't due for another three hours.

She looked around the huge, low-ceilinged room, which was illuminated by long stretches of neon lamps. It was filling up rapidly, and later she wondered if it hadn't contained far more than the four hundred people for whom it was planned. Almost everybody was wearing their gasmask, and the sea of alien, insect-like heads was grotesque and frightening. People were talking in low, muffled voices, the sheer number of them creating a soft cacophony, like an army approaching from afar.

At the far end of the cavern were extra rooms, she knew. These had beds in them, for people who were ill, or even expecting mothers. There was also a kitchen back there, and the washrooms.

She moved closer to Leo and searched for his firm hand.

'You look terrible!' she said.

'Do I? But this is my favourite piece of clothing!'

'It doesn't suit you! I hope it goes out of fashion soon!'

Emma turned to her neighbour.

288

A Normal Couple

'Are you all right, Frau Sonntag?' she asked.

'Yes, my dear, thank you. Oh!'

The murmured conversation of the people in the shelter stopped abruptly as the droning of the approaching aircraft became audible. Despite the huge building above them and the reinforced ceiling and walls of the shelter, the rumbling grew louder and louder, and Emma felt herself beginning to tremble. Now nobody was talking; the only sound came from the excited chattering of some small children and a wailing baby. She moved even closer to Leo, pulling Jo in his tent with her. The roar of the enemy planes seemed to be directly above their heads. The sudden clatter and boom of the anti-aircraft guns from a post somewhere in the vicinity added to the racket. She was anticipating the whining of the first bombs, the crash of the missile hurtling through a roof, the explosion, the thunder of disintegrating buildings above their heads, the screams of terrified women as the first whiffs of gas seeped through the crack under the iron doors, the heat of flames outside .... The planes roared on and on, their sound muted by the shelter around them, and gradually the droning faded away. The nearby guns stuttered and ceased, and after fifteen minutes there was silence. There was deadly silence too in the huge shelter. They waited.

'There go the bombs,' murmured Leo.

'What do you mean?' asked Emma.

'They've dropped their bombs. Can't you hear them?'

Olga Peters

'No, I heard nothing. It must be very far away. God help the poor people there, wherever it is.'

Now and then there were bursts of distant anti-aircraft fire, but they could hear no explosions. The danger seemed to have bypassed them. Yet it was almost three hours before the all-clear sounded, people began to pull off their gas masks, the heavy doors were opened, and the first hardy locals emerged cautiously up the stairs to street level. More and more people streamed out of the shelter. When Emma, Leo and Frau Sonntag reached the surface, they were relieved to see that nothing had changed – nothing at all. It was still a warm, late August night, or rather early morning. A slight breeze was moving the leaves at the tops of the lime trees on either side of the road, a black-and-white cat raced across the deserted street and ducked under a garden gate, the waning moon provided just enough light to demonstrate that life in Charlottenburg at 3.20am on this twenty-ninth of August was absolutely and completely normal.

Emma felt almost light-headed as they hurried back to their house. Leo invited Frau Sonntag in for a small brandy to settle their nerves, but she refused, knowing that the young couple needed to get back to sleep as soon as possible. Jochen had slept soundly through all the panic.

In the morning, Emma made sure to listen to the official army news bulletin on the radio. Severe bombing raids with many casualties

A Normal Couple

had taken place in the heavily industrialised Ruhr area in the west of Germany. A school and two hospitals had also been hit, an injustice which the report capitalised on with great indignation. The Berlin bombing came at the end of the report. Most of the bombs had fallen on open ground in the eastern part of the city, but one of the main railway stations had been demolished. Twenty-eight people had been injured, and twelve had been killed. It was the first time that destruction had hit Berlin, and these were its first casualties. Emma was shocked. Surely it was only a matter of time before their area would also be targeted. True, there were no major train stations in their direct vicinity, nor were there any industrial plants. She thought it through and came to the conclusion that, in fact, there was nothing that would justify (if one could even call it that) an attack on Charlottenburg. If both parties to the war continued to play a fair game, selecting to bomb only military infrastructure, then the three Gebhardts (and Frau Sonntag) should be safe.

During the day, she talked to her parents and Franzi on the phone, and they reassured each other that the areas they were living in were safe. That applied especially to her parents, whose house was on the south-west perimeter of Berlin, almost in the forest which grew around that area of the city. Her father was able to tell her that the station which had been bombed was about eight kilometres from her flat as the crow flies, which would explain why she hadn't heard the bombs.

Olga Peters

'Leo must have very keen hearing,' he commented, when she told him that he had heard them exploding.

But how would this go on? How often would the bombers come? Surely not every night? How were people to live under such conditions, how were they to work, to go about their business, to take care of their families – without sleep? Why had the anti-aircraft defence even allowed the British bombers to reach the capital? Hadn't Göring promised that this would never happen?

'I'll change my name to Meier if any enemy aircraft reach Berlin,' he is supposed to have boasted some time back. Now everyone was talking about Herr Meier under their breath.

Sure enough, only two nights later, the alarm sounded again. They had been fast asleep. It was two am. Yet both Emma and Leo had developed a lighter sleep after the past raid, and they had left the bedroom window open, so that this time they heard the first alarm, warning them that an attack might be expected. They had trouble staying awake for a possible second signal. But, once it started, there was no missing it. For two minutes the oscillating tone penetrated every wall, window, eardrum, urging sleepers to rise and run. Fear enveloped them instantly. Yet this time they decided it would do if they sheltered in the cellar of their apartment house, where one room had been converted to serve as an air-raid shelter. Again Emma looked after Jo, while Leo took their cases, which contained all

292

A Normal Couple

their important documents, small valuables, some clothes, food and money. He also grabbed the bag with the gasmasks and their steel helmets.

This time they didn't see Frau Sonntag. Emma even ran to her door and rang and knocked, but Leo bellowed at her to leave it and to go downstairs. When they reached the shelter, they found that two other couples from the floors above theirs had sought refuge there too.

The room was more intimate than the big shelter in the Post Office. Each apartment had contributed one or two old armchairs or deckchairs. There was a little table, and a radio on a shelf attached to the wall. Buckets of water lined one side, with a pile of old towels and blankets folded next to them. The walls of the cellar were clean and freshly white-washed after they had been reinforced the previous year, when detailed directives obliging all homeowners to carry out these 'improvements' had been issued. In the centre of the room, a newly constructed column of steel and cement added support for the ceiling, but it was commonly known that the arched ceilings of the old Berlin cellars were immensely strong. Should it come to the worst and the house collapse on top of them, they offered a good measure of protection. The former wooden door had been replaced by a strong steel panel within a rubber frame, to prevent gas seeping in, and a second exit had been opened to the courtyard at the back of the house. There were no windows to the room, and no ventilation

Olga Peters

system like in the public shelter, and Emma thought the air would get very stuffy if they had to stay there longer than a couple of hours.

Again Jo slept on while she fitted the gas tent around him. They didn't know these neighbours well, had only greeted them briefly whenever they'd met in the stairwell or in the lift. The middle-aged couple from the smaller apartment on the top floor hadn't bothered to pull on their gas masks, and were joking about 'laughing themselves to death' if gas should enter.

'That's not funny,' snapped Emma, and they both stopped sniggering immediately, and even indicated apologies. She snubbed them when they offered a friendly comment on Jo. She and Leo settled into their deckchairs as well as they could, and began to listen. After a moment their light-hearted neighbours fell silent too. The first floor had just taken their seats in grim silence. All were quiet, tense, and frightened – all except Leo. He moved his deckchair closer to hers, and searched for her hand.

'Try to sleep, dearest,' he said, 'I'll watch out.' He stroked her hand.

Emma almost smiled. Sleep? Now? In a few minutes? And he would watch out? He was sweet.

And then they could hear the aircraft approaching. At first they sounded very far away, but their deep roar drew closer and closer. The sudden outburst of the anti-aircraft guns pounding nearby made Emma

294

A Normal Couple

jump. The floor under her feet vibrated softly. The droning and rumbling grew ever louder, and when it seemed to be directly above them, Emma heard the whining sound she had been dreading. Louder and louder, closer and closer – and then a thunderous explosion. The floor under her feet trembled, crumbs of plaster fell from the ceiling and the cellar light flickered. Emma cried 'No! No!' and threw herself over the basket with Jo. Already Leo was beside her, throwing his arm over her.

'It's all right, Em, it's all right, it wasn't for us, we're all safe.'

Crying, she clung to him, and he pulled her close with his long arms wrapped around her. The other people in the cellar had also changed position – the joking husband was crouching on the floor with his arms shielding his head, his wife was clinging to the pillar in the centre of the room, and the other couple were cowering in a corner with their faces to the wall. Hardly had they all drawn breath when a further explosion followed, not so close, but this in turn was succeeded by an even louder bombardment which seemed to have struck their house. Everything vibrated. The noise was unbearable, the cracking, bursting, shattering. The cellar door shivered, and Emma thought she could smell smoke.

Leo firmly pushed Emma away from him and told her to sit on the floor. He took one of the blankets, folded it and placed it for her to sit on. Then he took three of the towels and steeped them in the water in the buckets,

Olga Peters

wrung them out and handed one to each of the women in the room.

'Wrap this around your head,' he told them.

Everybody was sitting on the floor by this time. Emma had taken Jo out of his basket and was holding him on her lap. He had woken and was yelling. She tried to calm him, but with the noise and the panic in the air, it was hopeless. She decided to ignore the strangers around her, and unbuttoned her blouse and her nursing bra, opened Jo's tent so that his head emerged, and laid him at her breast. Fortunately, when he realised what was on offer, he quietened down, producing only a yell of protest at intervals.

The thunder of the bombing, the explosions, the lifting of the floor and the grit showering from the ceiling, together with the shattering bursts of the anti-aircraft guns continued unabated for a further ten minutes. Then it all gradually subsided. Then suddenly ceased. They could hear crackling noises in the outside world, and Leo made out the wailing of a fire-brigade or an ambulance. But the bombers had gone.

They stayed where they were until they heard the all-clear. The joking man cautiously turned the lever which had sealed the door of their shelter. Emma anticipated that a load of rubble would tumble into the room, but it opened easily. The stairway outside was covered in dust, but otherwise clear. They climbed up into the lobby of their building. There was nothing special to be seen. Leo opened the door to the street and stepped

A Normal Couple

outside. Everything appeared unchanged. He walked to the corner and looked around into Dusseldorfer Strasse. Two houses down, on the far side of the street, flames were shooting from the top floors of a building, and the fire-brigade was already in action. All the windows of this house and the house opposite, on their side, were shattered. He could see no further damage. Where had the other detonations taken place?

He returned to their house and helped Emma upstairs, then went back down to the cellar to fetch the cases. Their flat was intact, except for a large, ornate, rather hideous vase a colleague of Leo's had given them as a wedding present. They had placed it on top of the glass cabinet, but now it was lying on the floor, shattered. The vibrations from the detonations must have caused it to shift.

'That's the silver lining on the edge of the cloud,' observed Leo, as he shoved the shards aside with his foot.

Emma was still shivering and crying, so Leo made her a cup of hot cocoa with a shot of rum in it. Then he made her undress and tucked her into her bed.

'Try to sleep now, my love,' he said, and placed a kiss on her forehead. 'We'll talk about all this in the morning,' he promised. 'It's not going to happen again.'

Power of Rural Electrification
Josephine McCann

He cycled north to visit his aunt and
to a dance on New Year's night.
She bussed south to her aunt and
to a dance that very same night.
Light footed pairs waltzed and whirled.
Floorboards creaked as many a heart missed
a beat. The rhythm of the music flowed
He met she, together the hours flew by.

The decades flew by. After the death
of their elderly mother, the bottom drawer
in her wardrobe to be cleared,
a roll of letters was found.

A young man from the south writing
to a young lady living in the north.
Emotions, palpable from the copperplate
scrawl that fills the now yellowed pages.
A power of energy must have flowed
as he wrote of the richness electricity
brought to his home and business,
local undertaker. Prospects further
enhanced, house also had indoor toilet.

Power of Rural Electrification

Years ago, when those words were
first read by oil-filled lamp, a current
of excitement, the handsome young man
with the shiny seat of his twill pants,
oiled from the saddle of his bike
now wanted to be her beau.
Her heart warmed but her bones
chilled as she made her way to
the water closet in her family's backyard.

Seven children later, and she not yet fifty,
her handsome young man breathed his last.
His brother claimed the business.
He too, was soon claimed by a local unwed
lass.
The young widow now left with a land holding,
acres of useless agricultural worth and
in permanent abide in the room above the
kitchen,
her late husband's bed-ridden uncle.

Sadness today, that the young lady
from the north didn't get to enjoy
the enhanced value of the acreage,
Its frontage having soared in value.

Old Loves
Deirdre Anne Gialamas

I ducked when I saw you
not wanting you to see me.
I spied you wearing gigantic
jowls around your neck, cosy
like a cashmere scarf,
your nose longer,
redder than I remembered,
ears furred with hair migrated down
from your shiny crown.

I ducked when I saw you because
I saw myself in you and not
wanting to make friends with time
who never waits for me anyway,
always thundering on.

I ducked when I saw you and bowed
To my nemesis who made you miss me
by a nanosecond...

A Step Too Far

Mary Hawkshaw

Trudging along the dark narrow lane, Bridget moved as if in a dream. She struggled with a barrage of thoughts flooding her mind – the kind of thoughts that bring a haunting restlessness, just by their presence. Her footsteps echoed on the gravel path, a reminder she was getting further and further away, away from her home. Tiny creatures scurried under bushes as she passed. The glaring eyes of a night owl watched her, from a high perch on an old oak tree. Its long branches swayed back and forth against the moonlit sky. She gasped for breath as a gusty wind blew hard against her face. Turning her back to the wind, she pushed the loose hair strands back under her scarf and pulled it tight around her head. The sun had set over an hour ago. But, daylight meant nothing now; darkness meant nothing now. Rubbing her face with her hands for the umpteenth time changed nothing. With downcast eyes, and her coat pulled tightly around her, she drifted aimlessly, a tormented soul.

Suddenly, startled by the loud shrill of a train whistle in the distance, she stopped in the middle of the lane and looked into the darkness. As the misty rain mingled with her tears, she turned towards her home. The lights were shining through her windows. Black smoke was rising

Mary Hawkshaw

from the chimney as the moonlight glistened on its slate roof. She sat on an outstretched boulder at the edge of the lane and looked at the cottage, her home the only one she knew.

'My home and yet, not my home,' she whispered. 'This whitewashed cottage with Granny's pink roses around the door. The notches Dad etched into the side of the house to measure how much I grew each year.'

She remembered rolling down the hayloft while Dad roared: 'Stop, stop, Bridget, you'll break a leg doing that!'

In her mind she heard the clatter of milk churns in the back of the van, as they returned home from the dairy.

She thought about the first time she brought Tommy home to meet her parents and to tell them they wanted to get married.

So many memories, so much of her life.

She covered her face with her hands as if to shield herself from the images tearing her apart. Crushing pressure, along with a tightening sensation formed in her chest. She convulsed into the depths of despair and roared up at the night sky: 'Why? Why? Dear God, why? This is our life.'

For the last three hundred years, their small dairy farm and cottage stood on its land. Its isolation protected it from the ravages of industry, and urban sprawl. Each generation passed it down to the next. Providing them with shelter and a living, it was the blood running through their veins and linked them in a common goal. Tommy moved into the cottage to live with Bridget after their marriage forty years earlier.

302

A Step too Far

They replaced and repaired it, just like Bridget's parents did before them. Piece by piece, an extension was added, the old and the new blending perfectly.

That morning began like every morning did for the last forty years. Tommy was up at dawn to milk the cows. Rover, his old dog and constant companion was at his side. Bridget stoked the fire in the range until a vibrant glow appeared from the dying embers. She carefully placed more logs and turf around it and closed the door. The old cast iron kettle was topped up with cold water. It started to hiss as it prepared to boil.

Bridget placed the frying pan on the range and began to get the breakfast ready. She looked through the thick roses around the door to see if Tommy was on his way back. Their sweet scent drifted around her as she clipped some of them away from the entrance and placed them in a vase filled with water and put them on the table. Looking again for Tommy through the open window, she heard the bickering of a robin and goldfinch in the thick ivy, on the north side of the house. They built their nests too close to one another. For the moment, neither one was willing to give up their space.

Tommy appeared in the doorway, holding an open letter in his hand. He looked over at Bridget, unable to speak. Moving slowly towards the table, he held the edge of his chair to steady himself as he sat down. Bridget stood by the range, her eyes full of sadness. She removed the frying pan and placed it on the side of the sink. Tommy was seventy-five years old, two years older than Bridget. His work on the farm was physically

Mary Hawkshaw

demanding, yet there remained a gentle refinement in his thin face. His receding hairline was rarely visible. On the odd occasion when he removed his hat, it looked like a part of him was missing. His gentleness was apparent by his tender respect for nature and for the animals in his care. He was a small man, but over the years a few extra pounds had accumulated on his once slim frame. Bridget was in the same situation; she also accumulated a few pounds. She was small like Tommy; this was one of the features she was attracted to when she met him first. She wore her hair tied back in a neat bun at the back of her head. Her glasses dangled from a delicate chain around her neck.

The letter lay on the table. Bridget looked over at a crisp white single sheet. Two perfect creases were dividing it into three equal sections. The centre was sitting firmly on the table with both ends standing in the air. An unwanted silence hung between them. Neither one was able to form the words needed to lift the shroud of darkness covering them. The whistle of the kettle called for attention, its piercing urgency sounding in vain. Rover lingered around the door. His eyes darted back and forth between both of them. He sensed the fear in the room and whimpered as he lay down at Tommy's feet.

Bridget lifted the boiling kettle and placed it on the side of the range. The hissing died down. She stood gazing at it. Somehow, it looked different. Leaning on the rail of the range, she looked up at the clock. Its ticking grew louder as it mingled with the pounding of her heart. Emptiness and tiredness devoured her spirit. She felt the sorrow

A Step too Far

that comes with an ending and the fear that comes with the unknown. The small amount of money they borrowed five years earlier to buy milking equipment had quadrupled. Then the price of milk dropped drastically. They had struggled to make the payments, but the compound interest crippled their efforts. The eviction letter sealed their fate. Moving to the table, she sat down. No need to read the letter. She knew the end was close. When would they begin this journey that was now inevitable? A journey to a place she didn't know. The letter had a date. An important date. A time when their lives and all they knew would change. Bridget slowly reached for the letter. She avoided reading the words and looked for the date. There it was. First of July, 2019. One short month from now. One month to gather their lives and move.

Tommy sat motionless and silent. His blue eyes were unable to look at Bridget. For the first time in forty years, he had to force himself to go to the fields and gather the rest of the cows for milking. Getting to his feet, he moved slowly towards the door. He reached for the door handle as a tear rolled down his cheek. Bridget sat for some time, the letter hanging from her hand. She didn't notice Tommy leaving. She was staring down at her hand holding the letter. She tried to get to her feet but fell back into the chair. Her old cat appeared at her feet, rubbing her head firmly against her leg. Bridget picked her up.

'What are we going to do, missy?' she said. Putting her head close to the cat's face, the old cat curled up on her lap and closed her eyes. Bridget rested her hand on the cat's back and

Mary Hawkshaw

looked around her kitchen. The walls were full of photographs from the beginning of photography over a century ago: smiling children and adults, wedding pictures, confirmation pictures, birthday pictures.

Then her eyes fell on her parents' portrait. Her father looking so proud and happy. A rose neatly placed in his lapel. Mam, holding her small bag, and linking dad. A big smile on her face. A small hat covering her head as her curls dangled around her small face.

'I'm so sorry, Mam,' she said, 'this shouldn't be happening'.

'I'm sorry,' she said again.

She wiped her tears away, and put Missy in her cat bed beside the range, and decided to visit her mother's grave. She went there many times during the year, bringing roses from around the door and placing them in the vase on the grave. This afternoon she picked the most abundant blooms for her mother. She remembered her words.

'Bridget,' she'd say, 'Roses are like memories in December.'

Sitting by her grave, she told her mother all about the eviction notice. The scent from the roses drifted over the grave and around Bridget. A robin landed on the top of the headstone, tilting his head slightly to one side he watched her cautiously. He remained in the same position until Bridget left.

That evening Tommy and Bridget had dinner in silence. Each was searching their mind for any solution to this tragedy – each careful not to make matters worse for the other by talking

306

A Step too Far

about it. Since Bridget's mother and father passed away, it had just been herself and Tommy in the cottage. Their bond was as strong as it was the day they married.

After dinner, Tommy and Rover went to collect the chickens for the night. Closing the chicken coop, Tommy felt a deep pain in his chest. Leaning against the chicken wire, he took a deep breath and sat on the large stone beside the coop. He looked towards the cottage as the sun was going down. He never saw it looking so beautiful. When he returned to the cottage, Bridget was still out on her walk. He knew she liked to have time to think on her own when she was worried about something.

'This too will pass,' he said, as he entered the cottage and closed the door.

By the time Bridget returned home, Tommy was already in bed. She sat and gazed into the fire, afraid to close her eyes. Afraid to sleep. As if staying awake would somehow confine the misery to this day.

The sun was rising when she opened her eyes. This morning there was no routine. Getting up from the chair, she moved to do what she always did. Then she stopped in the middle of the floor on her way to fill the kettle. The house had an eerie silence.

'Where's the dog, where's Tommy?'

On her way to the bedroom, she could hear every beat of her heart getting louder as she moved closer. Everything around her was slowing down with each step.

'Tommy,' she called, but there was no reply. She paused for a few seconds, listening for any

307

Mary Hawkshaw

sound. But the only sound was her heart thumping in her chest. Today was the first morning she could ever remember that Tommy was not up before her. Putting her hand on the door handle, 'Tommy,' she said again. Then closed her eyes tight for a few seconds, with a shaking hand, she opened the door.

The rising sun cast shafts of silver light into the cottage the following morning. The song of the morning dove drifted over the farmyard and surrounding fields. A calming peace settled around the farmyard. The cattle waited quietly in the barn. The chickens bobbed their heads up and down and looked around for the hand that would set them free.

A neighbour farmer arrived to ask Tommy if he could bring an orphan calf to his barn to suckle from one of his cows. He knocked on the door, but received no reply. He looked through the kitchen window; there was no sign of Bridget or Tommy. Sensing something was wrong, he broke the kitchen window and crawled through. Looking around the kitchen, he could tell nothing was touched for at least a day and a half.

Going to the bedroom, he found them lying together. The old dog was lying beside the bed on the floor. The cat looked up from the end of the bed when she heard the door opening. The farmer slowly pulled a long piece of string from his pocket and tied it onto Rover's collar.

Then he covered their faces with the blanket and walked their old dog outside. Missy, their cat, followed them.

The Stolen Kiss
Elizabeth Hannon

Proud, she waited, with bated breath
Watched him moving forward
with hands joined
Watched as he reverently
received the sacred host
Then silently returned to his place
With the other First Communicants.

Mass over she moved quickly forward
to claim the first kiss,
the holy blessed first kiss
from her wonderful son.

Unbelievably a neighbour stole it –
the special blessing
she had looked forward to receiving.

Never forgiven.

If the Prom could Talk
Josephine McCann

I'm too old for this coast, yet here I stand,
A permanence in hues of grey, gnarled,
and chipped by eons of tread.
My life trundles on; energetic runners
morning and evening outpace strollers
who embrace me throughout the day.
Emotions of the walkers betrayed
by the rhythm of their steps,
journeying to unravel life's woes.
I absorb their moans and joys.
Gossip and hard luck stories abound,
But who listens? High heels, battered boots,
sandals, and dog waste,
Never mindful of their impact on my slabs.
I, too, have feelings.
Just look at my decay,
cracks with water seeping through.
When it freezes, pressure deepens my fissures.
Yet I will not yield; I am steadfast.

While you're cossetted in the warmth of home,
I'm often bashed by debris thrown ashore.
Don't forget the stench, the slime, litter,
And the gunge of seaweed,
And those who blame their last drink.
The trees may have their wood-wide web,
But our inanimate collection of sand, pebbles,
rocks, and cement has ways to communicate.

If the Prom could Talk

We wobble, vibrate, and weave our message
along our pathways.
We know who you are and what lies you tell,
And who you have deceived.
We share the whoppers and whispers
We've overheard as walkers weave their path.

I do have my treats; night morphs into
morning.
Sunrise, grey mist, or storm horses at sea
Herald in a new day, always a joy to see.
Blue, violet, orange, and yellow,
Atmospheric sunsets of which I never tire.
How I love a full moon after a day of rain.
Each shimmering puddle reflects into the
black night,
Its own full, perfect moon.

Mug of the Month

Once a month, the members of the Write-on group have a bit of fun competing in a 50-Word Challenge. The rules are simple: write a short piece, no more than 50 words, containing two 'trigger' words which are assigned at the beginning of the exercise.

A specially engraved coffee mug is presented to the Write-on member whose entry garners the most votes from their peers. They also get the accolade of being known as: 'The Write-on Mug of the Month!'

September
Keywords – *HIDE* and *STEAL*

Escape
Anne McManus

That was a real steal she thinks as she hides yet another ring in her knicker drawer.

She now has a total of fourteen; her favourite is the ruby and diamond.

She has never worn and never will wear any of them. They will become her escape money.

Secrets
Anne Murray

I don't want to hide anymore.
I want everything out in the open.
That secret stole my youth.
I don't want it to steal my old age.

Mug of the Month September

Hide and Steal
Jutta Rosen

'Hide and Steal'
'Hide and Steal' –
Words lacking any
Creative appeal.

I offered Ger
A little deal.
But: 'No! My words
You will not steal!'

I scoured Thesaurus
With desperate zeal.
Shakespeare brought
No repeal.

So, here's my fifty
Words. I feel
I'm out of luck
With 'Hide and Steal'.

Mug of the Month September

Memory
Mary Hodson

Peek a Boo
Where are you?
He hides.
I'm coming to get you.
Where can he be?

I recall, the laughter, joy, and innocence of
that special time.
Unnoticed, the thief of time steals your time.

Seventeen years have passed.
Treasured moments now, locked in my
memory.

My Shyly Sweet
James Conway

'Go hide your love
My shyly sweet,'
He said,
'In your garden
of secrets under
a starlit sky.
Wrap it in the velvet
of ribbons, deep
in the Earth's heart.
And when the thief
of dreams wants your
soul draw quick your sword
engrave the words:
Thou shan't steal.'

Mug of the Month September

Hide there in the Barn
Ciara Keogh

Hide there in the barn
Wide black eyes of charm
Steal into the moonlit night
Silent beating wings aflight.

With a sudden quick glide
A drop and a slide
A mouse victim, it seems,
The woods echo her squeals.
Are you an ominous presence?
Or sent from the heavens?

Steal my Hide
Josephine McCann

You steal my hide?
The hide I so haggled for it was a steal.
I had considered to hide my hide prior to the
party, but foolishly thought no friend would
steal my hide.
Camera replay shows you tried to hide my
hide as you steal away from my house.

Mug of the Month September

Stolen Goods
Frank Fahy

In a quiet neighbourhood, a new burglar
entered a house, unknowingly selecting a
seasoned thief's stash.
Amidst luxurious items, he lifted a stolen fur
stole.
Now, he has to hide the already hidden hide.

Twilight Zone
Mary Rose Tobin

Autumn whispers, golden flight,
Overcast skies, dimming light.
Montbretia's flames begin to sway,
Fuchsia's brilliance steals away.
Crisp leaves crunch, children play.

Back to school: 'Come on, we're late!'
Write-on resumes, Thursday date.
Chilly breezes start to chide,
Approaching winter cannot hide,
The year is now an ebbing tide.

Mug of the Month September

Who Stole Her Stole?
Seamus Keogh

Did Noel steal her stole?
Who said it was stolen?
If it was, indeed, taken?
Was it the fur of a mink?
Or the brush of a fox?
Where would he hide it?
Probably somewhere about
In plain sight.
'Look, Noel's wife at the table
Is wearing my beautiful sable.'

You Hide Among Wildflowers
Molly Fogarty

You hide among wildflowers,
silent, dingy, a metal sleeper cell,
waiting out the hours pretending
you're a bit of bling someone once lost,
or, maybe, a noble seed, embracing earth,
averting famine,
when you know fine well you're a born killer
primed to steal life itself at the first footfall.

October
Keywords – *WILD* and *WONDER*

Imbroglio
Nollaig O'Donnell

Annie always has the good word:
Praising the neighbours for the warmth of
their welcome –
She commends their *'hostility'*.
She talks about their wonderful bungalows –
All with *'dormant'* windows -
And triple *'dazed'*.
She often mentions the police patrolling their
neighbourhood:
Sure, they cover at least 100 *'kgs'* per night!

Wild.

Mug of the Month October

Just Asking
Anne Murray

Wondering
If
Love
Died,

Would
Our
Nurture
Derive
Eternal
Repose?

Puppy Love
Frank Fahy

In a world both wild and wonder-filled, young *Cailín* embarks on a journey of discovery.

Her eyes, like glistening orbs of innocence, drink in each new sight and sound.

With every step, she finds a world bursting with marvels, all under the gentle guidance and protection of her human companions.

Mug of the Month October

Roselit
James Conway

What is it like
to live without the wonder
of the wild, without its silky
fur, without the colours of its
rustic heart?
Roselit in excitement,
I inhale the oxygen
of my years, I seek
life beyond my beginning
a thunderstorm moment
my first breath, a soul
minuetting at last.

Seasons of Life
Mary Rose Tobin

In my youth I was wild, a river unchecked.
Every occasion with magic bedecked.
Middle years' worries a long shadow cast,
Childish bright sunshine seemed all in the
past.
But now that I'm old, like a tree in full
splendour,
To the vast sky of wonder I once more
surrender

Mug of the Month October

The Old Bog Road
Mary Hodson

Wondering of generations past
following in their steadfast footsteps,
along The Old Bog Road.
Autumnal winds blow wild, soft and gentle,
scattering mosaic rustic leaves,
crunching beneath my feet.
Nature truly wonderful, predictable
heralding the coming of winter.
Sleep descends, nature rests.

The Power of Sound
Molly Fogarty

Hearing clumsy, flapping wings, she turned
to see the wild, crazy cockerel had launched
himself from a height,
his outstretched, bloodthirsty talons now
inches from her eyes.
Terror exploded,
instinctively releasing a wall of sound,
a wall he somehow ...crashed into.
Crumpled,
stunned,
He dropped earthward.
The wonder of it.

Mug of the Month October

What's It?
Seamus Keogh

Shure 'tis no wonder the Gods go wild, when
humans can't decide
if they are an 'IT' or not?
Shure 'tis no wonder men go to the drink,
while Irish women just prattle and think about
'IT'.
Shure 'tis no wonder me dog's
no longer a Doberman.
It's a Doberit.

Why I Must Die
Jutta Rosen

His jet-black eyes, his demon smile,
Caressing silken voice.
Though but a child I was his bride,
His touch left me no choice.

Oh he was wild, I but a child,
He laughed and would not stay.
Small wonder I am doomed to die -
He stole my soul away.

Why Migrate?
Josephine McCann

Wet, wild and windy
West of Ireland winter blues
No wonder birds flew

Mug of the Month October

Wild
Richard O'Donnell

Rest in the peace of the wild,
Where there is no wonder for the past or the future –
Just being present in the presence.

Wild with Wonder
Geraldine Warren

Wild with wonder at his touch.
God I miss him so much.
What a cruel twist of fate
That we ever had that date.
His texts I see and press,
Delete
His emails come and go,
Delete
All he ever did was cheat,
But how he made my heart beat!

Wild Wonder
Elizabeth Hannon

'That the world may wonder at your great fortune.'

This was an often-quoted greeting used by my husband's grandfather.

With it, he wished his many half-wild, highly amused grandchildren success in all examinations, business enterprises, love and marriage.

I think it's brilliant. I may start using it myself.

November
Keywords – *LIKE* and *BOSS*

An Influencer
Anne Murray

There was Frank, like,
in his Hugo Boss suit,
checking his socials like.
'I'm an online influencer like,'
says he.
'Like, you'll have to go to my page and give me
a like.'
'I will if I like,' says I, 'but like,
you're not the boss of me, like.'

Exception to the Rule
Frank Fahy

'"*What do you think of this boss?*" is completely
inaccurate,' said the Senior Editor, 'without
inserting a comma after the word *'this'!*'
'I'd beg to differ,' said the Junior. 'A hurley
manufacturer could ask someone did they like
the boss of a new hurley!'
The Senior Editor remained silent.

Mug of the Month November

Brutus
Kathleen Phelan

I remember you
barking at spiders and
greeting strangers.
You would have welcomed
Jack the Ripper.
Only in sleep you snarled,
chased cats and
showed the world the staffy
you were born to be.
Like you were the boss of everything.
I miss you buddy.
Sleep well in rainbow heaven.

Dancing in the Park
Mary Hodson

He appeared on a cloud of booming musical
beats,
We waited in anticipation, genuflecting at his
feet.
Lean toned body, chiselled face, muscles
pulsating,
Tight jeans we liked to emulate.
We wore his tee-shirt,
We danced in the dark.
We screamed his name,
We desired the Boss.

Mug of the Month November

Like and Boss
Nollaig O'Donnell

'Write 50 words,' you say,
'On any topic, you may.
Like and Boss must be included;
Omit, and you're excluded!'
So, I sit with pen in hand
To write a piece without a plan.
My brain, it aches;
My mind goes dim.
The light's gone out:
I must give in!

My Boss
Mary Hawkshaw

My boss, I like, he's bright and gay.
He ensures I work hard every single day.
But one day soon, I hope to take his place,
And be like him, so full of grace.
For every dog will have his day.
Then I, too, will take home the highest pay.

Mug of the Month November

Orders
Josephine McCann

I'd like you to clean the chimney.
Yes Boss.
I'd like you to shine the silver.
Yes Boss.
I'd like you to paint the parlour.
Yes Boss.
I'd like you to F... off.
You too Boss.

Ouch!
James Conway

Peck a peak
wraps a beak upon
my windowpane

'My tray is dry
not a gram
for my tum.'

Peck a peak
'What? You cheeky
bird, ordering me
about like a boss.'

'Yum, yum,' shrieks
the bird. 'I'll eat your
fat cheeks instead.'

Ouch....

Mug of the Month November

Outfoxed
Elizabeth Hannon

Chloe, my granddaughter has Chicken Pox
I, like a mother hen, have to keep her boxed.
Hands sheathed in cotton gloves
So she can't scratch spots,
Or pass the itch to granddad
Who fears shingles.
Paradoxically, she's the 'Boss'.
The little vixen demands comfort treats.
Tired out, I accede, outfoxed.

Planet Earth
Richard O'Donnell

Planet Earth is the boss –
Like it or not.
Gaia screams, 'I have had enough!
Humanity, you have too much.
You have stolen from creation.'
'Return what you have stolen.
Take only what you need,
Or I will destroy you...
To date is but a warning.'

Mug of the Month November

Shadows of Deception
Mary Rose Tobin

Late-night city lights, Ricky gets the call,
Boss says, 'Hit the vault – this time, get it all!'
Heart of the city,
trying to survive.
Orders are orders, but he doesn't trust the
vibe.

Crime's gone sideways, alarms blaring loud,
Ricky's in the shadows, like he's lost in the
crowd.

The Boss
Molly Fogarty

Though everyone called him The Boss,
he rarely graced the family business which
bore his wife's name
(for tax purposes).
A policeman, not much liked on the street,
he was the man of the house
and owned the lot.
He went first,
his name topping the gravestone –
Still The Boss.

January
Keywords – TUNE and FINE

Amadeus
Mary Rose Tobin

A young musician on the stage
Had the critics in a rage
Notes he struck, so wild and free,
Jangled, tangled like a stormy sea.
'Your tune's a discordant maddening mess!
The audience is in distress...'
Two hundred years later, it's a fine classic,
A masterpiece born from chaotic magic.

Haiku
Jutta Rosen

A fine white mist descends
the unseen sea heaving sighs
its never-ending tune

Mug of the Month January

January Aspirations
Elizabeth Hannon

May brightening days lighten our load,
returning tuneful birds dispel winter's gloom,
post-Christmas fasting yield to spring's
abundance.
May the simple enjoyment of snowdrops,
And pioneering daffodils remind us,
Despite war and wanton waste, the year cycle
continues.
May everyday things reawaken fine memories
of family and friends passed on.

Maybe
Anne McManus

During a lull in the bombing,
I try tuning in; the usual crackling noises.
Then!
Magically 'One Fine Day' comes through;
her voice coming from God knows where,
brimming with hope and love,
almost breaking, moves me to tears.
What chance is there of ever seeing my
beloved again?

Mug of the Month January

Saying Goodbye
Kathleen Phelan

He cycled down the lane,
His bicycle rattling,
Fine-tuned by the gentle rise and fall of the
surface.
At the entrance, workmen powered up their
machines.
Weeping,
He said goodbye to the dry-stone wall,
the vibrant nesting season,
And every living thing that called the
hedgerows their home.

To the Height of the Stars
James Conway

A poem has been the greenest
island of my imagination as Bryon
once said.
A special way of thinking,
A unique way of knowing the world
with cadences close to musicality.
A fine tune in colour chasing close
to the soul as it sparkles to the height
of the stars.

Mug of the Month January

The Deer Hunter
Mary Hodson

Fine-tuned, restrung classical Spanish Guitar
purred once more.
He strummed; smiled contented.
'The Deer Hunter,' I said.
'Yes,' he replied softly.
Nimble fingers plucked the new strings,
moving backwards and forward with renewed
confidence.
Rustic, tattered music sheet positioned.
I closed my eyes in anticipation, remembering.

February
Keywords – TIME and TIDE

Beach Walk
Frank Fahy

Time ticks, tide shifts, alongside my stride,
Beach walks, heart talks, my dog as my guide.
Each wave's retreat, a reminder to bide,
Life's fleeting moments, in nature, I confide.
My end, not a fight, but a merge with the tide.
In its depths, my essence will finally reside.

Diamonds
Mary Hodson

The day had arrived,
Picnic prepared,
favourite treats packed.
Tides checked.
Time for our adventure to begin.
We sauntered along the sandy beach.
We ascended the tall sand dunes,
We found our secret place.
Elated, they shouted in jubilant harmony,
'Nana, we found diamonds'.

Mug of the Month February

Fifties Childhood
Mary Rose Tobin

A warm snug kitchen, laughter aired,
Tins of Jacob's biscuits shared
Tide's bright promise, clothes agleam,
Golden syrup's honeyed stream.
Royal baking powder tin
Other tins within, within
Guinness' froth, a dad's retreat
'Listen with Mother' a daily treat
Childhood's rhyme and laughter's chime,
Nostalgic warmth, through sands of time.

Time and Tide
Mary Hawkshaw

Time, you are a fickle friend,
Measuring my days to their end.
Will my time be long or short?
You will not let me know.

But if I knew for sure,
Would my dreams and plans endure?
Or would I drift upon the tide?
Would the number be my guide?

Mug of the Month February

He Sees the Girl
Seamus Keogh

There is an instant when the Tide stops
between ebb and flow, like the first halved
second when he glimpsed the partner across
the room and he sees the girl he longs to get to
know. Then Time flies on as we all know and
celebrations of a Golden Anniversary.

No Chance
Anne Murray

It was always the same old story with him,
mooching around, doing nothing.
'Any chance of a few bob to tide me over till my
dole comes in?'
This time she's had enough.
'No,' she says. 'No chance.
Any chance you might get a job?'

Time and Tide
Elizabeth Hannon

Did you ride career foamy white breakers
During your professional high energy years?
Hit exciting stormy summits
Climax in glory.
Time wanes, life takes its toll.
Now floundering, wallowing in tide pools,
Busy circling, going nowhere.
Like me,
Waiting for Godot.

Mug of the Month February

Time and Tide
Richard O'Donnell

Time and tide – never still;
Like life itself – ever hurried.
Yet time will end, and so will tide.
And even life itself will end.
Slow down.

Be still.

Revel in this moment!

It,
too,
will end;

Oft
e'er
it's lived.

Trystan and Aoife
Deirdre Anne Gialamas

Trystan did not keep his trist,
Tripping, trying to taste a truffle.
Fair Aoife fell foul of frost.
Feisty fairies flung them far afield.
Wintry winds to wake their woe.
Soon siren sisters stole their ashes.
Still Trystan and Aoife tread the crill
As tides of time trickle and thrill.

Mug of the Month February

Waiting
Molly Fogarty

It's way past time.
I mean, how often
can the tide roll in and out
before the flotsam and jetsam
of a lost life
come home to roost?
Gulls circle, screaming
with arbitrary malice,
though no wreckage
of your final struggles
sloshes between
the wave-ravaged rocks
at my feet.
Yet.

Wash Day
Kathleen Phelan

She stands bowed over the slant of the
washboard,
A hunched silhouette against the sink's worn
surface.
A mountain of clothes on the flag floor beside
her.
With calloused hands, she battles the tide.
Time isn't on her side.
There are cows to be milked and chickens to
be fed.

Mug of the Month February

With Breath
James Conway

Precious seconds shadow
in the dance of silver light
by the fire of a golden sun

From the torch of birth
to the pull of death, seconds'
time sifts in and out with breath

then thumbs a ride with the tide

the two together, their blood
as one, thriving on!

Time and Tide
Nollaig O'Donnell

Sun, sea-sound, boats click.
Book and bike on Spiddal pier –
Time and tide are mine.

March

Keywords – *PITCH* and *GROUND*

A Smashing Cup of Coffee
Anne Murray

The rich aroma of boiling water on freshly
ground coffee beans,
While she practised her operatic aria.
Electrifying!
The perfect start to a day!
She'll never know if it was the boiling water,
or the pitch of her voice,
that made the glass shatter!

Mug of the Month March

Bread from Stones
Jutta Rosen

The sails grasp the wind
The cog-wheels whirr
The hoist heaves the sacks
The grain gets pitched
Down the chute
To the furrowed stones

Churning
Rasping
Crushing
Grinding

Milled powdery
Soft grey dust
Trickling into sacks:
Stone-ground flour

Sun, earth, seeds,
Wind, sails, wheels
Stones
Bring mankind
Bread and life

Mug of the Month March

Escaped
Anne McManus

The night is pitch dark
I don't know where I am.
My pulse is racing.
My mouth is dry.
I stumble on the rough ground.
I'm afraid to breathe in fear of being caught.
I'm out of that odious cellar
Where you locked me in.
God damn you to hell.

Leap Towards Infinity
Frank Fahy

In fire's embrace, he chose the leap –
Desperate flight from flames so deep.
His choice alone, to jump, to fly,
Extend his life, gravity defy.
With high-pitched scream, midst air he
soared,
Fear and courage through him poured
For ten seconds, freedom's hero,
On his tragic flight to ground zero.

Mug of the Month March

Lovers
Geraldine Warren

They sprang at each other
Clawing,
Drawing each breath heavily.
Their clothes hit the ground,
A mound of littered debris.
Their high-pitched cries
Broke the silence of the night.
Lovers...
Loving with all their might.

Terra Nova
Mary Rose Tobin

Tents pitched on unforgiving ground,
'Neath stars that mock with silent sound.
Oates, sick and weary, brave words chime
'I'm just going out, may be some time.'

Shattered dreams, a hero crowned,
In endless ice, his peace is found
Courageous heart meets Antarctic light,
His final act, a beacon bright.

The Abyss
Seamus Keogh

Oh!
That this too too solid ground would open up and pitch the Despots of this World into the Abyss of Darkness and Desolation that they have condemned the wretched unwanted displaced Souls into.

Should the Gods decide to smite and punish evil now is the time for true Justice.

The E-Factor
Elizabeth Hannon

Leo ground his teeth.
The euphoria of presenting the shamrocks in the White House
Evaporating.
Small country lecturing the de facto world leader on the ethics of war and famine, exhilarating.
Back home at the day job. Exhausting exasperation and ennui.
Decision.
Evacuate. Get off the pitch.

Mug of the Month March

The Little White Ball
Mary Hodson

Ground conditions ideal.
Trolly set, lead hand gloved,
weapons unsheathed,
lucky tees pocketed.
Only Pars, and Birdies today folks,
On the tee box.
Address the little white ball.
Swing lands in the drink.
Penalty.
Damn.
Swing reliable five wood.
Ball outside the green.
Pitching action into the cup.
Birdie.

The Singer
Mary Hawkshaw

She stood before a crowd,
all eyes and ears.
And opened her mouth
to sing, before her peers.
Her pitch went through the roof,
like a stick of dynamite.
And the crowd fell to the ground
screaming from the fright.

April
Keywords – WALK and LIE

Caught in the Act
Anne Murray

I cannot lie,
It's all my fault.
I got the code,
I opened the vault.
The cops arrived,
I heard the talk.
They're right outside.
No time to walk.
I could lie low
Make my escape.
CCTV,
They'll view the tape.
Hands up, it's me,
Enjoy the wake!

Mug of the Month April

False Alarm
Frances Dermody

The sun blinds my vision as I walk the footbridge over the river.

Breathing suddenly suspended, I see the child's body, face down in the shallow water.

I'm screaming, mind and body paralysed, Until the sun hides. It was all a lie, a shopping bag wrapped around a stone.

Once a Man, Twice a Child
Mary Hodson

Don't lie beneath it;
you might leave us too soon.
We are not ready to let you go.
Let's find your walking stick;
let's stroll together.'
Hesitant little steps are taken.
Strength and confidence return.
'Once a man, twice a child' –
In the fullness of time, she, went under,
Surrendering.

Mug of the Month April

Struck Down in my Prime
Frank Fahy

At seventeen, a strike so keen,
a hurley's vicious blow,
A hospital bed, where I would lie,
my heart and spirits low.
With crutches, I reclaimed my walk,
each step a victory scored,
Beyond playing fields, a love for books,
my zest for life restored.

Survivor Guilt
Mary Rose Tobin

Annually, when Valentine's comes around,
Stardust Memories once again resound.
While elsewhere, we partied, happily, securely
NEWSFLASH — What? A lie, surely?
Events of that night branded us,
Forty-eight flames have haunted us.
Those kids went out and never came home,
But we survived to walk paths of our own.

Mug of the Month April

Waiting
Anne McManus

I will lie in wait. I will not hurt her body,
rather her mind with hate filled words.
She has driven me to this action
by her betrayal.
Little did I realise her contempt for me.
Soon she will walk this way.
My heart is pounding but I am resolute.

What a Thought!
James Conway

He sleeps with sister one,
The man called... invisible love,
Then with sister two,
Their hearts become spinning tops.
He will lie with them again on different nights.

Later he decides to walk.
The sisters talk.
He ends up shot,
Carried to... the crematorium Without a
passport.
What a thought!

Mug of the Month April

Cosy Bedroom Vibes
Josephine McCann

Another grey day outside.
Cocooned, I lie, no need to stride.
Upon my bed, I'll rest my head.
Yet those I love must be fed.
Loving eyes look into mine.
Canine curls my fingers entwine.
Tender tones with which I talk,
No substitute for a doggy's walk.

Songs

The Write-on group encourages writing of all styles and genres. Here is a collection of songs from our songwriters.

Everything is Grand
Bill Geoghegan

Everything is grand, everything is grand.
Even sitting in the kitchen waiting for the ham.
Everything is grand, everything is grand.
Whether you like singing solo or playing with
the band.

Some like peanut butter, some say they like
jam.
Some like skiing snowy slopes while others
stroll the sand.
Doesn't matter what you like or where on
earth you am.
'Cause when all is said and done everything is
grand.

Everything is grand, everything is grand.
Even sitting in the kitchen waiting for the ham.
Everything is grand everything is grand.
Whether you like singing solo or playing with
the band.

Some folks they like reading books while
others prefer the glam.
Some like racing fancy cars still others walk
the land.
Doesn't matter how you go or what you may
have planned.

Everything is Grand

Just take the lead from Ireland cause
everything is grand.

Everything is grand, everything is grand.
Even sitting in the kitchen waiting for the ham.
Everything is grand, everything is grand.
Whether you like singing solo or playing with
the band.

You may live in faded jeans or don the formal
wear.
Or spending time at rock concerts or love the
Country Fair.
Swing the night out on the town or solo in a
chair.
Since when everything is grand, we haven't got
a care.

Everything is grand, everything is grand.
Even sitting in the kitchen, waiting for the ham.
Everything is grand, everything is grand.
Whether you like singing solo or playing with
the band.

Friends
Grit Metsch

It's that time of year again
And the streets are full of lights
Another winter night begins
One of December's silent nights.
For me it's time to sit back
And remember all my friends
Remember all they've done for me throughout
this year
And write these lines for them.

They're never far out of reach
Though we don't meet every day.
They stand by me, lend me their hand
Companions on my way.
They help me chase away my fears
When I have to start all over again.
We give and we take,
And I won't forget
What friends I have in them.

A candle in my window
Will be burning all night long
For all you dear ones that I know
To shine into your home
And maybe as I think of you
You might as well think of me
So tonight let's share our candlelight
And this song and a dream.

Friends

It's that time of year again
And the streets are full of lights
Oh, how I love these winter winds
Wishing you all were by my side
Maybe you, too, stay up tonight
Thinking of what this year has brought
And maybe somewhere in the night
We'll meet on crossroads of our thoughts.

A candle in my window
Will be burning all night long
For all you dear ones that I know
To shine into your home
And maybe as I think of you
You might as well think of me
So tonight, let's share our candlelight
And this song.

You help me chase away my fears
When I have to start all over again
We give and we take
So we shouldn't forget
We've got friends.

A candle in my window
Will be burning all night long
For all you dear ones that I know
To shine into your home
And maybe as I think of you
You might as well think of me
So tonight let's share our candlelight
And this song
And a dream, and a dream.

Christopher's Journey
Mary Rose and Peter Tobin

In a room filled with silence, a tiny boy plays,
Curious fingers finding each phrase,
Blue eyes piercing as golden curls shine
In a whole world of dreams each note he'd
define.

Christopher, Christopher, where did you roam?
Your heart hears a song and it's guiding you
home.
Through the twists and the turns, the highs and
the lows,
You'll find your peace where a melody flows.

In school, classes chatter, his spirit won't lift.
A wandering mind is a curse or a gift.
Alone in a crowd, he's there but he's gone
The songs of the mind, they just flow on and
on.

Christopher, Christopher, where did you roam?
Your heart hears a song and it's guiding you
home.
Through the twists and the turns, the highs and
the lows,
You'll find your peace where a melody flows.

Christopher's Journey

Oh Chris, Oh Chris, with your heart on the keys,
Fighting the tide, always trying to please.
Caught in the storm of what you should be,
The song of your soul sets you free.

Christopher, Christopher,
Heart on your sleeve,
You'll find your place if you just believe
In the power of music to heal and to mend,
Your journey's not over, it's just around the bend.

Christopher, Christopher, where did you roam?
Your heart hears a song and it's guiding you home.
Through the twists and the turns, the highs and the lows,
You'll find your peace where a melody flows.

Call Me Tomorrow
Frank Fahy

This time you say it's over
This time we're really done.
Can we ever recover
Feelings that are numb?

Let me be your knight again.
Let me make your day.
I'd like every minute to be ours,
For our love to find a way.

Call me selfish, call me cruel
Call me heartbreak, call me sorrow.
Call me stubborn as a mule...
But darlin', call me tomorrow.

Don't let the sun set
Upon an angry row
Never meant to forget
This was our marriage vow.

But you're hiding in your castle
While I'm fitful in my sleep.
How can I win the battle
When you're locked up in your keep?

Call Me Tomorrow

Let me be your knight again.
Let me make your day.
I'd like every minute to be ours
For our love to find a way.

Call me selfish, call me cruel
Call me heartbreak, call me sorrow
Call me stubborn as a mule...
But darlin', call me tomorrow.

About the Authors

Póilín Brennan is a recent addition to the Write-on group, bringing a diverse background in health, education, development aid, and biodiversity. She is dedicated to promoting well-being and respect for biodiversity through therapeutic horticulture, particularly with children who have special educational needs. Póilín's affinity for the written and spoken word began in her youth while growing up in the scenic surroundings of Bearna. Now residing in Dublin with her husband and young family, she continues to nurture her passion for storytelling by writing short stories and poems. Amidst a hectic lifestyle, Póilín has reignited her enthusiasm for writing, with a special fondness for bilingual poetry. Her inspiration stems from the enchanting beauty of nature, the richness of the Irish language, and its profound connection with spirituality and ancestral heritage.

Joyce Butcher is the author of six novels, two children's books and two books of short stories, all of which are available on Amazon. She is proud to have had several short stories included in three previous Write-on Group's Anthologies. She is a retired counsellor and lives in Melbourne, Australia.

Joyce took up writing after her retirement in 2016 and is now an established member of the

Write-on community. Living in Melbourne, Australia, she enjoys the camaraderie and creative infusion from the group's diverse membership, which has grown to include many new writers from Ireland and around the world. This year has been particularly prolific for Write-on, with the Anthology 2025 marking the third publication. Joyce is thrilled to contribute once again, sharing her love for storytelling and continuing to inspire and be inspired by the group's dynamic

Helena Clare was born and raised in Galway, Ireland. She lives in North Carolina with her husband Robert. Together they enjoy outdoor activities in the nearby parks and greenways. More accustomed to scholarly rather than creative writing, she is a recent addition to the Write-on group. The title of her first published short story *Gone the Heather – Gone the Hawthorn* was inspired by Patrick Kelly's poem *Waitin'* where he wrote:

But we'll play no more the rover,
Good rover you and I;
Gone the dew an' dead the clover –
An' we . . . we wait to die.

James Conway was born in Dublin. He founded the Rathmines Writers' Workshop in 1990. He was awarded the Jonathan Swift Poetry prize in 2019 and the Prose prize in 2017. One of his stories was short listed for the William Trevor Award in 2006. He holds an English Literature degree from the Open University and three diplomas in Creative Writing from The Open College of the Arts. His books include *Vertebrae of Journey* by Swan

Press, 2010 and *Purple Coat* by Lapwing of Belfast, 2017.

Frances Dermody grew up in East Galway and has lived and worked in Galway city since the late 1980s. She has been involved with several creative writing workshops in Galway city, since joining her first workshop in Galway Arts Centre in 2000. She worked on the publication of a creative writing anthology for GROW Mental Health charity in 2015. She took a break from creative writing to return to education as a mature student with TUS, Athlone during the COVID pandemic. She joined the Write-on group early in 2024, with the aim of improving discipline and working towards a routine of daily writing. She has since discovered that the group also provides an opportunity to constantly improve IT skills, without detracting in any way from the supportive and creative space that the group provides for its members.

Joanne Dowling is from Co. Galway. She lived in England for ten years. While there, she attended university and wrote a dissertation on the work of James Joyce. Back in Ireland, she was a teacher for a couple of years. She now lives with her husband and son in the parish of Athenry. She has two other sons, one who lives in Galway and the other in the south of England. She is a member of the School of Practical Philosophy. She's had work published in the *Galway Advertiser* and *Crannóg* magazine. Previously a member of other writing groups, she is delighted to be with Write-on at present.

About the Authors

Frank Fahy hails from Galway and is a talented teacher, journalist, publisher, and musician. He is a highly accomplished writer and songwriter and was awarded at the SiarScéil International Literary Festival for his short story *Western Medley Surprise.* In 2019, Frank published his first collection of poetry, *Building New Bridges,* which received critical acclaim. He followed it up in 2023 with the release of *A Father's Love and Other Stories,* a collection of twenty-two short stories that showcases his impressive range and versatility as a storyteller. His lifelong love for books has never waned. Frank is a founding member of the Write-on group and has been instrumental in editing and publishing this year's Anthology 2025, our third publication this year. With his passion for literature and dedication to the craft, Frank continues to inspire and delight readers with his work. He is also delighted that the group has welcomed many new members from Ireland and across the globe, enriching the community's diversity and creative output.

Molly Fogarty is from county Galway and lives in Galway city. She became involved with *Write-On* in 2023 as part of her efforts to improve her writing skills. A mother and homemaker, she has worked on a contract basis as an actor, workshop leader, scriptwriter and teacher.

Bill Geoghegan was born in New Rochelle, New York and now lives in Galway with his wife, Judith. His childhood dream was to sing, play and write music. 'I am so fortunate to be able to do that in both Ireland and the U.S.,' he says.

365

About the Authors

Prior to being a full-time musician, he worked for Barclays Bank and the American Automobile Association. Bill's other hobby is swimming. 'When not playing music,' he says, 'I compete in Masters Swimming for Swim West Ireland and Conn Masters in the States.'

Elizabeth Hannon, a retired teacher, originally from Donegal, has lived in Galway with her husband for almost fifty years. She is the mother of three and grandmother to six children. 'Working with Write-on has provided me with the incentive and inspiration to produce more writing and to improve with each effort,' she says. Elizabeth brings her experience and constructive criticism to every Write-on session. She was delighted to have her first book *Out of the Blue – Stories, Poems and Memories* published by the Write-on group in 2020.

Mary Hawkshaw, originally from Dublin, has led a life filled with diverse experiences across Ireland and Canada. Her career began in nursing, but she later pursued her passion for English literature at Memorial University in Newfoundland and York University in Ontario. Although she did not complete her degrees, these studies greatly enhanced her understanding and appreciation of the classics, providing a solid foundation for her literary pursuits. Now enjoying retirement back in Galway, Mary devotes herself to poetry and storytelling. As a proud mother of four, her works in the Write-on Anthology capture her deep love for literature and her enthusiasm for sharing this with others.

About the Authors

Mary Hodson is a retired Nurse Tutor. She resides in Leitrim and shares her life with her husband, John, their three children, and ten beloved grandchildren. Her life has been devoted to the dual pursuits of nurturing her close-knit family and advancing her fulfilling career. Mary's extensive tenure with the UK and Irish Health Service's respectively saw her excel as a compassionate nurse and a dedicated nurse educator, always advocating for equality and accessibility in education, a cause she pursued through her Doctorate in Education with The Open University.

Mary's love for the written word has culminated in a captivating collection of short stories, highlighting her skill in encapsulating the intricacies of the human experience. Since joining the Write-on community she has been an enthusiastic participant, appreciating the vast array of inspirations and the unyielding support from her fellow authors.

Ciara Keogh was born in Galway. She now lives in Moycullen with her husband and two children. Joining the Write-on group has helped her to give expression to the stories and poems that she feels passionate about. She hopes to write much more in the years ahead.

Seamus Keogh grew up on Fr Griffin Road in Galway. He attended Scoil Fhursa and the 'Jes' beside his grandparents' shop, Keogh's, (now Kai Café) on Sea Road. He now lives in Moycullen. He has been writing stories and children's stories for many years and he is an active member of the Write-on group.

About the Authors

Josephine McCann lives in Galway. Retired from careers in business and motherhood, she now enjoys grandparenting, albeit, mostly via Facetime.

Although, enjoying writing, art, golf and bridge, travels regularly to Australia. She is increasingly conscious of the earth we are bequeathing to the next generations, not only climate impact but economic policies and increasing imbalance in society.

She attended, for many years, poetry workshops facilitated by the late Kevin Higgins in the Galway Arts Centre. She has read her own poems at the *Over the Edge Open Mic* events in Galway Public Library and at the Westside Literary festival. Her work has been printed in both local and national publications; indeed an item or two has surfaced abroad.

Anne Henry McManus was born in Sligo between majestic Ben Bulben and regal Knocknarea. A retired teacher of Home Economics and German, Anne and her husband, Ray, moved to Galway as newly-weds in 1964. They have four children and twelve grandchildren. She discovered her love of writing through the Salthill Active Retirement Writers' group under the tutorship of Maire Holmes.

Grit Metsch born and raised in the German Democratic Republic, moved to Ireland in 2017 to live her dream busking in the street and mingling with the people of this country. Ireland with all its beauty, culture and history is the greatest inspiration she has ever found for her song writing. Having joined the Write-on circle, she eagerly takes every chance to learn and improve her writing skills as the basis for new songs and poems. Grit writes her songs and music from the heart. You can listen to her work on YouTube.

Anne Murray was born in West Cork, but she has lived in Galway for over fifty years. Married to Michael, a Galwegian, she is the mother of seven children and grandmother of eight. A retired postmistress, her interest in writing was sparked after retirement when she discovered the Westside Write-on Group. She hopes to continue to write stories and poems and to keep improving with the help of the group.

Nollaig O'Donnell is a Write-on member. Her book, *Something Within,* a collection of her reflections and sketches, was published by Veritas. A native of Ennis, Co. Clare, Nollaig now lives in Galway with her husband, Richard. A teacher of piano, French and English, she also enjoys writing, sketching and silk painting. She is currently completing her memoir, which she plans to publish soon.

Richard O'Donnell is a small organic farmer in the Burren in Co. Clare. He is particularly interested in ecological diversity in all its forms. Farming in the Burren, by working with nature, provides him with an extraordinarily rich opportunity to maximise the natural biodiversity of his farm and deeply appreciate and sense the Divine at play and work in his own life. Richard has only recently begun writing, taking his inspiration primarily from the wonders of nature and our responsibilities

About the Authors

and privileges as human beings to till and take care of it.

Kathleen Phelan is from Kilkenny by the banks of the river Nore. She began writing poetry in her early thirties. Over the years she has been involved in numerous workshops and writing groups. She studied English for Publication in Maynooth Outreach University with tutor and writer John MacKenna. For many years she studied in Kilkenny's Liberal Studies Group under the guidance of poet Mark Roper. A short course in art history by Catherine Marshall, then curator of The Irish Museum of Modern Art, led her to love the subject. Though her knowledge is limited, she hopes for the opportunity for further study. She has been happily married to Donny since August 1969. They have four children. She's vegetarian and passionate about animal welfare, especially the plight of feral cats.

Jutta Rosen grew up in Dublin and Kerry but returned to her native Germany to teach in the early 1970s. An extensive reader, she rediscovered her love of the English language while translating German city guidebooks. Her own writing was limited to extensive letters and emails until, encouraged by literary friends to develop her story-telling talent, she joined The Write-on group in early 2021. Her first novel was published by Write-on in 2024.

Mary Rose Tobin was born and raised in Galway. She moved to Dublin to embark on a fulfilling career in the public sector. Upon retiring, she returned to the scenic village of Barna. She continues to work with the Mental

370

About the Authors

Health Commission on a part-time basis.

Mary Rose sings with the Galway Choral Association and is also an accomplished writer. As a founding member of Write-on, she has contributed to the Anthologies since 2019. In 2023, Mary Rose won the Hannah Greally Award, an International Short Story competition. She published her first collection of short stories in 2024 – *The Life and Times of Jimmy Mullins and Other Stories.*

Her writings, much like her life, blend her love for family and community, her passion for public service, and her dedication to mental health. She cherishes her daily walks by the sea.

Geraldine Warren is a founder member of The Write-on group. Born in Galway, she is a former Television News Producer who travelled extensively to cover news for BBC and ABC Australia, while based in London, Frankfurt, and Berlin.

'We are all apprentices in a craft where no one ever becomes a master.'

Ernest Hemingway, *The Wild Years*

Printed in Great Britain
by Amazon